ANNA SAYBURN LANE

The Soho Jazz Murders

A 1920s murder mystery

To Paul,

STARLING
STREET BOOKS

First published by Starling Street Books 2023

Copyright © 2023 by Anna Sayburn Lane

This novel is a work of fiction. The names, characters and incidents portrayed in it (with the exception of historical characters) are the work of the author's imagination.

First edition

ISBN: 978-1-7395144-2-6

*This book was professionally typeset on Reedsy.
Find out more at reedsy.com*

Foreword

This is the second of a series of 1920s murder mystery adventures featuring assistant private investigator Marjorie Swallow. I hope you enjoy it.

A word about spelling: I'm a British author and the series is set in 1920s London, so I use British spelling and grammar.

You can find out more about the books, get free short stories and a prequel novella when you sign up to my Readers Club newsletter on my website: https://wp.me/P9ZyRq-20X.

Chapter 1

I twisted my hips to wriggle free, the weight of my assailant pinning me to the parquet floor. I could smell the carbolic soap used to mop it; feel grit against my cheek as I turned my head. The face above me flushed with anticipated triumph. My shoulders were held down, my ribs crushed by the young ruffian sitting astride me.

I could hear laughter from the crowd that had gathered to watch. No-one was going to help. They thought it a foregone conclusion. And a few weeks ago, it would have been.

But I was determined not to be beaten this time. I raised one knee, levering my attacker up and making a little space between us. Quickly I followed through, twisting into the movement and using my elbow as a fulcrum. With a last effort, I managed to turn her weight against her, flipping us over so that my forearm was across her neck and my knee trapped her bent leg beneath us.

'Hurrah!' A tiny woman in dark serge jacket and skirt applauded and held out her hand to pull me to my feet. 'There you go, Frankie. Miss Swallow is one too many for you now.'

Frankie grinned, sitting up and tucking her shirt back into her breeches. 'Next time, Marjorie. I demand a repeat match.'

I laughed, but I felt rather proud of myself. It was the first time I'd escaped from a hold when matched with Frankie O'Grady, the undisputed champion of the Golden Square dojo. And I'd only been learning jiu-jitsu for two months. After my escapades during our last investigation, my employer Mrs Jameson had insisted I learn the martial art, as taught by the legendary Mrs Garrud, for self-defence.

Edith Garrud had been instructress to the fearsome suffragette bodyguards of the Women's Social and Political Union before the War. Legend had it that this four-foot-eleven woman had once thrown a policeman over her shoulder outside the gates of the Houses of Parliament. While I had no plans to start throwing policemen about, I was enjoying the training. And it was a cheering thought, that one could throw a ruffian over one's shoulder if the occasion arose.

There was a knock and respectful cough from outside the hall.

'Come!' called Mrs Garrud.

Graham Hargreaves, Mrs Jameson's butler, put his head around the door. 'Sorry to interrupt, ladies. May I remind Miss Swallow that she has an appointment for luncheon?' He looked at my dusty skirt and blouse. 'You might want to come back to Bedford Square to change. It's the American ambassador.'

There was a chorus of oohs and aahs. 'Get you,' said Frankie. 'Don't let us keep you from your society engagements. All right for some, eh?'

I blushed hard and tried to tidy my hair, which had fallen down my back. 'Thank you, Graham. I'll come at once.'

'Let me help.' Lily Rose, Frankie's girl, took the hairbrush from my canvas bag and brushed out my dark locks, twisting them up into a bun. 'When are you going to get it cut, then?'

Her own brown hair curled prettily down her back, but she was adamant I should have mine shingled in the modern style. I wasn't sure I was ready for the chop.

'One day. I've been too busy.' Since concluding the case of the Bloomsbury blackmail murder, Mrs Jameson and I had been occupied with moving into her new house in Bedford Square, which required much furnishing and staffing. And then there was the task of informing her many friends and acquaintances of her new address, and of inviting them all to a Christmas Eve housewarming party in Bloomsbury. Most of this work had fallen to me, as Mrs Jameson's secretary. It was as well that we'd had no private investigations underway for the past two months.

But now Christmas was over, I could tell Mrs Jameson was getting bored. She claimed her work as a lady detective was to help achieve justice for those who might otherwise not get it, but if you asked me, it was mainly to keep her entertained. She'd complained non-stop about the dreary January weather in London and vowed that next year, she would spend the winter on the Riviera. I hoped that this appointment with the American ambassador to London – which had been postponed several times because of our house move and Christmas – would provide her with some new interest.

Hastily I brushed myself down, thanked Mrs Garrud for the class and promised Frankie I would beat her again next time. Graham was waiting on the steps of the hall, hailing a taxi-cab.

'You didn't need to come and fetch me,' I told him. 'I wasn't going to forget.'

He smiled, his knobbly face kindly. 'I know what you young ladies are like when you're enjoying yourselves,' he said. 'Besides, I like to see young Francesca. She was in the same class at school as my sister's daughter in Limehouse. A very original young woman. We always wondered what would happen to Frankie O'Grady. But she seems to find her own way.'

Frankie was indeed an original. I'd never met a woman who wore breeches, neck-ties, and waistcoats. But she carried off her outfit with swagger and assurance, and indeed you couldn't imagine her wearing a frock. It would look odd with her cropped hair, for a start. She and Lily Rose had rescued me from a particularly tight spot down a dark alleyway the previous autumn, demonstrating the power of jiu jitsu. I was delighted when Mrs Jameson suggested I should train alongside the two of them at Golden Square.

'She's saving up to get her own motor garage,' I said. Frankie had trained as a motor mechanic during the War and, somewhat to the surprise of the garage owner, refused to quit her job in 1919 when the soldiers came home. As she was more mechanically adept than most of the men he'd employed, not to mention earning lower wages, he kept her on. But she was determined to become her own boss.

'And I've no doubt she'll do it,' said Graham, admiringly. 'My sister says you never met such a stubborn child in all your life.'

The journey from Soho to Bloomsbury took minutes. I ran up the stairs to my room at the top of the house and changed into a navy and green plaid skirt and jacket, with a fresh white blouse. There was a smudge of dirt on my nose and a slight bruise on my cheek. I washed off the dirt and hoped the American ambassador would be broad-minded about bruising.

I pinned on a scarlet cloche hat and trotted down the stairs to where Mrs Jameson stood waiting, imperious in plum-coloured wool from Paris and crowned with a matching turban. She tapped her malacca cane on the parquet floor impatiently. Her ankle, broken in the autumn, was still weak.

'There you are, Marjorie,' she said. This was her habitual greeting to me. 'Now, sharpen your wits. Henry Caldwell is a most intelligent man, not to mention one of the kindest people I know. I owe him a great deal for help he gave me when he was the US consul in Rome many years ago. Anything I can do for him in return, I will happily do.'

Rome. My interest in the ambassador heightened. Was I about to discover the secret that Mrs Jameson guarded so closely, about what had happened to her in Rome – and the fate of her late husband? I jumped into the waiting taxi-cab with alacrity.

Chapter 2

'Iris, I'm so glad you could come.'

The ambassador was unusually tall, with a rangy build and a domed head topped with thinning grey hair brushed straight back from his long face. He smiled, the corners of his green eyes crinkling, and held out both hands.

Mrs Jameson stepped past the footman who had opened the door and took the ambassador's hands. She surveyed him for a moment, her sharp features softened with affection.

'Good to see you, Henry. How's Myrtle?'

His smile faded. 'She's having a bad day, I'm afraid. She won't come down for lunch. But perhaps you could go up to talk with her afterwards? I know she'd love to see you. She sends her apologies. Her head is wretched.'

Mrs Jameson had warned me that Mrs Caldwell suffered from painful headaches that kept her confined to her bedroom for days at a time.

'Of course. And Felicity?' The ambassador's daughter had just turned eighteen. She'd been invited to Mrs Jameson's Christmas party along with her father, but opted to stay at home and look after her sick mother instead.

He smiled with paternal pride. 'She's just fine. She'll be down soon with her cousin, the latest member of my household. It's so nice for Felicity to have someone her own age about the place. I don't think you've met my niece, Daisy Caldwell? My younger brother's eldest girl. She's very... well, you'll meet her soon enough.'

He broke off and shook my hand. 'My apologies, Miss Swallow, for neglecting you. I'm delighted you could come too.'

We stepped through the hall and a pretty young maid took our things. My gaze lingered on my new charcoal grey coat with red ribbon trim and shoulder cape. I'd picked out the fabric from my father's shop and my mother had made it up for my Christmas present. I was extremely proud of it. The only problem was that my indoor clothes looked rather shabby by comparison. I must learn to be satisfied, I reminded myself. I'd spent half of last year wishing for a new coat, and now I wanted a new day dress to go with it.

'Now.' Ambassador Caldwell stood and rubbed his hands together. He looked awkward. 'We'll go through in a minute and fix you some drinks. But I wonder if you would just step into my study for a moment, Iris? There's something I'd like to ask you about.' He smiled at me apologetically, and I prepared to make myself scarce.

'If this is something you want me to investigate, I need Marjorie with me,' said Mrs Jameson firmly. 'She is my right-hand woman, and you can trust her absolutely.'

I was surprised and rather pleased. My employer didn't dole out compliments readily.

The ambassador looked unconvinced, but I could see that he knew better than to argue with Mrs Jameson. Like Frankie, she could be stubborn in the extreme. He nodded and led us into a book-lined room off the hall, with a leather-topped desk and several deep red leather armchairs. Outside the tall sash windows, motor cars, omnibuses and carts trundled between Knightsbridge and Kensington. On the other side of the busy road, the horses and riders of the household cavalry made a splash of scarlet as they trotted through Hyde Park.

We sat. I balanced my notebook on my knee and uncapped my fountain pen. My first role was always to take notes and observe, as Mrs Jameson asked questions.

'So, Henry. Please speak as freely as you would if we were alone. Tell me everything.'

Ambassador Caldwell sighed, steepled his long fingers and looked at the ceiling. 'It's rather delicate. Family business.'

We waited. Family business was always delicate.

'I'd like to get your opinion on my niece, Daisy.' He hesitated again. 'She's nineteen, which I suppose is a dangerous age. I hadn't seen her since she was in the school room. I don't suppose I took much notice of her then, although she was a cute little thing. Lively, always up to something – putting on plays with her sisters and cousins, making up songs and dances.'

Charming as the domestic detail was, I didn't think his niece's theatrical tendencies were what Mr Caldwell wanted our opinion about.

'What are you worried about, Henry?' asked Mrs Jameson bluntly, tapping him on the knee.

There was a bit more throat-clearing before he finally came out with it.

'She got into some bad habits back in Manhattan. My brother begged me to take her to England. He thought London would be a safer environment for her. She'd been going to these nightclubs, dancing to jazz music, mixing with all sorts of people. And what with prohibition, the speakeasies in New York have gotten kind of wild.'

I brightened up. I was rather keen on dancing to jazz music myself. Perhaps lunch would be livelier than I'd anticipated.

'Henry, you didn't bring me here to advise you on Daisy's dancing. Spit it out.'

'She's been with us four months, and she's already found her way to most of the dive bars and late-night cabarets in the West End of London. It seems like London can be every bit as wild as New York.

'And recently, Felicity told me something very concerning. They have rooms next to each other, and sometimes they pop in and out – you know how girls are. She popped in one morning and found Daisy – well. She had some powder. White stuff, in a little gold box.'

Mrs Jameson exhaled. 'Ah. And it wasn't face powder for her nose?'

He shook his head. 'Felicity didn't know what it was, of course. But she said Daisy took a pinch from the box and sniffed it up her nose. It sounds to me like cocaine.'

Cocaine. I knew about it, of course. It wasn't so long ago that you could buy cocaine tincture for toothache at any chemist. We'd used it on occasion at the hospital, although morphine was more often prescribed. But since the War, there had been a big panic about drugs. Cocaine and opium were now illegal except for medical purposes, and there had been all sorts of alarming stories in the newspapers about people getting 'hooked' on drugs and driven to desperate measures to get hold of more.

'Have you asked her about it?' Mrs Jameson never sounded shocked. She took a pragmatic view of most things.

'No. Not yet. I mean, what if Felicity had misunderstood and got it wrong? I'm not Daisy's father.'

Mrs Jameson smiled gently. 'But if your daughter was staying in New York with your brother, would you not want him to ask Felicity, in your place?'

He sighed and stretched out his legs. 'I suppose. Not that Felicity has ever given me a moment's worry. She's a sweet girl; still a child, really.'

Mrs Jameson gave him a long look. 'Henry, you wanted my advice. My advice is to talk to the girl. Ten to one, she'll be mortified and drop it right away.'

He looked gloomy. 'Maybe. But won't you just take a look at her and tell me if you think I'm way off? Or maybe this young woman...' he looked at me, pleadingly. 'Maybe Miss Swallow would have a chat with Daisy and see what comes up?'

I bit the inside of my cheeks to prevent myself from giggling. I'm not sure what sort of girl-chat the ambassador thought English women indulged in, but none of my friends had ever dropped their cocaine use into casual conversation. Maybe I was moving in the wrong circles.

We agreed to 'take a look' at Daisy and give Mr Caldwell our considered opinion as to whether his niece was a dope fiend. And with that, we went through to meet the family.

Chapter 3

A tall, athletic-looking young man was hovering by the French doors that led from the drawing room to the terrace. He stepped forward, a curl of chestnut hair springing up from his forehead despite liberal use of brilliantine.

'This is my secretary, Mr John B Franklin,' said Ambassador Caldwell. 'Franklin, may I introduce Mrs Iris Jameson and Miss Marjorie Swallow? Mrs Jameson is a very old friend from my days at the embassy in Rome.'

'Not so much of the old,' said Mrs Jameson crisply, offering the young man her hand.

'How do you do?' said Mr Franklin. 'It's always a pleasure to meet a fellow American in foreign parts. And especially a friend of the Caldwell family.'

His American accent was low and attractive. Ambassador Caldwell introduced me next.

'I'm Mrs Jameson's secretary,' I told him. 'English as they come, I'm afraid.' It was a new experience for me, meeting a man as a professional equal. Even if his work might involve drawing up peace treaties, while mine tended more towards answering invitations to parties and luncheons.

'Good to know who the real workers are, Miss Swallow,' he said, shaking my hand in a manly fashion. 'We secretaries must stick together.' He smiled, his teeth very white and his fingernails clean and manicured. He seemed like an advertisement for American manhood.

He organised drinks – whisky and soda for Ambassador Caldwell and Mrs Jameson, soda water for the working secretaries. Minutes later, a tall young woman who I took to be Felicity, the daughter of the ambassador, slipped into the room. Although I knew that she was fully eighteen, she dressed as if she'd barely left the school room. She wore a long navy serge pinafore dress over a striped blouse, and a navy beret pulled over pale auburn hair styled in schoolgirl braids.

'Aunt Iris! How lovely to see you.' Her smile was wide and unaffected. 'I've missed you loads.'

'Felicity, dear. Let me look at you.' Mrs Jameson held her by the shoulders and did just that. 'You've grown tall, but you're a little pasty. This country is wretched in the winter. Henry, you should send Myrtle and Felicity to the south of France. Get some roses back in those cheeks.'

'I'm fine, honestly. I've been reading a lot, while Mamma has been sick. That's probably why I look pale,' she said.

She held out her hand to me. 'And you're Aunt Iris's secretary? That must be very exciting. Do you get involved with all her investigations? You must be very clever.' Her eyes were wide. I could tell her a few stories that would make them go wider still, I thought.

'Some of them,' I said, smiling. 'But Mrs Jameson is the clever one.' Out of the corner of my eye, I noticed my employer nodding her approval.

Felicity turned to her father. 'Mamma is feeling a little better. She says she will have some luncheon in her room, and asked if Aunt Iris could go up to see her afterwards.'

'That's good. Thank you, Felicity.' He patted her shoulder and turned to Mrs Jameson. 'Your goddaughter is a very devoted nurse. I don't know what Myrtle and I would do without her.'

Felicity took a glass of soda water from Mr Franklin. 'And Daisy says she'll be right down. Our maid is just helping her to fix her hair.'

I wondered how Daisy fitted into this household of hard-working men and devoted girls. The answer was plain a few minutes later as she rushed into the room. She didn't fit in at all.

'Sorry, sorry, blame me for everything,' she cried gaily. 'My stoopid hair was sticking up like a porcupine and Harriet couldn't find my curling irons. I borrowed Auntie Myrtle's, but they got too hot, and I frizzled my ends.' She turned a dazzling smile on Mr Franklin. 'John B, would you be an angel and pour me a very tiny whisky soda? Otherwise I'll fall asleep in the soup. I don't know what time I got in from the Sampsons' party last night, but it wasn't early. It wasn't early at all.'

As she swallowed the drink down, I took in this exotic apparition. She wore what seemed to be a golfing outfit in pink and yellow checks with a pleated skirt swinging from her hips. A diamond-patterned Argylle knit sweater was flung around her shoulders. On top of her bright ginger curls, which did look a bit singed, perched a jaunty tam o'shanter with a pink and yellow tartan ribbon. The whole effect was striking and rather comical, although her face was bonny as a baby.

'Hit the spot,' she pronounced, handing Mr Franklin her empty glass. 'Are we having lunch now? I could eat a horse.'

'My niece, Miss Daisy Caldwell,' said the ambassador, his

voice dry. 'Daisy, this is Mrs Iris Jameson and Miss Marjorie Swallow.'

She flashed us a grin. 'Howdy. I like your turban, Mrs Jameson. Very snazzy. Do either of you like jazz?'

Fortunately, I'd learned quite a bit about jazz over the past couple of months.

'I do,' I volunteered. 'One of my friends plays piano in a jazz band. He's been telling me all about it.'

She squealed in excitement. 'Isn't it just too much? I'm crazy about it. You must sit next to me, and we can have a proper talk.'

We trooped through to the dining room, its walls covered in purple damask. In the low January light, it gave the room a rather ghoulish air, like dried blood. We took our places around a long, formal dinner table that could have hosted a party twice the size.

Without Daisy, it might have been a rather dull affair. I certainly fulfilled the ambassador's request to chat to his niece, although the girl hardly needed drawing out. I didn't manage to get a word in edgeways during the first two courses of a most delicious luncheon.

Daisy barely paused for breath as she listed her favourite bands, the best tunes to dance to, the spiffiest singers and the newest dance trends from Chicago and New Orleans, periodically waving her wine glass at the handsome Mr Franklin for a top-up. He was talking knowledgeably with the ambassador and Mrs Jameson about the League of Nations, while Felicity ate in near-silence, listening to her vivacious cousin with an awed face. You would never have thought they were almost the same age.

Daisy moved on to her favourites among the nightclubs and

dance halls of the West End.

'There's the Blue Lagoon on Beak Street, and the Ham Bone in Soho. But my favourite is the Harlequin in Wardour Street on a Wednesday,' she said, as the remains of the beefsteak were cleared away. 'That's when the All Stars Jazz Orchestra play, featuring T-bone Tommy Lee on trombone and Sidney Harpo on clarinet. I'm just crazy about them. They're smoking hot, let me tell you.'

I grinned. 'I know. That's my friend's band. Freddie Gillespie is the pianist. I saw them playing one night at the Criterion Roof Gardens. Freddie's been on at me ever since to go to see them at the Harlequin.'

The sensation caused by this news was almost too much for Daisy. 'Hot patootie, Marjorie! Let's go tomorrow night. How about it?'

'Not without an escort,' said Ambassador Caldwell. 'Really, Daisy, I must insist…'

'Then Mr Franklin will come with us,' said Daisy. 'Won't you, John B? He's a responsible adult. And Felicity, too. That makes three grown-ups and me. We can make up a party. Ah, come on, Uncle Henry. Don't you remember what it was like to be young?'

Evidently, Ambassador Caldwell did remember, just about.

'Very well. But be home by midnight and don't order alcohol after ten o'clock. I don't want you all arrested for drinking outside licensed hours.'

'I'm not going,' demurred Felicity. 'I can't dance. Honestly, I'm terrible.'

'Then we'll teach you,' said Daisy. 'John B will show you, won't you, John? You need to have a good time, Felicity. You're only young once.'

15

Mr Franklin tried to laugh off his part in the plan, but took it gamely enough when he realised there was no escape.

'It will be my pleasure,' he said, looking past Daisy to me. I returned his warm smile, wondering what on earth we were letting ourselves in for.

Chapter 4

Mrs Jameson was delighted that I had the opportunity to observe Daisy in her natural habitat. She announced she was giving me a dress allowance, to be spent on clothes I would not have required if it hadn't been for our investigations. Apparently, that included evening wear for going to nightclubs, which suited me very well indeed.

I spent a happy afternoon searching through the racks at Liberty, the fashionable retailer on Regent Street, looking for something appropriate. There was no time to get an evening frock made, but ready-to-wear was perfectly good if you chose quality materials and fitted a standard size.

I picked out a cream sleeveless crêpe de Chine dress with black beading over the square-necked bodice and a black silk sash around the hips. Waists were lower this year, the sales assistant told me, although I was dubious. But the dress went perfectly with my black t-strap heeled shoes and needed only a sequinned cap to finish it off. I stood before the looking glass, rather pleased.

'You know what would set it off properly, Miss?' asked the sales girl, tentatively.

I loosened my hair, gathered it in one hand and pulled it back. 'This?'

She beamed. 'You'd really suit it, Miss. There's a hairdressing salon on the top floor, you know. Why don't you go up while I wrap these things for you?'

Heart fluttering, I approached the salon. A kindly looking lady my mother's age was in charge, which was a relief. In all the films, hairdressing salons were run by temperamental Frenchmen intent on creating their artistic vision, rather than asking the clients what they wanted.

'I've been thinking of getting my hair cut into a bob,' I told her, noting that her own grey locks were worn in an elegant chignon. 'What do you think? Would it suit me?'

She sat me down, brushed out my hair and regarded me critically with her head on one side. Then she gently twisted my hair in her hand and pulled it back, so it was about chin-length.

'Yes, I think that would look very nice,' she said. 'You've got a bit of a wave, which will give it body, and that chestnut colour has plenty of shine. What you don't want is to have it looking dull and lank, hanging down like a pair of curtains. But you'll be fine. If you're sure?'

I nodded and closed my eyes. 'Yes, but I don't think I can watch.'

She spun the chair around, so I was facing away from the glass, divided my locks into sections and snipped away for what seemed like hours. Finally, she used heated curling irons to twist a few strands into pin-curls and spun me back round to look.

'Golly.' My face looked exposed and somehow younger, framed by two wings of shiny hair.

'Do you like it?' The woman sounded anxious.

I turned my head one way and another, running my hands

over the very bare back of my neck.

'I think so. It's a big change. But yes.' I smiled decisively at my reflection. 'I like it very much.'

My haircut caused a mild sensation back at Bedford Square, but by the time I was dressed in my new outfit, with a tiny bit of eye-lash black and a dab of pink on my lips, I knew I'd got it right. Not, I supposed, that anyone would be looking at me in the Harlequin. Not with Daisy Caldwell in the room.

Nonetheless, I was pleased to see John Franklin's surprised smile when Graham showed the Caldwell party into the drawing room. Mr Franklin was looking rather dashing in grey-striped trousers and black tails with white waistcoat, holding his top hat. Felicity Caldwell wore a girlish light-blue velvet dress without a belt, which accentuated her pale colouring and thin frame.

'Oh! You've cut your lovely hair,' she said. 'That's very brave.' I felt a twinge of annoyance. I didn't want to be brave; I wanted to be stylish and pretty.

'I rather like it,' I said, trying to keep my voice light.

She blushed peony-pink, realising she'd said the wrong thing. 'Oh, so do I. It's lovely. Very modern. I don't think I'd dare. Papa wouldn't like it.' She had twisted her pale auburn braids over her ears, like a pair of giant hairy ear-muffs. I tried to think of something nice to say about her hair-do, but was saved by Daisy's arrival.

When she strolled in, for a moment, I thought she'd for-gotten her dress and come in just her chemise and bloomers. Her canary-yellow spangled chiffon had a scooped neck, a low back that showed most of her spine, and the zig-zag hemline revealed her legs to the knee. She wore white stockings with correspondent black and yellow Mary-Janes, and a feathered head-band. Dangling gold earrings and a string of pearls that was far too long to be real completed the outfit.

She looked me up and down, and for a second, I saw disgruntlement that my transformation had taken the wind out of her sails. She recovered quickly.

'Gee, Marjorie, look at you! Isn't that the bee's knees?' she cried. 'I thought you were kidding when you said you planned to bob your hair. But you look fine. Doesn't she, John B? Doesn't Marjorie look fine?'

I hoped I looked a little better than fine, but smiled and took the compliment. At least she hadn't called me brave.

'You all look marvellous,' said Mrs Jameson, who had come to review the troops before our departure. 'Now, Mr Franklin, be sure and take good care of these young ladies. I'll expect Marjorie back by midnight at the latest. Enjoy your evening, Felicity. Have fun, all of you!'

Chapter 5

The music from the Harlequin could be heard all the way up into Wardour Street. I pulled my new coat around my shoulders, shivering in the cold as Mr Franklin paid the taxi driver. Daisy was wrapped in an enormous cocoon of silver mink, while Felicity wore a dark brown mink in an old-fashioned style that she said belonged to her mother.

'Mamma says I may as well have it. She never goes out any more.'

Felicity didn't look as if she was used to going out much either. She peered apprehensively down the grilled metal steps to the basement of 27 Wardour Street. The red door to the club had the motif of a carnival mask painted over it, but no name.

'Is it down there? Are you sure?'

'Come on, Felicity! Don't hang around like a wet weekend.' Daisy charged down the steps. I followed, my pulse quickening as I heard the syncopated rhythm of the drums.

Through the red door, the Harlequin was very smart and modern. The walls were lacquered in red, with angular gold-framed mirrors catching the light from electric lamps on the tables. The floor was shiny and black, the round tables draped in diamond-patterned red and gold cloths. The theme was the Italian Commedia dell'arte, with Harlequins, Pierrots and Columbines weaving their way through the crowd.

A cloakroom attendant wearing a Harlequin costume took our coats, then a young woman dressed as a black and white Pierrette ushered us to a table on the edge of the dance floor. Our progress was slowed by Daisy, who seemed to recognise everyone and stopped to chat at every table. It was all rather thrilling. I recognised one very junior member of the Royal family, an American film actor and a table occupied by several members of the Surrey cricket team. The cricketers were especially voluble in their appreciation of Daisy's 'get-up', as they called it. She only escaped by promising several of them dances 'after I've had a spot of the old giggle juice.'

Giggle juice, it turned out, was the main ingredient in the gin cocktails with which Daisy fuelled a night out. Mr Franklin ordered bourbon and Felicity asked for lemonade. Feeling very sophisticated, I requested a French 75, which was Mrs Jameson's favourite cocktail. I'd had one in the Rivoli Bar at The Ritz, when we celebrated my engagement as her secretary – and the conclusion of our first murder case.

To my disappointment, the Harlequin's version was nothing like as good. The gin caught in my throat, the lemon was too strong, and the 'champagne' was nothing of the sort. However, I sipped it gamely and sat back to enjoy the band.

T-bone's trombone wailed; Freddie's piano jangled and the drummer's beat was infectious. The clarinet player and trumpeter took their lead from T-bone, swinging into an up-tempo two-step. Freddie looked around, caught sight of me and grinned, his eyebrows shooting up his forehead as he noticed my short hair. I'd go and talk to him in the break, see what jokes he had to make about my shearing. I hoped he'd like it.

Daisy couldn't sit still. She jiggled on the black leather seat, swinging her legs like a child and craning her neck to look around the club. She caught at the arm of a passing Pierrette.

'Say, where's Vi tonight?'

The young woman, who was carrying a tray of drinks to a party of men seated beside the band, paused. 'Hello, Miss Caldwell. Miss Crumb isn't in. She's had the 'flu. Can I help you with anything?'

A second round of drinks arrived at our table, sent over by the Surrey cricketers.

'No, I'm good,' said Daisy, raising her cocktail to the players with enthusiasm. 'That hits the spot!' she shouted in my ear. 'A dirty martini. Why don't you have one?'

I looked at the oily liquid sloshing around her glass with a battered-looking tinned olive.

'I think I'll stick to this,' I told her, lifting my own drink. 'Better the devil you know.'

She found this hilariously funny and repeated it several times to John Franklin and Felicity. Mr Franklin smiled the first time, but Felicity just looked confused, which may have been why Daisy felt the need to repeat my supposed witticism.

'Deaf as a post!' she yelled in my ear. 'Needs to get out of the sick-room and onto the dance floor. Don'tcha think?'

To my relief, one of the cricketers came and whisked Daisy away to dance. She clung to him far too closely, sticking her elbows out at exaggerated angles and gazing into his eyes. He looked as if he was trying not to laugh. I caught a glimpse of the rest of the fellows on his table, who were watching with unrestrained amusement. Oh dear, I thought. Poor Daisy.

'Do you like the music?' I asked Felicity, hoping to distract her attention from the exhibition her cousin was making of herself.

Felicity was trying to tap her feet in time, but kept missing the beat. 'It's lovely,' she said politely. 'Is that your friend playing piano?'

'That's him,' I said. Freddie was whooping it up, reaching from one end of the keyboard to the other with a big grin, perspiration shining on his face. I smiled fondly, but realised he didn't look like a particularly respectable sort of friend for a young woman to have.

I was trying to think of a way to continue the conversation when another of the cricketers – one I recognised from the cigarette cards that my brother used to collect – walked over and bowed.

'Excuse me, Miss. Would you care to dance?'

I hesitated, then saw John Franklin had got to his feet and was holding out his hand to Felicity. She looked both terrified and delighted. Maybe it would do her good to dance. I thanked the man and let him lead me onto the dance floor.

'Your friend over there is a bit of a live wire,' he said, by way of introduction.

'She's very keen on jazz,' I said, diplomatically. 'How about you?'

'It's all fun, isn't it? You've got to enjoy yourself.' Something about his tone told me that he wasn't enjoying himself that much, really. He looked to be about the age my brother James would have been, had he not been killed at the Front. I wondered where he'd seen service.

'I always try to,' I told him, a little more gently. 'But one doesn't always feel like it, of course.'

He regarded me for a moment with a grave look of understanding. 'I should have introduced myself properly. I'm Wilders, Geoffrey Wilders. And you?'

'I know. I'm Marjorie Swallow. I've seen you play at The Oval,' I told him. My old school friend Evelyn was very keen on cricket, and we had watched several county matches together before she went off to Cambridge University.

'Have you, now? I hope I put on a decent show.'

We concentrated on dancing after that, fox-trotting quite companionably. I caught glimpses of Daisy, trying to chivvy her partner into a new dance that involved kicking up the legs from the knees and swinging the arms. At one point I saw him grimace as she stepped back firmly onto his foot.

John Franklin was steering Felicity around the floor as carefully as if she was an invalid. She hadn't been being modest about her dancing – she seemed to lack all natural rhythm. I wondered if she was enjoying herself. Then I caught a glimpse of her face, lit up with a radiance that had been entirely absent so far. Good, I thought. All she needed was a handsome chap to take a bit of notice of her.

My cricketer delivered me back to the table at the end of the dance, just as Daisy arrived on the arm of hers.

'Say, we've got half the team here!' she said, laughing. 'Maybe you fellows could make us cheer-leaders.'

The men exchanged baffled looks. 'I don't think they have those for cricket,' I told Daisy. 'But it's a nice idea.'

She gasped and clutched my arm. 'Look! It's Lucky Li! I must go and say hello.'

She charged across the dance floor to a table in a corner where a man in evening dress sat alone, smoking a cigar. He was Chinese, his shiny black hair brushed straight back from his forehead, a gentle look of amusement on his face. He stood as Daisy approached and took her hand, bowing low over it. At least he had manners. She sat and gabbled away. His polite smile stayed in place.

The dance number came to an end, and the clarinet player took the microphone. 'Thank you very much, ladies and gentlemen. We're the All Stars Jazz Orchestra, and we're here all night. But we're going to take a little break. Don't go away!'

Freddie closed the piano, grabbed a beer from a passing waiter and made a bee-line for our table.

'Nurse Swallow! You're looking very spiffy. What happened to your hair?' He was pink in the face from exertion, his sandy forelock falling into his eyes. 'Can I sit with you?'

'Of course. But don't call me that. And my hair has been styled in the latest fashion at Liberty's emporium, I'll have you know. Unlike yours, which is all over the place.'

We grinned at each other. We'd met years ago, when I was nursing with the VAD at the Maudsley Hospital in south London and he was a neurasthenia patient in a rather bad way. He was much improved since getting his job with the jazz orchestra. We'd met again the previous year and he'd called for me enough times on a Sunday afternoon for my mother to ask if there was anything she should know. I liked Freddie a lot.

'You look perfectly splendid, Marjorie. I'm so glad you came. I think it's going well tonight, don't you?'

John Franklin and Felicity arrived back at the table, and I introduced them. Felicity's cheeks were flushed pink, her eyes were sparkling, and she looked quite pretty. She just needs some properly cut clothes and a good hairdresser, I thought. And an intensive course of dancing lessons.

Mr Franklin hailed a waiter to refill Freddie's glass and bring

Felicity another lemonade.

'What about you, Miss Swallow? Can I get you another of those French things?' he asked.

I shook my head. 'I'll have lemonade, too.' I knew my limits and was mindful of the fact I was on duty.

'Where's Daisy gone?' asked Felicity, glancing around.

I swivelled my head. The Chinese gentleman was sitting on his own. 'She went to talk to someone. But she's not there now. Maybe she's in the cloakroom.' She seemed to have been gone quite a long time. 'Perhaps I'll go and see,' I said.

Chapter 6

The ladies' powder room was tastefully appointed in pink and gilt. Young women perched on pink velvet stools facing big mirrors lit up by electric bulbs, fixing their maquillage or tidying their hair. None of them was wearing canary yellow or had bright ginger hair.

A maid in a ribboned Columbine dress sat behind a counter on which were all manner of aids to modern living – hair brushes, safety pins, bottles of scent, handkerchiefs and sewing kits. I took a seat on one of the stools, re-applied my pink lip tint and waited for Daisy.

I didn't have to wait long. She emerged from behind the swing doors at the end of the powder room, pink-cheeked and fanning herself with her hand.

'Say, it's hot in here. I need another of those martinis. With ice, this time. More giggle juice, what do you say?' She sneezed three times in swift succession and buried her nose in her pocket handkerchief.

'Let me just sit down for a minute. My hair's got all mussed up,' she said.

I waited while she titivated her curls.

'Who was that man you went to say hello to? The Chinese man in the corner,' I asked.

28

'What? Oh, you mean Lucky Li. Don't you know him? He's an absolute darling. His name's Li Chang Taio or Dao or something, but everyone calls him Lucky. He owns this place, and I don't know how many other places besides.'

Daisy searched through her yellow velvet bag for lipstick. She pulled everything out, including a gold-coloured hinged box about the size of a powder compact, with a scallop shell design engraved on it. Was this the box that Felicity had told her father about?

'Lucky's got a restaurant down on Piccadilly where they have the most divine Chinese food. The Lucky Lotus. Did you ever eat Chinese? Say, you've got to try it. Tell 'em you like it hot. You do, don'tcha?'

I smiled politely and said I did indeed.

'Atta girl. Now, how do I look?'

Her face looked hectic, the colour high and her eyes enormous and glittering. I got the feeling that she wasn't just on the giggle juice.

'You look fine,' I said. Then I had an idea. 'Say, Daisy, I've come out without my powder compact, and my nose is all shiny. Do you mind if I use yours?' I indicated the little gold box.

She whooped. 'I knew it! You might look all serious, but I knew you were up for a good time, the minute I saw you. Go on, take it. Have a quick toot.'

I locked the lavatory door, sat on the closed lid, and carefully prised the top off the little round box. My ruse had worked better than I'd expected. The box was half full of a crystalline white powder, glittering in the light. I scooped out a little with a small paper envelope, which I sealed and tucked away in my handbag. Mrs Jameson had impressed upon me the need to carry these envelopes for collecting evidence everywhere we went.

I'll admit, I was quite tempted to give it a try. How dangerous could it be, if Daisy took it so casually and until a few years ago, you could buy it for toothache? But I was on duty, and I'd already found out more than enough. Besides, who knew what effect it might have on me? I decided not to take the risk.

I wondered if I should ask Daisy outright where she got it from. But, given that she'd talked to the mysterious Mr Li just moments before disappearing to the ladies' room, I thought I had a shrewd idea.

Daisy and I headed back to our table arm in arm, bosom friends now that she thought me a fellow dope fiend. Freddie was on his feet, T-bone next to him.

'Well, hello, boys,' trilled Daisy. 'Have you come to visit?'

'I came to see Marjorie,' said Freddie. 'But then she disappeared.' He looked a bit put out.

T-bone grinned. 'Very lovely to see you again, Miss Swallow, Miss Caldwell. I hope you'll be doing us the honour of dancing again tonight?'

Daisy squealed and clutched his arm. 'You bet! Say, Tommy. Do you know how to dance the Charleston? Did they have it in New York when you were last in town?'

'Nope, don't know that one, Miss Caldwell. Maybe you should teach it to us,' said T-bone, straight-faced. I wasn't sure if he was teasing her. I'd heard of the scandalous new dance myself, although I'd never seen it done. But I was pretty sure T-bone and the band would keep up with all the latest trends.

'You bet I will! I'll need you to play rag-time in four/four time, nice and quick. Marjorie, you'd better come with me.'

To my alarm, she grabbed my arm and dragged me to the

dance floor.

'Don't worry, you'll pick it up. No partner required – just follow my lead. Turn your toes out and your knees in. Say, this is fun!'

Which was how I found myself dancing the first-ever Charleston to be performed in London, to the amazement of minor royalty, the American ambassador's daughter, the All Stars Jazz Orchestra, and half of the Surrey cricket team. Half-way through, I looked up, mortified, to see Mr Li watching with his expression of detached amusement, beating time in the air with his cigar.

Chapter 7

Mrs Jameson took the news of Daisy's little powder compact more seriously than I'd expected. She'd tasted a tiny dab of the powder on her tongue and confirmed that it was cocaine. I told her my suspicions about Mr 'Lucky' Li and Daisy's disappearance to the ladies' cloakroom shortly after talking to him.

'But you can't be sure the drug came from him,' she said, as we reviewed the situation before lunch. We were in the detective agency office: a large, bright room with long windows onto Bedford Square. She sat at a pretty rosewood bureau with a green leather blotter, while my more utilitarian desk was topped with an Olivetti typewriter and stacked with correspondence. I stifled a yawn. My late night escapades had worn me out.

'No, but it seems quite likely,' I protested.

'Why? Because he's Chinese? Really, Marjorie. I'd expected better of you.' Mrs Jameson capped her pen, set it down and frowned at me. 'It is very lazy thinking to assume a man is guilty of a crime because that crime has been linked to his countrymen. It's not even logical. Mr Li owns profitable restaurants, nightclubs and bars all over the West End. Trafficking in illegal drugs on the premises would risk closure, fines, and imprisonment. If he wanted to supply cocaine, he'd be better off opening a chemist shop.'

I was abashed. I supposed I associated Chinese men with Limehouse opium dens, exotic and dangerous places where English girls languished on couches, drugged into oblivion, before being kidnapped for the white slave trade. Scenes, I admitted, that owed more to detective novels and sensational movies than reality.

'You're right. I'm sorry.' But the thought of Mr Li, his amusement as Daisy and I danced the Charleston, still made me shiver a little.

'My main concern is what to do with this information,' said Mrs Jameson, pensively. 'Henry will be in an invidious position, knowing that someone in his household is in possession of illegal drugs. The house is officially United States territory, and the ambassador's household has diplomatic immunity from prosecution. But if it came out, it would cause a terrific scandal. The United States pushed hard for cocaine to be included in the international regulations for dangerous drugs. It would be more than unfortunate if cocaine was found inside the American ambassador's London residence.'

Uncharacteristically, she put off making a decision. 'Let's have lunch. I can't think properly on an empty stomach,' she announced.

We had a light lunch during the week. Today was just oxtail soup followed by poached salmon. Mrs Jameson had announced no more pudding on working days, after discovering she had gained five pounds while staying at The Ritz.

I was enjoying the last of the hollandaise sauce on my potatoes when Graham entered, looking grave.

'Mrs Jameson, Ambassador Caldwell is on the telephone. It seems to be rather urgent.'

She rose at once and followed him. I hovered by the door to the office, until she beckoned me in.

'Henry, I am so sorry. How terrible for you. Yes, of course. Right away. Have you called the police?'

She listened a moment longer, then replaced the receiver and turned to me, her grey eyes sombre.

'We're to go to Prince's Gate at once,' she said. 'Daisy Caldwell is dead.'

Chapter 8

The footman opened the door. Immediately, John Franklin came through from the study, his face white.

'Ambassador Caldwell is making a telephone call. Will you wait in the drawing room, Mrs Jameson?'

His manner was distracted; his eyes slid over me as if I wasn't there. I felt awkward, conscious that the last time I had seen him, I'd been making an exhibition of myself on the dance floor with poor Daisy. Our jolly night out had come to a desperately sad conclusion.

We went through to the drawing room where I'd first met the family only two days before. The hearth needed sweeping, the roses in their heavy crystal vase were drooping and abandoned tea cups sat on the gilt side table. The room spoke of the household's shock, and indeed, I was struggling to believe that Daisy would not come breezing down the stairs wearing one of her startling outfits. It seemed impossible that such a force of nature could be truly dead.

Mrs Jameson took an upright chair by the window and beckoned Mr Franklin to join her.

'Please, sit down and tell me what has happened. Mr Caldwell has asked me to help.'

I took out my notebook and pen. Mr Franklin sat, smoothing down his unusually dishevelled hair.

'I'll do my best, ma'am. It's all rather ghastly. I just wish I'd been able to shield poor Felicity from the worst of it. Miss Caldwell, I mean.'

'How is Felicity?' asked Mrs Jameson. 'She must be very upset.'

He nodded. 'Hell of a thing. She found the... she found her.'

'Felicity found Daisy's body?'

He nodded. "Fraid so. She's with Mrs Caldwell and the doctor. He was going to give her something for the shock. Calm her nerves a bit.'

'The doctor's here now?'

'Dr Spink, who attends Mrs Caldwell, was visiting when... when it happened. He did what he could, of course. But in his opinion, she had been dead for several hours.'

Mrs Jameson leaned forward and tapped his knee. 'Mr Franklin, it would be most useful if you would outline the events in order from when you arrived home from the Harlequin club last night. Which would have been shortly after midnight, I think?'

He exhaled and stared at the floor for a minute, then examined his perfect fingernails. This seemed to encourage him, and he straightened his back.

'Yes. Right. Well, like you said, I got back with the girls – Miss Daisy and Miss Felicity – at about ten past midnight. Miss Felicity went straight up to bed. I don't think she's used to late nights.'

'And Daisy?'

'The ambassador's light was still on in his study. I went to see if he wanted any help. We've been working on the Allied debt repayment schedule, and he had a lot of work to prepare for a meeting with the Foreign Office...' he paused and realised, '...today. The meeting is this afternoon. I'll have to cancel.

'He said no, he was just finishing up and was about to have a nightcap. He asked if I wanted to join him. Well, of course, then Daisy had to have one too. So, the three of us sat in his study for about half an hour, drinking whiskey and soda, although honestly I thought she had already had enough liquor for one night.'

He looked up and caught my eye, then looked quickly away. 'I don't mean to speak ill of her, Mrs Jameson. But it was getting late. Anyway, the ambassador went to bed, and I followed not long after. Miss Daisy didn't make an appearance over breakfast, but that wasn't unusual. She often sleeps in until midday or later. Henry and I worked all morning. We often work from the residence. He says he thinks better in his study than at the embassy with lots of people around. At lunchtime, when Daisy hadn't appeared, Miss Felicity offered to go and wake her.'

He sat back, shook his head. 'I've never heard a scream like it. Fit to wake the dead.' He winced, realising his inappropriate phrase. 'Sorry. We all charged up the stairs, and Felicity was standing at the end of the bed, just in pieces. Daisy was lying on her back. There was a gold box open on her bedside table, with white powder in it.'

'Oh!' I exclaimed.

Mr Franklin turned to stare at me.

'Miss Swallow has seen that box before,' said Mrs Jameson. 'But please carry on, Mr Franklin.'

He gave me a wary look. 'Mr Caldwell told the maid to telephone for a doctor at once. Then Felicity said Dr Spink was already with her mother, so I ran to get him. He tried to awaken Daisy, checked her over and pronounced her dead. He says it was a cocaine overdose.' Mr Franklin shrugged helplessly. 'That's about it.'

The door opened and Ambassador Caldwell walked slowly towards us. He looked grey from head to toe, and about a hundred years old. Mr Franklin jumped to his feet solicitously.

'Henry.' Mrs Jameson rose and took the ambassador's hands.

He disengaged himself and sat heavily in the chair Mr Franklin had just vacated.

'I've asked the embassy to wire my brother,' he said. 'I need to write to him.' He looked up, his eyes hollow. 'What on earth am I going to say? He entrusted her to me. His little girl. And now this.'

'It's ghastly, Henry. I'm so sorry. I promise you I will do whatever is in my power to help you.'

'I know you will.'

She hesitated. 'The question is, what do you want me to do? When we spoke on Tuesday, you had a specific request for information. I have that information, but the situation has changed. Henry, do you want me to investigate Daisy's death?'

'Yes, of course I do.'

'Are you sure?' Mrs Jameson's voice was steady. Her question seemed to hold some special message for him, but I couldn't tell what.

Ambassador Caldwell looked puzzled. 'That's what you do, isn't it? I want to know who gave her that dope. Who is responsible. And for them to be brought to justice.'

'Ah.' Mrs Jameson patted his knee. 'I cannot promise you justice, Henry. I will investigate, and I will tell you what I discover. But I warn you, that may not be comfortable information.'

He shook his head, slow and weary. 'An innocent girl is dead. There's no comfort to be had anywhere but the truth.'

Chapter 9

John Franklin accompanied us to the door of Daisy's bedroom. It was on the second floor, at the back of the house.

'Mr Caldwell asked me to lock it after the doctor had finished,' he said. 'This is pretty much how we found the room.' He took a key from his pocket, turned it in the lock and opened the door.

'Thank you, Mr Franklin.' Mrs Jameson paused. 'Where did that key come from?'

He frowned at it, as if trying to remember. 'It was on the inside of the door. She'd locked it. We went in through Miss Felicity's room, then I unlocked this door to go and fetch the doctor.'

Mrs Jameson nodded. 'Leave us to it. There's no need for you to stay.'

Daisy's room, like Daisy's life, was colourful and chaotic. Someone had pulled back the pink curtains and the drab January light filtered into the room. The spangled yellow frock of the night before lay crumpled on the white fur rug beside her bed. Her white stockings were beside it, the yellow and black shoes kicked over towards the dressing table. The table itself was crowded with an array of bottles and pots of face cream, brushes choked with hair, strings of pearls and brooches spilling out of jewel boxes.

On the baby-blue satin eiderdown in the middle of it all, Daisy's ginger curls shone brightly. She was lying on her back, one arm flung out, her cold bare feet sticking out of the end of a pink feather-trimmed peignoir. She wore pink and yellow striped pyjamas beneath her robe. Fleetingly, I wondered why a girl with forcefully ginger colouring would make those her signature colours.

I'd heard somewhere that people looked peaceful in death. Not Daisy. No more peaceful in death than in life; her pretty face wore an expression of complete surprise. Death, it seemed, had crept up on her unawares.

The connecting door to Felicity's bedroom stood ajar, giving a glimpse of a neat, simple room kept in good order. Mrs Jameson stepped over the discarded clothes to the door and closed it, then returned to the bedside. Delicately she put a hand to Daisy's face and carefully raised one eyelid. She frowned, checked the other eye, then gently lifted and dropped her outstretched hand.

'Marjorie, make a note. The time is two fifteen in the afternoon. The body is cold, the limbs not yet stiffened. Her finger and toenails have a blue tinge. The pupils of the eyes are dilated. Although the bedclothes are disarranged, there is no sign of thrashing about, convulsions or anything of that sort.'

She turned to the gold box on the bedside table and tasted a crystal or two on her little finger. 'The box contains cocaine, as did the box you took the sample from last night. Come and look. Is this the same box? And how much was there in it when you saw it last?'

I tiptoed over to the bed. Taking white cotton gloves from

my handbag, as Mrs Jameson had taught me, I picked up the gold box by the edges and closed it. It had a familiar scallop shell design on the lid.

'It looks the same,' I said. I opened it again. 'There's about half of what was in the box when I saw it last night. So, I suppose she must have used it again.'

'Make a note of that. I estimate the box contains less than one-tenth of an ounce. We will ask Henry to weigh it, if he has scales that will accommodate such small quantities. Now, we need to take an inventory of the room.' She pulled on her own pair of gloves.

I looked around in dismay. Listing all the articles in Daisy's untidy bedroom would take ages. But Mrs Jameson had been insistent that I learn her system of noticing and recording everything about a crime scene – if indeed this was a crime scene. From what I could see, everything suggested an unfortunate overdose of cocaine.

We moved around the room together, Mrs Jameson pointing out objects for me to write down. Pretty lace-trimmed undergarments lay where they had been kicked under the bed, gathering dust. Underneath them were the curling irons that the maid had been unable to find on Tuesday. A pile of paper-backed books teetered beside the wardrobe. I recognised a few of my own favourites: detective novels from Arthur Conan Doyle and the latest Agatha Christie. Mrs Jameson sorted through the wastepaper basket, pulling out used cotton-wool pads, a bottle of eye drops and various scrunched-up papers.

'Put them in your bag, Marjorie. There may be something of use in them,' said Mrs Jameson. Gingerly, I did so. It felt wrong, to be removing the dead girl's letters with her body lying cold in the room with us.

Most poignant of all was a big floppy Pierrot doll lying on a cushion in the corner of the room. It was dressed in loose white silk pyjamas with black pom-poms and a black skull cap, a tear-drop painted on its white porcelain face. It reminded me of the hostesses in their costumes at the Harlequin. Daisy may have cultivated the image of a sophisticated flapper, but she was not too old to have cherished a doll.

Mrs Jameson paused before the dressing table, going through the bottles of scent and cosmetics. I saw the yellow velvet bag Daisy had carried the previous night. She appeared to have turned it upside down on the glass-topped table on her arrival home, spilling out the contents. I noted down the pink lipstick, coin-purse, nail file and scent bottle.

Mrs Jameson picked up the bottle. 'Guerlain's Mitsouko,' she commented, sniffing it and holding it up to the light. 'Empty. But she hasn't thrown it away.'

I pointed to various other empty or half-empty jars and bottles on the table. 'I don't think she's very good at tidying up,' I said.

'Indeed not,' said Mrs Jameson, thoughtfully.

The door was flung open. A middle-aged man with a bald head and a fierce expression stood in the doorway.

'What the blazes are you doing?' he asked.

Mrs Jameson drew herself up to her full height, which was half an inch taller than him.

'I am investigating the scene of this crime, on behalf of Ambassador Caldwell. And you?'

'Nonsense. There's no crime,' he said. 'I don't know who you are, but I don't like people taking advantage of a newly bereaved family.'

'Are you the doctor?' I asked, noting his bag.

'I am Dr Spink, the family physician. And who are you, young lady?'

'Ah, Dr Spink, that's splendid. I wanted to ask you some questions,' said Mrs Jameson. 'I am Mrs Jameson, private detective, and this is my assistant Miss Swallow. Now, tell me what you moved when you were called into the room. Was Miss Caldwell in exactly this position on the bed?'

'I most certainly will not,' Dr Spink exploded. 'This unfortunate young woman has indulged in the dangerous practice of cocaine sniffing. It's a great pity, but that's what happens when the fairer sex is allowed to roam wild, meeting unsuitable people and going to dances unchaperoned, when they should be kept at home with their mothers,' he continued, slightly incoherently. I could see he and Mrs Jameson were not going to get along.

Chapter 10

We were rescued by Mr Franklin, who asked if we were finished and would like to join the family downstairs in the drawing room. It was unclear whether the invitation included Dr Spink, but he came anyway in his self-appointed role as protector of the Caldwell family.

Mrs Caldwell was seated on a chaise longue near the fire with a fur rug tucked around her legs. This was my first sight of the invalid. Her face was thin and drawn, and her dark grey hair was braided down her back in a style that reminded me of her daughter. She was wrapped in an Indian cashmere shawl, plaiting the fringe with her nervous fingers.

'Hello, Myrtle. What a dreadful business.' Mrs Jameson bent to embrace her friend. They were about the same age, she'd told me, but Mrs Caldwell looked far older than her fifty years.

'I know… that poor, foolish girl,' murmured Mrs Caldwell. 'And Henry feels wretched, of course.'

Ambassador Caldwell stood by the windows, looking out onto the dull January garden. He barely seemed aware of our entry.

'You should be in bed, Mrs Caldwell,' said Dr Spink, reprovingly. 'As should your daughter.'

Felicity looked up from the armchair beside her mother,

where she was sipping from a cup of what looked like Horlicks. 'I'm all right,' she said. 'Thank you, Dr Spink. I feel much better now. And Mamma wanted to come downstairs to see Papa.'

'Hello, Felicity. I'm so sorry about Daisy,' I said.

'It was a horrible shock,' she said. 'Poor Daisy. I can't believe it. I just wish I'd told Papa sooner. Maybe we could have stopped her from taking that horrible stuff.'

Her eyelids were pink, and she looked tired, but she was composed.

Mrs Jameson took the seat next to her. 'How do you mean, Felicity? What did you know about what she was taking?'

Felicity set down the cup and looked up, anxious. 'I don't like to tell tales. But I don't suppose it matters now. I went into her room after breakfast a couple of weeks ago – she'd asked to borrow a book – and she was sniffing up powder from that little gold box she had. She got flustered when she saw me and sneezed five times, then said it was medicine for her sinuses. But I hadn't heard of any such thing, so I asked Papa. He didn't tell me, but it was cocaine, wasn't it?' She shuddered. 'I've read about it in the newspapers.'

'So, you think she took cocaine last night?' asked Mrs Jameson, gently. 'From the box that was in her room?'

'I suppose so,' said Felicity. 'When… when I went in, I saw it by her bed. It was the same box that I'd seen before. And Dr Spink tasted some and said it was cocaine.'

Mrs Jameson nodded. 'I see. Felicity, my dear, would you mind very much telling me what happened? I know you won't want to dwell on it. But if you could just run through what happened, to the best of your memory, since you got home last night?'

'Really, I don't think that is appropriate…' Dr Spink barged in. Finally, Henry Caldwell left off his contemplation of the gardens and strode to his daughter's side.

'Doctor, I've asked Mrs Jameson to investigate Daisy's death. I would be grateful if you – and everyone in the household – would offer her every assistance.'

He turned his gaze to his daughter, while Dr Spink fumed.

'Felicity, if you're feeling well enough?'

The girl looked up at her father, her eyes anxious. 'All right. I'll do my best. I want to help, Papa. It's just so horrible to think about.'

She folded her hands in her lap. 'We got home after midnight, I suppose. I don't usually stay up that late. I was terribly tired, so I checked on Mamma then went straight up to bed. Harriet, my maid, helped me undress and I fell asleep almost immediately.

'I woke up at nine, but I was very sleepy. So, I was still in bed when Harriet brought in my tea. She was brushing out my hair when we heard Daisy snoring through the door.'

'What time was this?' asked Mrs Jameson, sharply. I sat up with my pen poised.

'Harriet usually comes in at nine. But this morning it was more like half-past, I think. I suppose she let me sleep in. I… I made a joke about Daisy's snoring, because it was really quite loud.' She looked embarrassed.

'Harriet asked if she should go through and wake her. She does for Daisy as well as me, you see. I said to let her sleep.' She looked at Mrs Jameson, and tears welled in her eyes. 'I should have woken her, shouldn't I?'

Mrs Jameson patted her shoulder. 'You weren't to know, Felicity. Go on. What happened next?'

'Well, I dressed and went down to breakfast. There wasn't

anyone around. Then I went in to see Mamma and be sure she had everything she needed. Her head was bad, and she asked me to call Dr Spink to see if he could come by. So, I did that, then got on with various things. I'm trying to learn French, and I was reading a novel by Mr Proust. But I kept getting in a muddle with it. I'm not much good at languages. Eventually I heard the doctor's voice in the hall, so I took him up to Mamma. And then Papa came out of his study with Mr Franklin and wanted to know if Daisy and I were joining them for luncheon. That was when I realised how late it was, and that Daisy still wasn't down. I said I'd go to see if she wanted to eat with us.'

She paused and looked up at her audience. 'Must I go on?'

'You're doing splendidly, Felicity,' said Mrs Jameson. 'What time was this, Henry?'

'Just after one,' he said, shortly. 'Franklin and I had been working all morning. There's an important...' he gasped. 'We have to call the Foreign Office. The meeting...'

Mr Franklin placed a reassuring hand on his arm. 'I've already made our excuses. A family emergency. I said we would call to rearrange in the morning.'

Mr Caldwell nodded. 'Good man. Thank you.' His voice was brusque.

'Now, Felicity,' said Mrs Jameson. 'Tell us the rest, if you would.'

The girl looked up at Mr Franklin, her eyes shining with tears. 'It's so awful. I hardly dare say it.'

'Just tell them what you saw,' said Mr Franklin, his voice coaxing. 'You're being very brave.'

She seemed to gain strength from his encouragement and took a deep breath.

'I couldn't hear snoring, or anything else. I knocked, of course, but there was no answer. Her door was locked. She... she's been keeping it locked, since I interrupted her with the powder. But we both have a key to the door between our rooms, so I unlocked it, opened the door a crack, and called her name. Again, nothing. I went through.'

She paused and looked down at her hands. Her voice was very quiet.

'At first, I thought she was asleep, but she didn't stir when I called her. And then I went over and saw that her face was quite white. It was scary. I saw the box of powder on her bedside table. I called her again, then shook her by the shoulder. And – oh! It was horrible. Her arm was quite cold and her head sort of flopped around on her neck. I suppose that's when I screamed.'

She took a long, shuddering breath. 'Mr Franklin came running in, followed by Papa and Harriet. Papa shouted about getting a doctor, and I remembered that Dr Spink was already here with Mamma. So, Mr Franklin went to get him, and then... and then...' She put her face in her hands and began to sob.

'There, I said Miss Caldwell should not be up,' said Dr Spink, jumping to his feet. 'Are you satisfied now, Mrs Jameson? This poor child should be distracted from her dreadful experience, not required to repeat it.'

'I'm very sorry, Felicity. But well done. Thank you for helping me,' said Mrs Jameson, ignoring the doctor. 'One more question, please. Where did you keep your key to the door between your rooms?'

'Mine is kept in my bedside drawer.'

'And did anyone else know where it was?'

49

Felicity bit her lip. 'Well, Daisy knew. And Harriet, of course. It was easier for her to go between our rooms than around, so I told her to use it when she needed to.'

'Thank you. That's all. Do you want to go up to your room now?' asked Mrs Jameson.

Felicity looked up at us, her face white and frightened. 'How can I go back to my room, when I know that she is just the other side of the door?'

'Go to my room,' said Mrs Caldwell. 'Dr Spink, will you take her up? Have a lie down, dear. You've been very courageous.'

The doctor took poor Felicity by the arm and steered her out of the room, throwing reproachful glances at me and Mrs Jameson all the way to the door.

Chapter 11

Before we could go any further, there was a loud rapping on the front door. After a moment, the butler appeared, looking grave.

'Two gentlemen from the Metropolitan Police have arrived to see you, Ambassador.'

The ambassador looked startled for a moment.

'I called them,' Mr Franklin said. 'At your request, Sir?'

'Of course. Yes. You'd better show them in, I suppose.'

Two uniformed officers appeared, one young and the other a solid-looking veteran of the streets. The young man seemed rather over-awed by his surroundings, but the elder was determined not to be impressed by the residence's grand rooms. He knew, I supposed, that he was only allowed on the premises at the ambassador's invitation, and perhaps resented the curtailment of his usual powers.

'I'm Sergeant Borden, Mr Caldwell, and this is Constable Lloyd. We have received a report of a suspicious death on the premises. Will you be so good as to explain, and show us the evidence?'

'It's not suspicious,' said Dr Spink, reappearing at the door. 'I've already told the ambassador. His niece has died from an overdose of cocaine. The question for you fellows is, where did she get it? Hey?'

Sergeant Borden regarded him phlegmatically for a moment. 'With all due respect…' I've noticed that whenever people begin a sentence like that, whatever comes next has little respect in it, '…I will be asking the questions,' he concluded. 'Mr Caldwell, can you tell me what has happened here?'

The ambassador and Mr Franklin filled the policemen in on the events of the morning.

'I will inspect the unfortunate young lady,' announced Sergeant Borden. 'You say there is a box containing the drug? With your permission, Mr Caldwell, we will remove it and have the powder analysed.'

'Better fingerprint it, too,' said Constable Lloyd, showing the first signs of animation. 'And the unfortunate lady, to eliminate her prints.' He was clearly keen to exhibit his knowledge of modern forensic procedures.

Oh, goodness. An unpleasant thought occurred to me. I looked at Mrs Jameson, but she was sitting by Mrs Caldwell, quietly holding her hand. The ambassador's wife looked quite faint at the intrusion of the police into their well-regulated lives.

'Um… you had better take my fingerprints, too,' I said. 'I handled the box last night. Miss Caldwell showed it to me. My prints will be all over it, as well as hers.'

Sergeant Borden turned slowly to look me up and down. 'Thank you, Miss…'

'Swallow. Marjorie Swallow,' I said. Constable Lloyd wrote down my name in his notebook. 'We were all out at the Harlequin last night,' I continued. 'Miss Daisy Caldwell, Mr Franklin, Miss Felicity Caldwell and me.'

Sergeant Borden's eyebrows rose slightly. 'That nightclub

owned by the Chinaman?' he asked. 'Lucky Li, or whatever he calls himself. Did you see the fellow?'

I nodded. 'Mr Li. Yes, he was there.' I glanced at Mrs Jameson, but her face was a bland mask. 'Daisy talked to him for a while. Then I followed her to the ladies' cloakroom. That's when she showed me the box.'

'And did this box contain cocaine at the time you saw it?' he asked.

I nodded, nervously. 'Yes. That is, it contained white powder.'

'And did you take any yourself?' The sergeant's voice was stern. I swallowed hard.

'Well – not like you mean. But yes, I took a tiny bit.'

Mr and Mrs Caldwell looked beyond shocked, and John Franklin stared at me with frank disgust. They all started to talk at once, Dr Spink adding his outrage from the door. I sensed that Sergeant Borden was readying himself to whip out the handcuffs and march me off to jail. Thankfully, my employer's clear voice cut through the babble.

'Miss Swallow abstracted some of the powder at my request,' said Mrs Jameson, coming to my rescue at last. 'I am a private investigator. Mr Caldwell had asked me to look into whether his niece was taking cocaine. Marjorie went to the nightclub with the Caldwell party as my employee, with the intention of finding out. When Daisy showed her the box, she very resourcefully put a small sample in an envelope and brought it to me to be analysed. I sent it to the laboratory at Scotland Yard this morning.'

I breathed again.

'And I suppose Scotland Yard will confirm this story?' asked Sergeant Borden, sounding rather disappointed.

'They will. Ask for Inspector Peter Chadwick. And, of course, it is sensible to take Marjorie's fingerprints so they can be eliminated, along with those of the deceased.'

The footman led Constable Lloyd and me through to the kitchen to carry out this rather messy procedure. I'd never seen it done before, so I was most interested. Constable Lloyd firmly grasped each of my fingers in turn, rolled them on an ink pad, and then on a sheet of paper marked out for the purpose, which he'd extracted from his pocket book.

'Are you really a private detective?' he asked. 'Like in the Sherlock Holmes stories?'

I forced a smile. 'Mrs Jameson is the detective,' I said. 'I'm just her assistant. But she's very clever. She'll find out where that cocaine came from, I bet.'

Constable Lloyd waited as I attempted to scrub off the ink. 'The sergeant won't like it. Borden says women have no place in the criminal justice system, unless they are a victim, a witness, or a crook. He took on something terrible when they introduced policewomen during the War.'

He should get on well with Dr Spink, I reflected. Of all the horrors inflicted by the War, some men seemed to think that the introduction of women into the workplace was the worst.

'Oh! Sorry to disturb, Miss.' The pretty young maid I'd noticed on our first visit stopped in the doorway. The footman, standing like a sentinel at the side of the door, jumped as if he'd been electrocuted. A deep flush rose from his neck, covering his freckled face. She frowned at him. 'What are you gawping at, Thomas?'

He looked at the floor.

'Nothing to worry about,' I said. 'We're finished now.' I thought for a moment. 'Are you Harriet?'

'That's me, Miss.' She really was remarkably pretty; her pink cheeks the exact colour of a wild rose and her glossy brown curls escaping from under her cap in a most becoming way. Her hazel eyes were large and fringed with long dark lashes. I could see why the footman was so overcome.

'So, you were Daisy's maid, as well as Felicity's? It must have been a shock for you.'

'Yes, Miss. Nasty business,' she said.

'Mrs Jameson, my employer, may wish to speak to you about it. Is that all right?' Mrs Jameson said it was always a good idea to interview domestic staff during an investigation. There was little they didn't know about their employers.

'Of course, Miss. But I didn't see Miss Daisy until after Miss Felicity found her this morning,' she said.

'You didn't help her undress last night, or take in tea this morning?'

She shook her pretty head. 'She was very late turning in last night. She'd told me before not to wait up for her. I went to my bed after seeing to Miss Felicity and slept like a log all night. And I knew Miss Daisy would want to sleep late. I heard her snoring when I was doing for Miss Felicity,' she said. 'Very loud, it was.'

There was nothing exactly wrong with the girl's words, but I knew what my mother would have said. Harriet was pert. I thanked her, filing the knowledge away.

She whisked away, smiling. The footman watched her retreating back. His gormless expression had changed into a puzzled frown. For a second, he looked as if he would speak, but settled his features back into a professional blank.

Back in the drawing room, Ambassador Caldwell had recovered his powers of speech and was using them to the full.

'I thought London would be a safer place for my niece than Manhattan. But it turns out that London is nothing but a cesspit of vice, unsafe for innocent young girls.' He was almost shouting at Sergeant Borden. 'I demand you investigate this Li fellow. I want that nightclub closed down. I want the whole rotten trade in dope finished. If the London police allow these drugs dens to flourish, they are personally responsible for each and every tragic death that ensues. Do you understand?'

'Henry, dear…' Mrs Caldwell's voice was pleading. 'You'll make yourself ill.'

Sergeant Borden quivered with suppressed rage. 'As I have said before, Mr Caldwell, I am asking the questions. Now, if you have finished, I would like to inspect the deceased.'

The indispensable Mr Franklin took the police officers to view Daisy's bedroom. I saw Dr Spink hesitate between going with them or staying to protect the Caldwell family from further assault by me and Mrs Jameson. Professional pride won out, and he trooped up the stairs with the police.

I perched on the sofa. Ambassador Caldwell had subsided into an armchair beside his wife. Mrs Jameson was sitting on her other side. Although it was not their child that had died, the Caldwells seemed as distraught as any bereaved parents.

'You should have told me.' Ambassador Caldwell gestured towards Mrs Jameson. 'About Daisy's cocaine.'

Mrs Jameson sighed. 'I was going to call you this afternoon. I'd been unsure how to proceed. I knew it would put you in a difficult position. But you're right, I should have called as soon as I knew.'

'It wouldn't have made any difference, I don't suppose,' said the ambassador. 'Spink believes the poor child was already dead by mid-morning.'

Mrs Jameson stared into the fire, her eyes veiled with the deep thought I had come to recognise. 'And yet she was alive at half past nine,' she said. 'If only Felicity or the maid had gone to her then. It might not have been too late.'

'Don't say that.' Mrs Caldwell struggled to sit upright. 'Or at least, don't let Felicity hear you saying so. I won't have her carrying that burden. It was hard enough on the child to have discovered her cousin's body.'

Mrs Jameson nodded her assent.

The ambassador had been sitting with his face in his hands. Now he sat up, and I could see streaks of tears on his cheeks.

'Find them, Iris. Find out who gave Daisy that dope and get me the evidence. I helped you in Rome. We did what was right, remember? I've never had much faith in the police. If the ones here are anything like the cops back home, they're all too happy to look the other way for a dollar bill slipped into their pocket, especially when it comes to dope and licensing laws. Find out who that Chinese fellow is paying off, and we'll bring down the whole rotten system.'

'I will do my best,' she said. 'Now, Henry, if you don't object, I would like to speak to the domestic staff, starting with Daisy and Felicity's maid.'

Chapter 12

Mrs Jameson was in a sombre mood as we returned home. The interview with Harriet had yielded little that the girl had not already told me. She'd been Felicity's maid for over a year, since the family arrived in London, and had been happy to take on Daisy too, when she joined them. Miss Felicity needed little looking after, but Miss Daisy was very particular about her clothes and hair, she'd said, with the hint of a smirk. She said she'd seen Daisy's gold box before, but didn't know what was in it and had never seen her use it. I wondered how true that was. Daisy hadn't exactly been secretive when I asked her about it. And if Harriet knew about the box, did she also know how the cocaine inside it arrived?

For myself, I felt quite lucky not to have been hauled off to the police station for questioning about my handling of illicit drugs. Sergeant Borden had given me a stern lecture about the perils of cocaine before we left. There was no need: I was passionately grateful that I had resisted the temptation to take any of the beastly stuff myself.

'What did you make of Harriet?' I asked, rousing Mrs Jameson from her reverie in the taxi.

'Hmm?' She had been staring out of the window in silence. 'Oh, she's a bit of a minx, isn't she? That poor footman is a fool over her. He's protecting her from something.'

I'd come to the same conclusion myself. Thomas had said he'd gone straight to bed after Mr Franklin and the ladies returned and had seen nothing until Daisy was found at lunchtime. But the flush creeping up his neck had told another story. He'd answered all Mrs Jameson's questions in monosyllables, his eyes on the far wall.

'I think you should try him again, Marjorie. On your own, this time. See what he knows.'

Mrs Jameson relapsed into silence. Not even Graham Hargreaves's announcement of afternoon tea when we got home could cheer her. She left the cake untouched and sipped her tea in silence, staring out of the window as darkness fell over Bedford Square. I nibbled at a scone, thinking it was a shame to let them go to waste, but my heart wasn't in it.

Graham removed the tea trolley with a heavy tread. It wasn't like either of us to pass up a good tea.

'Perhaps I could talk to Freddie Gillespie,' I offered, as much to break the silence as anything. 'The band plays there every week, and they seemed to know Daisy. They might know what's going on in the Harlequin.'

She looked up and gave herself a little shake. 'Yes, why not?' she asked. 'Good idea. Although I have a job for you in the morning. You'll need to go to a pharmacy on Wigmore Street. I'll write the message down for you. Just give it to the chemist and ask him to write the reply. Please don't read it.'

I felt a little affronted that she was keeping something back from me, despite her protestations to Ambassador Caldwell that I was completely trustworthy. But I was her assistant, not her partner. I was wise enough not to think of us as friends. Perhaps it was nothing to do with the case, and she had some embarrassing ailment she didn't want me to know about.

She stood and went to the window. 'You know, Marjorie, I owe almost everything to Henry Caldwell. When we met, it was the worst time in my life. I could have lost everything – my position, my fortune, my liberty – even my life. He bent the rules for me. More than bent them. But he was intelligent enough to see that natural justice stood on my side, and he was kind enough to believe that everyone deserves natural justice. And a second chance.'

To my astonishment, I saw tears in her eyes, quickly brushed away. I had never seen Mrs Jameson exhibit such emotion before. Despite my intense curiosity, I didn't feel able to break into her thoughts to ask questions.

'And now he has come to me for help, and he too stands to lose everything. This will be a terrible affair, whatever the outcome, Marjorie. He may well have to resign, simply because of the scandal associated with Daisy's death. A drug addict, a dope girl, in the American ambassador's own residence. I think that's why he is so fixated on finding the source of the cocaine. It enables him to point the finger back at London.'

She turned to face me. 'I would like to deliver natural justice for Henry, but that may be very hard to do. So yes, Marjorie. Please go to your friends in the band and see what you can discover about drugs in the Harlequin. See if anyone knows where Daisy was getting her supply. There may have been suppliers on the premises, pushing their wares without the knowledge of the owner. Or perhaps you are right, and the owner was complicit in the trade. Either way, it will be good to be sure. And it will be something to offer Henry.'

She sat in an armchair and closed her eyes. 'Please leave me now, Marjorie. I feel very tired. I would like to be alone.'

Quietly, I picked up my handbag and slipped out of the room. Feeling in need of company, I wandered down to the kitchen. Graham and our cook, Mrs Smithson, were tucking into the untouched Dundee cake.

'Hello, Miss. What's happened to your appetites?' asked Mrs Smithson. 'Mrs Jameson usually loves my fruitcake.'

I sat at the scrubbed deal table and Graham poured me another cup of tea. 'It's this case we're working on,' I said, cutting myself a thick wedge of cake. 'Mr Caldwell is an old friend, and she feels badly for him.'

Graham shook his head. 'Such a sad affair. She was very young, I understand? The lady who died.'

'Nineteen,' I said. Even after seeing her lifeless body, I found it hard to believe. 'Dreadful, isn't it?' The last nine years should have inured me to untimely death, but somehow, they hadn't. How much cocaine had been needed to cause Daisy's death? If I had taken a sniff of it myself, would I now be lying cold in a mortuary? I shivered.

'Have another cup,' said Mrs Smithson. 'You're looking quite peaky. I'll warm up one of those scones for you. It won't take a minute. This new gas range is a marvel.'

As I ate, I remembered the scraps of paper we had collected from Daisy's wastepaper basket. I opened my handbag and took out the envelope I had placed them in. Would they give us a clue about Daisy's addiction? I smoothed them out and started to read.

The first paper was banal – a shopping list of lingerie, cosmetics, and other fripperies in an untidy hand. The second was a crumpled letter from America from an old school friend: 'You'll never guess! Jimmy Stoddard and Irene McIntyre spent two hours sitting in his car outside the country club Saturday night – can you imagine, with her teeth? She said he was showing her the stars or some such line. But her dress was buttoned up all wrong and he had that LOOK about him. Now, Daisy dear, do write me about your adventures in England. Is it very dull staying with your uncle? Did you find an English lord to marry yet?'

I sighed. That letter would never receive an answer.

The third piece was a torn scrap of pink writing paper, which seemed to be part of a letter with no address or signature. I frowned over the scrawl, trying to make it out.

'... speak to you. There's no point in pretending it hasn't happened, darling. We'll just have to face the music! Uncle Henry will come around. It's too late to cry over spilt milk.'

I read it over again, nerves tingling. Was this Daisy's handwriting? The reference to Uncle Henry suggested as much. I compared the writing to that of the shopping list. It looked to be the same.

So, who was the 'darling' she was writing to? Did she have a sweetheart, or did she just use the term indiscriminately to every acquaintance? And what exactly was the music that had to be faced?

Chapter 13

I hopped off the train at Brixton Railway Station and descended from the high-level platform into the bustle of Atlantic Road. The street market was in full swing, traders' noisy patter competing for attention. Hand carts and barrows cluttered the kerbside and I stepped into the road to avoid the litter of discarded vegetables and sacking. Children rushed around, dogs barked and women with baskets jostled and called their orders to the vendors. The place pulsed with life; something of a relief after the sombre atmosphere that had settled over Bedford Square.

I checked the address on Freddie's card and turned south towards Coldharbour Lane, past the big shoe shop and the crowd peering into the windows of the 'bargain emporium' of household goods tucked under the railway arches.

Freddie's digs were above a greengrocer, who was busy with customers picking over Brussels sprouts, battered-looking cabbages, and turnips. January was such a gloomy time of year for vegetables. My eye was caught by a pyramid of bright oranges, newly arrived from Spain with their glossy green leaves still attached, and my mouth watered.

I knocked on the door to the left of the shop front, wondering if anyone would hear above the noise of the market and the trains screeching by. How Freddie managed to sleep here I could not imagine. Eventually a sour-faced woman in a housecoat that had seen better days opened the door. I asked for Mr Gillespie, hoping that eleven o'clock would be late enough for him to have woken up. She looked me up and down in an impudent way.

'He's asleep. Blooming musicians sleep till all hours. What do you want with him, anyway?'

I was about to retort that was none of her business, when I heard footsteps clattering down the stairs.

'Well, if it ain't Miss Swallow! Hey, what are you doing down this way?' T-bone Tommy was all smiles.

The woman turned her aggression to a new target. 'I've told you before about making a racket. Don't think I wouldn't turn you out for tuppence. There's not many round here that would have your sort under their roof.' She slammed through a door behind the stairs.

Embarrassed, I turned back to T-bone. 'How rude of her,' I began.

His smile didn't waver. 'She's just talk,' he said. 'You here to see Freddie? Let me see if I can rouse him out.'

'Thank you so much,' I said. 'I didn't know you both lived here.'

'Well, I needed a place to stay, after the Harlem Swingers sailed back to New York and I decided to stay put awhile. Freddie put in a word for me with his landlady. We have rooms on the same floor. Wait there a second, Miss Swallow.'

A couple of minutes later, they were both on the street, dressed in wool caps and jackets against the chill of the day. I realised it was the first time I'd seen T-bone out of the evening suit he wore to perform. He looked comfortable, more himself, with a bright red kerchief around his neck and his shirt collar open. He loomed over Freddie, his lanky stride covering the same ground as two of my paces.

'I'm going to have myself some breakfast,' said T-bone. 'Want to come, or is this a hot date?'

'I'm starving,' said Freddie. 'Marjorie, do you mind if we go to get breakfast together? I suppose you had yours ages ago.'

I had, but I was quite ready for elevenses, so the three of us headed together to the Bon Marché café around the corner on Brixton Road. They ordered tea and thick door-steps of bread with fried eggs, while I chose coffee and an iced bun.

'Now,' said Freddie, his face serious, 'I have an important question for you, Miss Swallow. When did you learn to dance The Charleston, and will you promise never to do it again? I almost sprained something, trying not to laugh.'

I set down my coffee cup. 'You haven't heard.'

He saw the look on my face and dropped his facetious manner. 'Heard what?'

'Daisy Caldwell. The woman I was with, in the yellow frock. You remember?'

'I could hardly forget,' he said with a grin. 'She's quite the girl.'

'She's dead. She died yesterday morning,' I said. 'A cocaine overdose.'

'Oh, Miss Swallow. Say it isn't so. The poor kid.' T-bone put down his knife and fork. 'That's too bad.'

'Oh, Lord,' said Freddie. 'That's bad news.'

I took another sip of coffee. 'It's pretty awful,' I agreed. 'We were at the house yesterday. She's the niece of the American ambassador, you know. And he's a friend of Mrs Jameson. That's why I was there with them in the first place. Mr

Caldwell has asked us to investigate.'

'Investigate what?' asked Freddie. 'I thought you said she OD'd.'

'He wants to know who gave her the drugs,' I said. 'He thinks it must have been someone at the club.'

'Uh-oh.' T-bone looked uneasy. 'I can see where this is going. Soon as a white girl gets herself in trouble, folks start looking for a coloured fellow to blame. Well, I never gave her nothing, Miss Swallow. I give you my word.'

I was shocked. 'Of course you didn't. That didn't even cross my mind.'

He laughed, and for the first time I saw bitterness in his smile. 'Then you're the first white woman not to suspect the nearest black man, Miss Swallow. Mostly, you people can't help yourselves.'

'Hey, now.' Freddie put a hand on his arm. 'That's not fair. Marjorie doesn't suspect you, and nor do I. We're band mates, and musicians stick together. But, Marjorie, what he says is true. Some people will make that assumption if the police come sniffing around the Harlequin looking for drugs. And the police are not beyond planting them on a fellow, either.'

I saw from the solemn expressions on their faces that they spoke from experience.

'In that case,' I said, 'it makes it all the more important that I investigate and see if I can find out where she really did get them from.'

They exchanged a dubious look.

'I mean,' I said, 'what about all the other clients of the Harlequin? There were all sorts of people there. And then there's the owner...'

'No,' said Freddie, flatly.

'No, what?'

'Don't go pointing the finger at Mr Li, just because he's Chinese. That's as bad as assuming it was Tommy here.'

'I'm not assuming anything!' I protested. 'But I thought you might have some ideas. Given that you're there every week.'

Freddie pushed his tea away. 'More than that, from now onwards. Mr Li has offered to beat the screw we were getting at the Criterion. We start tonight, Friday to Saturday, then Wednesday and Thursday. The band will get two hundred quid a week.'

I gasped. 'That's a fortune!'

T-bone grinned. 'It's pretty good, ain't it? You can see why we took it.'

'I certainly can.' It also put them in a very good position to help me investigate any drug-dealing at the club. 'Congratulations.'

'It's a good gig,' said Freddie. 'So, we don't want any trouble at the Harlequin. I know what you're like, Marjorie. Sometimes I think trouble follows you around. Or you go looking for it.'

I was about to protest, but thought back over the past few months. He did rather have a point.

'So, you don't have any ideas, then?' I asked. 'About who might have sold Daisy cocaine?'

Freddie shook his head, although he didn't look straight at me. 'Search me. Could have been anyone. Probably not even at the club.'

T-bone looked like he wanted to say something, then stopped himself. He looked over at Freddie, then shrugged his shoulders.

'Say, Miss Swallow,' he said. 'You're serious about wanting

to investigate Daisy's death, are you?'

I leaned forward and held his anxious gaze. 'I certainly am. It's very important to Mrs Jameson.'

'Well, listen. They need a new dance hostess at the Harlequin. One of the regular girls is getting married to one of those cricketer fellows. Which is nice and all, but Vi says they're one down and the clients will run the girls ragged. And she can't stand the thought of having to audition a load of no-hopers again. How about we suggest you as a replacement?'

Freddie's jaw was hanging open. 'Are you out of your mind, T-bone? Marjorie can't be a dance hostess!'

'And why not?' I asked, hotly. 'I can dance, can't I?'

He laughed, rather cruelly. 'You can trot around the floor, but I don't know if you're up to Vi's standards. She usually picks them from the chorus line at the West End shows. She used to be a hoofer herself. And it's not just dancing. It's a different world, Marjorie. The men who come to the Harlequin... they don't always treat the girls with respect.'

My mettle was up now. 'I've handled ruffians intent on strangling me, Freddie,' I said, haughtily. 'And I've been told that I dance very well.'

Although not, perhaps, The Charleston. I was suddenly seized with horror.

'Who is Vi?' I asked, remembering Daisy enquiring about her on Wednesday night.

T-bone grinned. 'Miss Violet Crumb. She's the manageress, and by lucky chance, she was indisposed on Wednesday.'

'But it's too risky,' protested Freddie.

'Nah,' said T-bone. 'Miss Swallow can take care of herself, can't you? And we can help you get up to the mark. We're rehearsing this afternoon, three o'clock at the club. Why don't you come along and practise before we introduce you to Vi?'

Freddie still looked dubious, but I was delighted to have the opportunity to snoop on the Harlequin as an undercover agent. I hoped Mrs Jameson would approve.

Chapter 14

The Harlequin felt like a different place, out of hours. The shiny dance floor smelled of carbolic. The round tables, stripped of their red and black diamond patterned cloths, were revealed as cheap, roughly cut circles of wood. The mirrors threw back gloomy shadows, without brilliant lights to toss the glamour from place to place. Perversely, it felt smaller without crowds of people thronging it.

Freddie led the way to the upright piano and lifted the lid. He ran up and down the scales a couple of times, while T-bone unpacked his trombone, buffing it softly with a cloth. I perched on a stool by the side of the stage while the rest of the players assembled. First to arrive was the clarinettist, a small, ferrety-looking man with a toothbrush moustache and receding hairline.

'Say hello to Mr Sidney Harpo,' said T-bone. 'Harpo, this here is Miss Swallow. She's a friend of Freddie's, and she's going to try out for the dance hostess post. We said we'd let her have a little practice before Miss Crumb gets here.'

'Howdy-do,' said Mr Harpo, flashing a gold-toothed smile. 'Been in the business long?'

'Hullo.' I tried to look stage-struck. I'd discussed my supposed pedigree with Freddie and T-bone. They said enthusiastic amateur was likely to go down better than pretending to be a professional, which would certainly be rumbled. 'Not really, no. I was in the chorus at the Lewisham Apollo pantomime with my dance school one year,' I said. 'And I was very keen on amateur dramatics at Sydenham High. But I love to dance more than anything. I'm auditioning for the shows.'

His smile softened. 'Good luck with that, Miss Swallow. It's a hard business, but there's nothing like it.'

The trumpeter, Mr Goldberg, and Mr Sampson, the drummer, arrived together, and I gave them the same story. Mr Goldberg rolled his eyes, and I could see he would have preferred to rehearse without my presence. I promised to keep out of the way and just run through my routine at the side of the stage.

I already knew the fox-trot, quickstep and waltz, and Freddie showed me how to adapt those to a syncopated rhythm. We worked up a quick demonstration dance for me to show Miss Crumb, and I ran through it time after time while the musicians briskly trotted through their set. At first, I felt terribly exposed, dancing by myself in front of five top-class musicians, without so much as a partner to rely on. But I soon lost my self-consciousness, realising that the musicians were focused on their rehearsal, not on what I was up to. When we stopped for a cup of tea after an hour, I was perspiring freely.

'You're all right, Miss Swallow,' said Mr Harpo. 'Most of these kids who want to dance, they get all hung up on the exact sequence of the steps and don't listen to the band. But you've got rhythm, and that's the thing. You just relax and let the music carry you. I reckon Miss Crumb's gonna be blown away.'

Relieved, I poured the tea and checked that everyone had a cup. 'Mr Goldberg, can I get you anything?' I could see he was the band member I had to win around.

His look was scathing. 'I tell you, if I had a daughter, I wouldn't let her run around with a lot of musicians and stay out dancing half the night. What does your father think of all this?'

I flushed. 'He's very glad that I am pursuing my dreams,' I said, firmly. My father would be appalled to know I'd stepped over the threshold of the Harlequin, let alone that I was applying for the post of dance hostess. Both of my parents had been proud as punch when I landed a role as private secretary to a wealthy lady. I did my best to shield them from what this job sometimes involved.

'You might want to sit the next one out, Marjorie,' said Freddie. 'We're working up a new number and there'll be a lot of stopping and starting.'

I perched by the side of the stage, fascinated, as Mr Harpo, who was the band leader, and T-bone, who had come up with the main melody, put together the backbone of the piece. Mr Sampson, a young fellow whose clothes looked slightly too big for him, listened to them run through the melody twice, then started to tap out an underpinning rhythm with his drumsticks. T-bone gave him a big smile and raised his thumb. Freddie began a low rumble with his left hand, a simple repetitive series of notes that echoed the drum beat, then picked out the melody on top. Mr Goldberg nodded his approval and joined the trombone and clarinet.

My feet were tapping, my shoulders swaying. As they ran through it again, swinging joyously into the main chorus, I slipped from my stool and tried out my little sequence, fitting it to the provocative rhythms, letting the music carry me as Mr Harpo had said. T-bone flashed me a grin, Freddie turned around and smiled. Even Mr Goldberg didn't look too disapproving as I swung my arms and twirled on my toes.

Finally, the band reached a crescendo and the new number finished on a big fanfare. Laughing, I curtsied to them and sank to the floor, as exhausted as they were.

The overhead lights on the dance floor snapped on. A short, dark-haired young woman walked through the club, clapping slowly. I scrambled to my feet, panting. Oh, goodness. What a way to be discovered.

'Not bad,' said the woman. She was talking to the band. 'Who wrote that, Mr Harpo? Another of your compositions?'

'Joint effort, Miss Crumb. T-bone here came up with the melody, and I helped him put it together,' said the little man, wiping his brow with a handkerchief. 'If we can get it polished up, we'll play it tonight. I'm going to call it the Harlequin Shimmy. What d'you say?'

The woman switched her gaze to me. She had bobbed hair with a heavy fringe that gave her eyes a smoky, half-asleep look. Her mouth was painted a dark red, even at four in the afternoon. She wore a practical tweed suit in relaxed tailoring, which I was impressed to see appeared to be by Mademoiselle Chanel.

'Well, what d'you say, Miss? Is it danceable? Or am I to expect all my clients to collapse at the end of the number?'

I drew myself up. 'It's extremely danceable, Miss Crumb,' I said. Confidence, Mrs Jameson always says, is half the battle. 'I would be happy to demonstrate the steps to your other dance hostesses.'

She raised an eyebrow. 'The other hostesses?'

'I am Miss Marjorie Swallow, and I am ready to fill the vacant post tonight,' I said recklessly. 'You've seen I can dance. I'm sure I can pick up whatever else is required in the job.'

She laughed, a raucous hoot that was rather infectious. 'Oh, boy. That's the funniest thing I've heard all day, and I meet a lot of comedians. All right, Miss Swallow. Come through to the office and tell me about yourself.'

The office was a tiny, cramped space with an empty grate, two armchairs and a desk covered in paperwork. Miss Crumb pushed the papers aside and sat on the desk, silk-clad legs crossed at the knee and one smart patent-leather shoe swinging. She lit a cigarette, blew a perfect smoke-ring, and looked at me enquiringly.

'Well?'

I began my spiel about amateur dramatics at school and the Lewisham pantomime.

'I've worked at the Lewisham Apollo,' she said immediately. 'Which dance school were you at?'

Fortunately, I had wangled a couple of years of dance lessons, despite my father's disapproval. 'The Flora Fratelli School on Sydenham Rise,' I said, with as much dignity as I could muster. The Apollo had used the school's students for their pantomime chorus some years, although I had never been selected to be among those glittering few, and I doubt my parents would have allowed it if I had.

She nodded, with a condescending smile. 'And where were you educated, Miss Swallow? My clients like a girl who can talk intelligently, without being vulgar or causing embarrassment.'

I was on sounder ground here. 'Sydenham High School for Girls. I won a scholarship,' I said, proudly. 'I was there until

I was sixteen. And I worked as a VAD nurse during the War, then studied shorthand and typing.' I felt it was best to stick as closely as possible to the truth.

She sighed and extinguished her cigarette. 'Then why on earth, with such an array of talents and skills at your disposal, do you want to be a nightclub hostess?'

I leaned forward with as much solemnity as I could manage. 'I love to dance, Miss Crumb. I want to work in the theatre, one day. I've been going to auditions, but I know I need some proper professional experience. Won't you help a girl follow her dream?'

She laughed again, for quite a long time. 'Most of 'em want me to rescue them from a nightmare. This one wants to follow a dream,' she hooted, to no-one in particular. 'How much experience do you have of nightclubs, Miss Swallow? What do you know about what happens here?'

I thought. 'Well, I've been here as a guest. There's wonderful music from the band, and dancing, and lots of people having a jolly time. Having drinks, and so on.'

'And so on. What do you mean by that?'

I flushed. 'Just… enjoying themselves. I mean, the girls like to look pretty and be admired, the men like to dance with pretty girls. And everyone likes to have a glass of champagne and listen to good music.'

Miss Crumb gave me an appraising look. 'And what would you do if one of those men who enjoyed dancing with you offered you money to go home with him?'

'I'd tell him my father would be here to pick me up at closing time, after he finished his boxing match,' I said, promptly.

'And if he gave you a box of chocolates and wanted to see you outside of the club?'

'That I didn't much care for chocolate and was busy practising when I wasn't working.'

'And if he sent you roses?'

'I should tell him my mother liked them, but they gave me hay-fever.'

Miss Crumb laughed, then leaned forward. 'And if he said he was a producer of a show who could get you a part in the chorus?'

I wavered. 'I'd ask your opinion as to whether he was who he said he was, Miss Crumb. Some men will say anything to get what they want from a girl.'

She grinned. 'They certainly will. I like you, Miss Swallow. If you stick to your guns, you should do all right. Be here at eight o'clock sharp. Bring a needle and thread, in case you need to adjust your frock. But you're about the same size as Miss Smith, so I should think it will fit you well enough.'

Elated, I thanked Freddie and the band for their help, and rushed back to Bedford Square with the news.

Chapter 15

To my relief, Mrs Jameson had recovered from her despondency of the previous evening. When I got back from Soho, she was at her desk, poring over the scrap of letter I had retrieved from Daisy Caldwell's wastepaper basket.

'There you are, Marjorie. The question is,' she said, barely glancing my way as I came into the office, 'whether this was part of a letter she had sent, but which had been returned to her, or written but decided not to send, or if this was an early draft of a letter that was sent later.'

'But where's the rest of the letter?' I asked.

She looked up and smiled. 'Good question. I have asked Mr Caldwell's housekeeper what happens to discarded paper. She says the ambassador's wastepaper is burned for security. The rest of the household waste is collected by the maids and removed by the municipal services. She's going to see if anything remains uncollected. Would you like some tea? I was about to ring for some.'

'Rather.'

'As to the rest of it, the situation seems clear. I wonder who the man in question was, and how far things had progressed. Poor Daisy. Now, how did you get on today? Do you have an answer from the chemist shop?'

I produced the sealed envelope that the Wigmore Street chemist had given me that morning before my trip to Brixton. She opened it immediately and read the contents, then folded the letter back into its envelope and secreted it in her crocodile-skin handbag. Her eyes had the faraway look she got when trying to fit a new piece of information into the jigsaw puzzle of a case.

I was dying to ask. The man in the shop had gone through his book, and then written down and sealed the answer, as requested. I was no closer to knowing what the question had been.

'Is the response satisfactory?' I was never able to keep my mouth shut for long.

She looked up, as if surprised to see me still there. 'What? Oh, yes, thank you. Perhaps we shall find out more at the inquest. Henry says it has been scheduled to open on Monday. We shall attend, of course. In fact, it's possible you may be asked to give evidence about Daisy's little gold box.'

I hadn't thought of that and was rather intimidated by the idea of appearing before the coroner. Still, Monday was days away, and I had more immediate concerns.

Over tea and Dutch butter cake, I described with triumph my visit to the Harlequin and my new role as a dance hostess, starting that very evening.

'Oh, well done. That's splendid. You must have a rest after tea, so you're fresh for your evening,' said Mrs Jameson. 'Did your musician friends have any ideas about where Daisy might have sourced her cocaine?'

So that hadn't been the question to the Wigmore Street chemist.

'No.' I thought back to my morning elevenses in Brixton and

remembered Freddie's evasive look with disquiet. 'Not that they were willing to tell me, anyway. But T-bone was worried that he'd be blamed. He says black men always get the blame when white girls are found with drugs.'

Mrs Jameson sighed. 'He's right, of course. That's certainly the way it goes in the States. And he's from the US, isn't he?'

I nodded. 'From Harlem, in New York. He came over with another jazz orchestra, but stayed behind when they went home, because he was making so much money playing with Freddie's band. He sends all his money back home to his family, he says. And he's worried about losing his job if the club gets a bad reputation.'

'Well,' Mrs Jameson took another bite of cake and masticated with enthusiasm, 'we'll have to make sure that you find out who really did supply those drugs,' she said, echoing my words of the morning. 'But do be careful, won't you? You're there to keep your eyes open and report back, not to put yourself in danger. Don't go off on any wild goose chases. Stay in the club, and I'll send Graham in a taxi-cab to collect you at closing time.'

'There's no need,' I protested. 'I can find a taxi. And what if they want to know who he is?'

Mrs Jameson laughed. 'Tell them he's your father. It's only for a few nights, until you have a better idea of what's going on at the club. I'll sleep more easily if I know Graham is going to see you home safely.'

I went up to my room to lie down for an hour. Secretly, I was rather relieved to know that nice, reliable Graham would be waiting to collect me after my night at the club. Despite my protestations to Miss Crumb, I had little enough experience of night life and the characters I might encounter in my undercover role.

Chapter 16

I hadn't expected the job to be so completely exhausting. The Harlequinettes, as Miss Crumb called us, were on the go from the moment we arrived until the club closed at two o'clock in the morning.

Our costumes were all variations on the Harlequin theme. The frock I inherited from the retiring Miss Smith was a Pierrette dress, white satinette with black pom-poms down the front and around the hem of the skirt, and a floppy black ruff. The fabric was a little grubby around the neck and armpits and could have done with freshening up. I resolved to take it home and launder it before Saturday night. I touched up my face with my usual pink lipstick, brushed my bobbed hair until it shone, and hoped for the best.

The other Harlequinettes arrived in a rush just before half past eight. There were five of us in addition to Miss Crumb, who looked extremely sophisticated in a plain black taffeta dress of impeccable cut, silk stockings and high-heeled black suede shoes. Our role, Miss Crumb informed me, was to sit at tables by the dance floor, dance and chat with customers, ensure they ordered plenty of drinks and had a good time. Diplomacy and tact were needed to ensure this good time did not encroach too far on one's own person.

The regulars all had their favourite hostesses. Miss Tierney, a round-faced blonde woman in a Columbine costume with multicoloured ribbons, said it was important not to poach another girl's admirers.

'I've got a factory owner from Manchester very keen,' she confided. 'He's coming tonight, with his colleagues. I'll look out for any likely prospects for you. They're not short of a few bob. Make sure they buy you a bottle of champagne. And don't drink more than one glass. Miss Crumb will pick up the bottle later and they'll use it to sell single glasses from behind the bar.'

She gave me a keen look. 'I recognise you. You were in two nights ago, weren't you? With that Daisy Caldwell. You danced The Charleston together.'

I groaned. 'Was it too awful?'

She laughed. 'Well, you can't go around doing that and not expect people to notice.' Her face went serious. 'Is it true, though? About Miss Caldwell, I mean. Is she really dead?'

I nodded, looking at the floor. 'It's awful. Her family are so upset,' I said.

'And it was an overdose?'

I feigned ignorance. 'That's what it said in the newspaper.'

Miss Potts, a comfortable-looking plump woman with twinkling dark eyes who also wore a Pierrette dress, promised to point out the more troublesome clients. 'Most of them are gentlemen, but there's some that you mustn't be left alone with. If you have any trouble, tell Miss Crumb. Vi's a good sort. She doesn't take any nonsense.'

The other two were Harlequin sisters, tall and willowy in slim-fitting sequinned frocks patterned with red, black, and silver diamonds. Their bobbed hair was glossy black, and their profiles were patrician.

'Miss Edith Proudfoot and Miss Hester Proudfoot,' said Miss Potts. 'Hester is the elder; you can tell them apart by the beauty-spot on Edith's lip. They're very popular with foreign aristocrats. Don't let that classy exterior fool you. Their father is a Newcastle miner, and they can swear like you wouldn't believe.'

They smiled in unison, a superior, barely-there smile. 'Gan away with you, pet,' said Miss Hester Proudfoot. I can't repeat what she said after that. I wasn't sure I understood, or indeed if it would be physically possible.

Miss Edith Proudfoot turned her gaze on me. 'Eee, it's the Charleston lass. Are you going to teach us? Because I don't think this frock would allow me to waggle my knees like that.'

To my relief, distraction arrived in the form of the band clattering down the steps. Mr Harpo and T-bone seemed to be especial favourites of the girls, who crowded around them. Freddie gave me an enormous wink.

'Ooh, is he your fellow?' asked Miss Potts. 'Don't let Vi see. She doesn't like us fraternising with the band. Puts off the clients, she says.'

After all the warnings, I was quite anxious by the time the doors opened at nine and the first customers appeared. Miss Crumb sat me with Miss Tierney at the foot of the stairs, so we got a good view of people as they descended.

The first to arrive was a distinguished-looking gentleman of about sixty, with receding white hair and a bristling military moustache to compensate. He was accompanied by a blonde woman half his age in a spangled black dress and a dazzling diamond necklace.

'Good evening, Colonel,' simpered Miss Tierney. 'Will you

have your usual table?' She installed them and brought whisky for him and champagne for his companion.

'He tells everyone she's his niece,' she muttered to me as she sat back down. 'Which is a coincidence, because she worked here a couple of years ago, before Vi Crumb threw her out for getting too fresh with the clients.'

After that, the customers poured in. A big party of men and women wearing black eye-masks struck languid poses, laughing raucously and drinking pretty fast. Miss Tierney's Manchester industrialist and his colleagues arrived, sweeping her off to sit with them. Two dark-haired men in white tie and tails descended the stairs together and made a bee-line for the Proudfoot sisters.

'They're ninth and tenth in line for the throne,' whispered Miss Potts, passing by on the arm of a young man who had captained the successful Cambridge team at the previous year's boat race. Which throne, she did not explain. They bore no resemblance to the British Royal Family that I could see.

Several of the Surrey cricketers came down next. Mr Wilders, the man who had danced with me on Wednesday, stopped before my table and gave me a quizzical look. Bother. With my costume, I had hoped to go unrecognised by the customers. He held out his hand, and we stepped onto the dance floor.

'You're working here now, Miss Swallow?' he asked.

I nodded. 'It seemed like a nice place,' I said, rather lamely. 'Thought I'd give it a go.'

'I heard about your pal,' he told me. 'I'm sorry. I know she was a bit wild, but she seemed like a good kid.'

I felt grateful that someone had noticed. 'She was,' I said. 'Thank you.' Our quickstep was coming to an end, and the band swung into an up-tempo foxtrot.

'Shall we have another?' asked Mr Wilders. 'Don't look now, but Lucky Li's just come in,' he murmured. 'Have you met your new boss yet?'

Chapter 17

He swung me around and I saw Mr Li traverse the club with Miss Crumb. While she greeted the men, Mr Li bowed low over the hands of parties of excitable young women, who all seemed delighted to see him.

The foxtrot finished and Mr Wilders and I returned to my table. I saw Miss Crumb steer her companion in our direction.

'Mr Li, I believe you have met Mr Wilders, the noted cricketer? And this is Miss Marjorie Swallow, our newest dance hostess. I see she is already making herself a favourite with the Surrey team, like her predecessor,' she said. 'Miss Swallow, may I introduce Mr Li Chen Taio?'

Mr Li shook hands with Mr Wilders, then took my hand and bowed politely. I saw a gleam of amused recognition in his face. Oh, golly. He knew me from my scandalous Charleston.

'Miss Swallow, I am pleased to see you return to the Harlequin and become part of our family here.' His voice was soft, his English accent faultless. 'Perhaps you would do me the honour to sit with me a moment?'

Both Miss Crumb and Mr Wilders looked surprised. Mr Li led me to the table at the corner of the room where he had sat on Wednesday night. He looked at me in silence for a moment, studying my face. His skin was smooth, his eyes a rather beautiful deep brown and his sleek hair brilliantined to a high shine. It was hard to know how old he was – thirty, perhaps, or forty. Up close, I could appreciate the perfection of his tailoring. The silk lapels of his tailcoat gleamed, his dress shirt dazzled white, and his pale yellow waistcoat, gloves and buttonhole rose gave the most refined touch of colour.

'Miss Swallow, I am surprised to see you here so soon after your last visit. I wished to offer my condolences on the untimely death of your friend, Miss Caldwell,' he said.

I should have realised he would have heard about Daisy's death. Now, I supposed, he would pump me for information about it. Well, two could play that game.

'Thank you. It was a great shock.'

'A very great tragedy,' he said, shaking his head sorrowfully. 'She was a young woman with much to live for.'

How much did he know? I wondered. I decided to push him a little and see how he reacted. Mrs Jameson always said you should throw in an unexpected question, then leave a good long pause until your interviewee felt they had to answer.

'She died of a cocaine overdose,' I said. 'Her friends all wonder where she got it from. I don't suppose you can help?'

He watched me in silence for a moment. 'Of course, that is natural. I expect her friends are well-placed to find out,' he said, a slight emphasis on the word 'friends'. I wondered what he meant by that. I continued to wait.

He sighed. 'Miss Swallow, I too am anxious to know if anyone is selling illegal drugs in my club. I imagine that is what you and Daisy's friends are wondering about. I hope that if you discover anything of that nature, you will come and tell me. I must protect my business, you understand. And my employees.' He smiled kindly. 'Will you do me that courtesy?'

I stammered that I would. This was hardly what I'd expected from him, but I supposed he was my employer now, every bit as much as Mrs Jameson.

'Please convey my regards to Mr Franklin and Miss Felicity Caldwell, and my deepest sympathies to Ambassador and Mrs Caldwell.' He bowed again, and I was dismissed.

So, he knew of Daisy's family, and the names of the party that had visited on Wednesday night. I supposed it was his business to know about his customers. Did he know, or suspect, that I was there on behalf of the ambassador? And what was I to do about his request to report any evidence of cocaine selling to him? If I had two employers now, it might be impossible to be loyal to them both.

I walked across the room thinking, as the band launched into the toe-tapping new Harlequin Shimmy. The number was an immediate hit; customers poured from the tables onto the dance floor. A young man of barely twenty grabbed me rather too enthusiastically and swung me into a quickstep.

'Hot band, don'tcha think?' he brayed into my ear. His hair was in disarray and his tie skew-whiff. I could smell whisky on his breath.

'They're very good.' I focused on trying to keep my dainty shoes from under his feet.

'Pretty wild stuff, ain't it? I'd be sent down if my pater knew I was here,' he slurred. 'He can't bear this jazz. Monkey music, he calls it.'

I stiffened. 'That's rather rude. I think jazz music is wonderful. So refreshing, so different from what we had before the War.'

'Oh, the War. Everyone goes on about it. Time we moved on, don'tcha think? Let bygones be bygones. I get so bloody bored hearing about the bloody War.'

Easy for this young pup to say. He hadn't experienced the hell of the trenches, or dealt with the grinding, numbing losses of friends, fathers, brothers. I said nothing and hoped the dance would be over soon.

But Mr Wilders, who had been standing close to the dance floor smoking with his team-mates, had heard all too clearly. He attempted to cut in.

'Miss Swallow, allow me,' he said, putting a hand on my shoulder. 'You shouldn't have to listen to that nonsense.'

My young partner wasn't about to relinquish me without a struggle.

'Push off, matey,' he said. 'We're having a nice dance. Find someone your own age.'

Mr Wilders laughed. 'I would say the same to you, my boy, if there was anyone from the nursery in tonight. Come along, give way.'

I stepped back, unsure how to deal with this situation. Unfortunately, the young man decided to deal with it by swinging a punch.

'Oh, don't be ridiculous,' I said.

Mr Wilders caught the boy's fist in his hand, while another of the players grabbed him from behind around the waist. The blow had been ill-aimed and lacking in power, but that cut no ice with the Surrey team.

'You need to learn some respect,' Mr Wilders snarled. He slapped him hard across the face.

'Stop it,' I pleaded. 'He's just a kid.'

The band played on, but people had noticed the kerfuffle and were gathering to watch. Where was Mr Li? I wondered. Or Violet Crumb? I looked around and saw Mr Li at the table where the Proudfoot sisters were entertaining foreign royalty. Miss Crumb was nowhere to be seen.

'Apologise,' said Mr Wilders. 'Kids like you, pretending to be grown-up. Laughing at those of us who saw action while you were tucked up in your cot.'

The boy struggled on, valour getting the better of any discretion he might once have possessed. 'Bunch of old soldiers,' he sneered. 'And you fight like a load of old women.'

He broke loose and set about the players indiscriminately. Other men, picking sides according to age and cricketing allegiance, gleefully piled into the brawl while women screamed and backed away.

I glimpsed T-bone and Mr Harpo confer with furrowed brows, then the band burst into a nice soothing waltz. It didn't stop the fighting, but gave it a bizarre accompaniment, like a battle scene from a film with the organ playing the wrong soundtrack. Miss Crumb bustled across the floor with Johnnie, the large gentleman who generally stood on the door outside. Thank goodness someone was going to stop this. He waded into the melee.

Over the general noise, I heard a drumming sound that wasn't coming from the band. Looking behind me, I saw the boy who had started the whole affair. A dark-haired man in an ill-fitting suit held him up against the wall, his elbow across the boy's throat. The noise came from the boy's heels, kicking against the wall as he struggled to get air into his lungs. I went cold. A moment longer and the boy would be dead.

Weight. I heard Mrs Garrud's voice in my head. Use their weight against them. And the man would not be expecting my assault.

I delivered a sharp kick to the back of the unknown man's

knee, at the same time pulling his shoulder back. His knee buckled, and he half-turned, grabbing my sleeve to break his fall. I heard my shoulder seam rip, and he went down awkwardly. I grasped his wrist and twisted like Frankie had shown me, forcing his elbow up his back. He bellowed as I used the purchase on his arm to pull him away from the boy, who collapsed onto the floor.

I shouted for help, but the doorman was fully occupied in breaking up the battle on the dance floor.

'Let go of the lady, Vince,' said a handsome-looking fellow, shouldering his way through the crowd. Vince wasn't about to point out that the lady had hold of him, but he shook himself free.

'Apologies, Miss,' said his friend, grasping the man's arm. 'He gets a bit over-excited when there's a ruckus. Oh, Vince. You've torn the lady's pretty costume. Come on. Let's go and sit down.'

The man allowed himself to be led away.

I knelt beside the boy. He was gasping for breath, his throat rattling. He looked up with frightened eyes.

'Stay there,' I said. 'I'll get some help.' I scanned the room and saw with relief Miss Crumb hovering by the side of the dance floor. I waved my arm, and she hastened over.

'Someone strangled him,' I said. 'He needs water, and to sit quietly and recover.'

She looked at the boy's face and her eyebrows disappeared into her dark fringe. 'Help me to get him to the office. Lucky you spotted him, Miss Swallow. His father is the Duke of Suffolk.'

Chapter 18

We settled the boy in one of the tired armchairs and gave him water to sip. I explained what I'd seen.

'I didn't recognise the man who strangled him. He was a bit rough-looking. His friend came and took him away. He called him Vince.'

'Oh, Lord,' said Miss Crumb. 'The Armstrong brothers. I didn't even know they were in tonight. Johnnie should have warned me. Did you see how it started? Was it deliberate? It's like them, to start a fight so the police will be called, and the club gets a bad reputation.'

Embarrassed, I told Miss Crumb about the altercation between the Duke of Suffolk's son and the Surrey cricketers. 'I didn't see either of the brothers until the fighting was well underway. They didn't start it,' I said.

The boy muttered that he would get his father onto them and see the so-and-sos hang.

'Hush now, Lord Sebastian,' said Miss Crumb. 'I don't suppose your father knows you're here, and I doubt he'd be pleased if he did. You thank your lucky stars that Miss Swallow was here to save you.'

Lord Sebastian didn't look very grateful, but subsided. I supposed being rescued by a woman about put the cap on a bad night for a twenty-year-old boy.

Miss Crumb glanced at her wristwatch. 'Would you believe it's only midnight? Two hours to go. Johnnie should have brought it under control by now. How are you feeling, Miss Swallow? Do you have enough pep for the next round?'

My feet ached, my shoulder hurt from pulling Vince Armstrong off his victim and my head was spinning from exhaustion. But I mustered a smile from somewhere and told her I felt fine.

'You get yourself tidied up and go back, then. I'll put Lord Sebastian into a taxi home and powder my nose,' said Miss Crumb. 'Won't be a tick.'

I brushed my hair, grateful it took so little managing now it was short, did what I could to stitch up the sleeve of my dress and returned to the fray. The main troublemakers had been ejected from the club, including most of my cricketing friends. The Armstrong brothers, however, were sitting quietly at a table in the corner, drinking beer. The band was playing a slower number, the hostesses were darting around soothing ruffled tempers, and the bar was doing a roaring trade.

'Are you all right, duckie?' Miss Potts bustled over, pompoms bouncing. 'I saw you were right at the heart of it.'

I smiled, although I still felt quite shaken. 'I'm fine, thank you, although my frock came off badly. Luckily, I've been training in jiu-jitsu.'

'Have you really? Maybe you could teach us. It sounds very useful.' Miss Potts looked impressed.

'I'm still a beginner. You should come to Golden Square. Mrs Garrud gives the lessons. She trained the suffragettes, you know.'

Miss Potts' face changed. At first, I thought it was the

mention of the fearsome suffragettes, then I saw she was looking over my shoulder.

'Evening, Miss.' It was the same East End voice as earlier, but now it was trying not to be. 'I wondered if you would like to join us for a drink.' His expression was docile, penitent. 'I wanted to apologise properly on behalf of my brother and myself. I'm Edward Armstrong, and my brother is Vincent. I hope you haven't come to any harm.' The care with which he aspirated his aitches was a dead giveaway.

Curious to find out more, I allowed him to lead me to their table and asked for a lemonade. I felt I needed my wits about me.

Vincent Armstrong was slumped in his chair, staring at his shoes. The two men were superficially alike, although Edward's handsome features, coarsened into brutality in his brother's face, were subtly different.

'Vince, what have you got to say to the lady?' he asked.

'Sorry. Got carried away,' said Vince. He looked up and stared at me with red-rimmed eyes, like a starving dog outside a butcher's shop. I suppressed a shudder.

'That's better. What's your name, Miss?' asked Edward.

'Miss Swallow.' His expression remained quizzical. 'Marjorie. I'm new. Just started at the club today.'

His face relaxed into a smile. 'I hope we'll become friends, Miss Swallow. Me and Vincent like this club, you see. We like all Lucky Li's restaurants and nightclubs. We'll be coming in regular. Maybe you can make sure we're well looked after?' He tucked a pound note under my lemonade glass.

Miss Crumb had told me that tips were part of the salary, and that it was quite usual for girls to be given money by the clients. But something about his tone of voice made me feel that this was dangerous money. I wasn't sure what would be expected of me in return.

'I'm sure you'll be looked after whether I'm here or not,' I said. 'There's no need to pay me extra for doing my job.' I tried to keep my voice pleasant, to take any sting from my words.

He looked surprised, then laughed. 'Can tell you're new,' he said. 'Most of Li's girls would have that in their pocket before you could wink. Go on, take it. Call it damages for ripping your frock. Never turn down money, Miss Swallow. You never know when you might need it.'

I picked it up and put it in the purse looped over my wrist. I'd give it to Miss Crumb at the end of the evening. She could decide what to do with it.

As if she'd heard me, Miss Crumb came rushing across the floor with a tray. 'There's a bunch of policemen on their way down from Vine Street,' she said, rapidly. 'Gentlemen, glasses on here, please. Marjorie, help me clear away. Miss Potts and Miss Tierney will distribute lemonade.'

The brothers handed over their glasses. 'We'll be off then, Vi. See you again soon,' said Edward. The brothers sauntered towards the exit.

Chapter 19

Miss Crumb and I rushed around the tables, removing glasses and bottles. We poured alcohol from the glasses down the sink in the men's cloakroom while Johnnie the doorman heaved wooden crates of bottles out of the back window and into the area, assisted by the band.

'You all right, Marjorie?' asked Freddie, passing out crates with a practised air. 'Bit of a baptism of fire, ain't it?'

I gave him a quick smile. 'It's certainly lively.'

T-bone squeezed out of the window and lifted boxes over the wall between the back area of the Harlequin and the Italian grocery store next door, where unseen hands received them. When the last one had gone, he pulled himself up onto the wall, where a black cat had been watching proceedings with equanimity, and dropped down the other side.

'He doesn't like policemen,' explained Freddie. 'And he's not completely sure his work permit hasn't run out.'

'All right,' breathed Miss Crumb. 'Now, don't panic. We want everyone on the dance floor. Nice sedate after-theatre tea-dance, that's what we want them to find.'

Freddie and the remainder of the band started up a genteel waltz. The regular customers were all on their feet, the hostesses wheeling decorously around the dance floor. A gentleman in his middle years with an unruffled demeanour held out his hand to me. There was a shout from up the stairs at the front door, and a dozen police officers in uniform clattered down, truncheons drawn.

'Keep going,' said the man I was dancing with. 'It annoys them like anything.' I wasn't sure that I wanted to annoy policemen wielding batons, but what else was there to do?

We waltzed until the policeman in charge yelled at the band to shut their noise, then circled to a halt.

'How can I help you, gentlemen?' asked Miss Crumb. Mr Li appeared behind her, an unperturbed smile on his face. Only the nervous way he smoothed his hair with his hand betrayed his anxiety.

'We've reason to believe you are infringing alcohol licensing regulations by serving alcohol after hours,' said the man. 'Go on,' he told his officers. 'Search the place.'

They began a rather half-hearted search, looking under the tables and tasting the lemonade that had been hastily distributed. Someone had found time to make coffee; those customers who were not dancing were sitting at tables sipping from steaming cups.

It must have been obvious that we'd had warning of the raid. The policeman in charge announced his intention to record everybody's names.

'You are welcome to take my name, Sir,' said Mr Li in his quiet voice. 'But may I ask on what grounds you propose to take the names of my friends? I don't believe you have found any evidence of alcohol being sold illegally on the premises?'

The policeman drew himself up to his full height. 'On the grounds that I suspect that there are people here in possession of illegal drugs, under the auspices of the Dangerous Drugs

Act,' he said. 'And I shall search them until I find them.'

This announcement caused a ripple of concern. 'Dammit,' murmured my dance partner. 'Is there a back exit to this place?'

Miss Crumb's face froze. I suddenly recalled her words about pep and powdering her nose. Miss Tierney looked equally dismayed. Only Mr Li remained unruffled.

'I believe you need a warrant to search my guests, as you are on private premises,' he said. 'May I see it?'

The look on the policeman's face made it clear he had no such warrant. 'You may not,' he said. 'Right. I'll let you off this time, Li. But don't think it's the end of it. We're under orders to find out who supplied the cocaine that killed a young lady yesterday. And that's what we'll do.'

Their boots tramped heavily back up the stairs. At a wave from Miss Crumb, the band resumed their set, but no-one's heart was in it. Mr Li announced free drinks for all remaining customers, but even so, the guests started to collect their coats and drift away. By one o'clock, the club was empty apart from the musicians and staff.

'Golly,' said Miss Potts, flopping into a chair as Freddie closed the piano lid and Mr Harpo disassembled his clarinet. 'What a night.' She kicked off her shoes and massaged her toes.

I sat next to her, my feet throbbing. 'Is it always like this?'

She laughed weakly. 'What, a brawl and a police raid? No, thank goodness. Beginner's luck, I'd say.'

Mr Li walked into the centre of the room. 'Thank you, everyone, for your efforts tonight. I know it has been a difficult evening. But you remained calm, and all is well.'

He beamed at the staff, but there was warning in his eyes. 'You heard what our friend from the Metropolitan Police had to say. We are under scrutiny, because of the sad death of our customer Miss Caldwell. If you are aware of any attempts to bring illicit drugs into this club, please alert Miss Crumb or me immediately. We will not tolerate such things on our premises. That's all. Goodnight.'

I changed out of my Pierrette dress and wrapped it up to take home. I'd need to launder and mend it for the next evening. I glanced at the clock. In half an hour, Graham would be outside to collect me. It was a relief not to have to negotiate the streets on my own.

Miss Potts and Miss Tierney yawned their way up the stairs, calling their goodbyes. The Misses Proudfoot slipped into matching fox-fur jackets, hats and muffs.

'Wish us luck,' said Hester. 'We're ganning to The Savoy for a nightcap with Count Rostokovich and his brother. We may be in Moscow by Monday.'

Miss Crumb smiled indulgently and shook her head as they disappeared up the steps with the remaining musicians. 'Still here, Miss Swallow?' she asked.

I explained that I was waiting for my father to accompany me home.

'That's good. I'm glad he looks after you. Come and sit with us in the office while you wait.'

The black cat had insinuated itself inside and was curled up by the fire, purring with contentment. I crouched down to scratch it behind the ears. I'd always been fond of cats. I liked their independence and admired the way they always seemed to find the cosiest corner and the best things to eat.

'That blinking moggie's had another litter of kittens,' said Miss Crumb. 'I saw them out the back.'

Mr Li sipped slowly at a glass of whisky, his face showing

exhaustion now that there was no audience to impress. Miss Crumb sat on the arm of his chair and patted his hand.

'All's well, like you said,' she told him. 'No arrests, no serious injuries.'

He shook his head. 'We are vulnerable, Violet. The Armstrong brothers bring trouble wherever they go. I have spoken to our neighbouring clubs and to the other West End restaurants. They are tightening their grip. A brawl here, a raid there; then the brothers step in and offer their protection. And where the Armstrongs go, illicit drugs go too.'

'We keep a clean club,' said Miss Crumb, a little too brightly. 'Nothing to find. We won't let them get a foot-hold.'

'I fear they may already have a foot-hold,' said Mr Li. 'But I will not let them bring their filthy trade here.' He watched me over the rim of his glass. 'And then there is the tragic death of Miss Daisy Caldwell. She wasn't a chorus girl or a hostess, Violet. She had important friends. Didn't she, Miss Swallow?'

Miss Crumb's eyes flashed towards me. 'You knew her?'

I nodded. 'Not very well. But we had friends in common. We came here together on Wednesday night.'

She drew her dark brows together. 'Wednesday? The night before she died? And you arrived on Friday looking for a job. Miss Swallow, I don't believe this is a coincidence.'

I thought quickly. 'Actually, that's why I was here on Wednesday. She'd told me one of the girls was leaving. She suggested I came along with her cousin and...' I hesitated, wondering how to describe Mr Franklin without involving the ambassador.

'And her boyfriend?' said Miss Crumb. 'That dandified young man that used to hang around with her, I suppose. Not seen much of him recently.'

'No, Mr Franklin. He's just a colleague of her uncle,' I said. 'He works in the office. He was only there to make up the party.'

So, who was the young man who used to go to the Harlequin with Daisy? Another mystery to clear up, and an important one. I thought of the fragment of letter in her wastepaper basket. Was he the 'darling' she was writing to? I wondered if Felicity would know.

'So anyway,' I said, picking up my story, 'she'd been practising steps with me. The Charleston, and so on.' I saw a ghost of a smile on Mr Li's lips. 'She's... she was very keen on anything new. And she knew I wanted to find a job that involved dancing. She was just being kind, really. And after she died... well, I thought I might as well press on.'

They were both watching me, their faces solemn. Did they believe me?

Mr Li nodded. 'I think I understand. And you did well tonight, Miss Swallow. Didn't she, Violet?'

Miss Crumb's face softened. 'You did. Now, make sure you get plenty of sleep. Be back here at eight-thirty pip emma, ready to go again.'

Chapter 20

Thankfully, Saturday was much less eventful than my first night at the Harlequin. The Armstrong brothers did not make an appearance, the customers concentrated on dancing and drinking, and the only policeman I saw wished me a good night as I trotted up the stairs into the taxi-cab that Graham had waiting.

But even so, I was exhausted. Dancing and being pleasant might sound like an attractive way to make a living, but I wasn't sure I had the stamina to do this full-time. The club was closed from Sunday until Wednesday; time to rest and recover.

My admiration for the professional dance hostesses increased. Each had their own style, I saw. The Proudfoots – who had reappeared on Saturday night looking refined and polished as ever – specialised in foreign aristocracy, who thought their Geordie accents exotic. Miss Potts mothered the younger men; Miss Tierney played the flirt with older customers.

And Violet Crumb, despite being no older than thirty, was the undisputed queen of the club. I liked her style, confidence, and ironic humour. It gave me hope, to see a woman running things with absolute competence and being accorded due respect. I wasn't sure where I fitted in at the Harlequin yet, but was still disturbed at having been singled out by Edward Armstrong on my first evening.

Mrs Jameson left me to sleep in until almost midday on Sunday, then plied me with an enormous pile of eggs and bacon on my descent to the breakfast room. I'd been too sleepy on Saturday to tell her much more than the bare bones of my adventures, but now she wanted to know all about the club.

'There is something odd going on,' I said. 'I think Miss Crumb knows more than she's saying about cocaine. She looked anxious when the police threatened to search everyone. So did one of the other hostesses.' Not to mention the customer I'd been dancing with.

'But then Mr Li gave this speech, saying that it was important anyone told Miss Crumb if they suspected drugs were being brought into the club. And he asked me to tell him if I found anything out. It's confusing. And then there's the Armstrong brothers. Where they go, illegal drugs follow, he said.'

Mrs Jameson tapped her chin with a pen. 'Perhaps Mr Li doesn't know everything that's going on in his club. He's not there all the time, I suppose. Tell me more about these gangster types. They sound rather worrisome.'

I explained about the Armstrong brothers, and their insistence on giving me money. I'd offered it to Miss Crumb, but she'd told me to keep it. She said that it would get complicated if some of the girls shared and others didn't.

'The other girls seem scared of them,' I said. 'And one of the brothers, Vincent Armstrong, looks like a nasty piece of work. He would have killed that boy if I hadn't stopped him.'

Graham coughed apologetically as he refilled my coffee cup.

'If I might add my tuppence ha'penny?' he asked. 'I know something about the Armstrong family. Most of us that grew up in Limehouse do, for better or worse. Usually worse.'

Mrs Jameson made him sit down at the table and drink a cup of coffee with us, while she grilled him for more details. The Armstrong family started out at the racecourses, running betting syndicates, he told us. But they terrorised their neighbours.

'That family is the reason I left the East End, Mrs Jameson. I grew up in my parents' pub, the Red Lion. It wasn't a fancy place, but my old dad ran it beautifully. Never any trouble, and the place was so clean you could see your face in the brasses.'

I could see where Graham had got his pride in things being done properly. His face had taken on a glow, like the gas had been lit inside.

'Then Jasper Armstrong – that's Ted and Vince's father – decided he wanted the Red Lion for himself. Dad had barred Jasper for getting drunk and starting fights. He wouldn't have it, see. And Jasper went crying to his brothers, and between them they made my parents' lives a misery until they finally agreed to sell. Brawls, break-ins, hiding stolen goods on the premises and tipping off the police. Arson attacks. Telling everyone the beer was watered down – which it most certainly was not. You name it.

'The day my parents sold the Red Lion, I left to wash plates in a hotel in the West End. I decided I'd rather do that than stay and watch the Armstrongs lord it over the old place. It broke my dad's heart. They moved right out to Essex and bought a bungalow. Then Jasper Armstrong drank himself to death within the year.'

His kindly face was flushed pink, his voice indignant. This

was the most information I'd ever heard about Graham's life, and I was fascinated.

'And what about this illegal drugs business?' asked Mrs Jameson. 'Have you heard anything about that?'

He shook his head. 'I don't go back, except to see my sister and her children every now and then. But you know what it's like at the docks. All sorts of goods coming in and going out. I wouldn't be surprised if the Armstrongs were mixed up in something like that.'

'What about Frankie?' I asked, remembering how he'd told me that his sister's children had grown up with her. 'She still lives in Limehouse, doesn't she?'

Graham considered. 'She might know something,' he agreed. 'That girl knows everyone in Limehouse and beyond. She used to be involved in one of those girl gangs...' he tailed off, glancing quickly at Mrs Jameson. 'Nothing to speak about, though. Just kids' stuff. A bit of minor pilfering. But she's out of it now, with this motor mechanic business. Back on the straight and narrow.'

Mrs Jameson pushed back her chair. 'That's useful, then. Marjorie, you can follow up that lead.'

I yawned again. It was time I went south of the river for my Sunday afternoon in Catford. I would take the Pierrette costume with me. Jenny, our housemaid, had done what she could, but my mother was the best seamstress I knew. I'd tell her it was a costume for a fancy dress party.

'Don't be too late back,' Mrs Jameson said. 'Remember the inquest opens tomorrow. I want to be there before it starts so we can talk to Henry and the family solicitor. You should be there too, Marjorie, in case they need you to take the stand.'

In all the excitement, I'd quite forgotten about Daisy's

inquest. I hoped I would not be called. If I was outed as Mrs Jameson's assistant, my cover at the Harlequin would be completely blown.

Chapter 21

Monday dawned cheerless and chilly, a raw easterly wind whipping up Horseferry Road from the river. Mrs Jameson and I emerged from the taxi-cab onto the pavement, pulling our coats and scarves closely around us. Mrs Jameson was all in black, her coat and hat sombre and more old-fashioned than most of her clothes. Unsure whether I should be in mourning or not, I'd buttoned a black jacket over my skirt and blouse and pulled on the hateful black hat I'd worn for a year after the telegram came about my brother. I hoped my grey coat with the red trim would do; I didn't have any other.

We hurried towards the handsome red-brick building, where a porch offered some shelter from the wind. Groups of people huddled around, including several press photographers. I kept two paces behind Mrs Jameson, my head down, hoping I would not be photographed. Policemen stood at the gates. Daisy's death was big news.

Ambassador Caldwell strode out of the courthouse to greet Mrs Jameson. He seemed calmer than when we had last seen him, but his face was still a shocking shade of grey.

'Come inside quickly. Ignore the vultures,' he said, throwing the press a contemptuous look. 'The police will have to let them in when the court opens, but they have been kind enough to offer us a modicum of privacy before then.'

Inside, Mr Franklin stood with Felicity, both looking solemn. They were in full mourning. Felicity's new black hat rather suited her, with its polka dot half-veil. She was pale but composed, her auburn hair out of the habitual braids and twisted into a French pleat. For once, she looked like a young woman, not a child. Perhaps the tragedy had forced her to grow up. Standing a little awkwardly behind her was Harriet, wearing her maid's uniform underneath a black coat and hat.

'Thank you for coming early,' said Ambassador Caldwell, taking off his hat and pushing his hand through his hair. 'It's all pretty grim. The police will be called first, then the doctor. Unfortunately, they are insisting that Felicity needs to give evidence, as she found Daisy. They even want to talk to the maid.'

'Of course. I'm sorry, Felicity. That will be difficult, I'm sure,' said Mrs Jameson. 'And how have you been, Henry?'

He shrugged his shoulders, looking helpless. 'It's a nightmare. I had a wire from my brother. He says he'll come over on the next boat. It was almost as if he'd been expecting it.'

He drew a long, quivering breath. 'I've had to leave most of the work to Franklin. Thank God, he's been wonderful. Dealt with the Foreign Office and all the arrangements for the debt conference.' He glanced towards the young man talking to Felicity, who gazed up at him, her face trusting.

'I had my doubts about Franklin at first, I'll admit,' said the ambassador quietly. 'He left his last posting in Paris rather suddenly, and I never heard a good explanation for it. But I've had no complaints. He works hard and is pleasant company.'

Mrs Jameson nodded, flashing a meaningful glance at me. I knew her well enough now to interpret. We would need to investigate Mr Franklin's previous post.

'Before we go in, I wanted to tell you that we are making progress with our investigation of the Harlequin club,' she said. 'Marjorie is working there, undercover. It would be most helpful if her relationship to me could be kept quiet, while we continue the investigation.'

He turned and grasped my hand, his green eyes lighting up eagerly. 'I'm most grateful, Miss Swallow. What have you found out?'

I wished I had more to tell him. 'Not much yet, I'm afraid. But two men with criminal connections have been visiting the place, and they seem to have links to the illegal drugs trade. I hope to find out more this week.'

But that was unlikely to happen if my photograph was on the front of the *Westminster Gazette* with the caption 'Miss Marjorie Swallow, undercover assistant to lady detective Mrs Jameson.'

'Good.' He nodded firmly. 'And this Chinese character. Have you met him yet?'

I nodded. 'Mr Li. I have, but I don't think he's involved.'

The ambassador gave a short laugh. 'Believe me, they're always involved. Very well, young woman. Keep at it. And take care of yourself. We don't want any more casualties.'

A clerk bustled up, his watch in his hand. 'We're about to start, Ambassador. Perhaps you and your party would like to come through before the public is admitted?'

'I'll wait,' I suggested. 'I'll be less conspicuous if I go in with the rest of the crowd.'

The Caldwells, Mr Franklin and Harriet disappeared through the courtroom doors with Mrs Jameson. Moments later, the lobby was flooded with people. I let myself be swept along as they flowed into the wood-panelled courtroom and took their seats on the hard chairs. The Caldwells were in the front row. I managed to find a seat three rows back, between a newspaper reporter with his notebook and two girls who seemed to be there to gawp. One opened her handbag and extracted a paper bag of boiled sweets, which they crunched noisily.

I kept my hat low over my face and took out my notebook. Mrs Jameson had asked me to take a shorthand record of the proceedings.

'You in the newspaper trade?' asked the young man to my left, with surprise. I shook my head.

'Not yet, but I'd like to be,' I said. 'I'm taking a course in shorthand. This is good practice.'

That seemed to satisfy him. 'Good luck to you, Miss. Going to be a nice juicy one, this,' he confided. 'My guvnor is keeping back half a page for a verbatim account. Wayward American flapper, dope, Lucky Li's nightclub – you couldn't make it up.'

I suppressed a shiver. It sounded like the newspapers had already made up their minds about the story before the inquest had even started.

'All rise,' called a voice at the back.

Chapter 22

We stood as a short man in black legal robes walked briskly to the centre of the bench at the front of the courtroom.

'Sir Leonard Tebbings,' whispered my reporter friend. 'Firm but fair. He doesn't take any nonsense.'

'You may be seated,' said Sir Leonard, looking at us mildly over the top of his spectacles.

He began by addressing a few kind words to Ambassador Caldwell and Felicity.

'An inquest is a necessary but difficult procedure for a grieving family,' he said. 'Discovering the truth about an unexpected and untimely death can be painful and you may hear evidence that you find distressing. However, I hope the process will help you to make your peace with Miss Daisy Caldwell's demise. I will try to ensure your ordeal is not more difficult than it need be.'

He stared hard at the reporters on the benches around me. 'And on that note, I wish to remind the gentlemen of the press that I will tolerate no ill-manners, no harassment of witnesses or the bereaved inside or in the environs of this courtroom, and no rudeness to the officers of the court. I will not hesitate to clear the court if these rules are not followed, and anyone who makes a nuisance of themselves can expect to be held in contempt.'

The first witness to be called was Sergeant Borden. I sank down in my seat. I hoped he would not need to discuss who had handled Daisy's gold box of cocaine.

The policeman was sworn in, took out his notebook and began droning away about the circumstances which led to his arrival at Ambassador Caldwell's residence in Prince's Gate.

'I was informed that the deceased had been found unresponsive at just after one o'clock, when her cousin went to call her for the midday meal,' he said. 'The family doctor, who was already in attendance on the deceased's aunt, confirmed death had occurred some hours previously. When I arrived, Dr Spink told me the death was due to an overdose of cocaine, and a box containing the drug was on the bedside table. I removed the box and the contents have been analysed and confirmed to be cocaine. Miss Caldwell's possession of this substance was in contravention of the 1920 Dangerous Drugs Act,' he said, stolidly.

'Thank you, Sergeant Borden. I believe you have submitted the report of the laboratory which analysed the substance? Ah, yes, here it is.'

Sir Leonard looked over his glasses again. 'So, you have confirmed that the unfortunate young lady was found dead beside a box containing cocaine. Have you confirmed that it was her box?'

Sergeant Borden swelled with pride. I wondered if my moment of unmasking was at hand. 'We have, Sir Leonard. The box was identified by several parties, including Miss Caldwell's cousin and her maid, as having been in her possession previous to the morning in question.'

Sir Leonard made a note. I held my breath as he asked the

next question.

'And what does the post-mortem examination tell us about the cause of death?' He rifled through his papers, a frown creasing his brow. 'Where is the report? I expected to see it here this morning, but I don't believe I have it.'

For the first time, the sergeant looked uncomfortable. 'There wasn't any need for a post-mortem examination,' he said. 'The doctor said the cause of death was clear.'

There was absolute silence in the courtroom. Sir Leonard looked up from his papers, an expression of incredulity on his round face. Colour began to mount in his cheeks.

'There wasn't... any... need?' he asked, his voice rising an octave with each word. 'Who, exactly, decided that the unexpected death of a healthy young woman – a death with potential criminal connotations – did not require a post-mortem?'

'Well, Sir,' the policeman swallowed hard, 'the doctor was very clear about it being cocaine. So, I made that recommendation to my superior. I didn't want to cause the family any more distress, Sir. Like what you said.'

The silence following his words lasted almost a minute. It must have been the longest minute of Sergeant Borden's life. But Sir Leonard's voice, when it came, was back to its usual mild tone.

'The fundamental purpose of an inquest, Sergeant, is to establish as far as is possible the cause of death, and a post-mortem examination is necessary for that purpose. While I aim to spare the family any unnecessary pain, my duty is to His Majesty the King. I, too, will be making a recommendation to your superior. Please be seated, Sergeant Borden, but remain present. I may wish to speak to you again once I have heard evidence from this doctor.'

The sergeant made way. I was relieved that my connection had not been discussed. It was also, I had to admit, quite satisfying to see the bumptious policeman taken down a peg.

'The doctor's for it now,' whispered the reporter, with a grin. He turned a page of his notebook and sat up with anticipation.

Poor Dr Spink was indeed in for a rough time. Sir Leonard led him through his evidence, pausing only to allow his incredulity to register.

'Had the young woman been heard to cry out in pain?' No. 'Had she complained of a bad headache?' No. 'Did her body show signs of convulsions?' No. 'Were the bedclothes disarranged in a way that suggested she had become too hot and thrown them off? Had she vomited? Did she exhibit any of the symptoms which are usual in the case of an overdose of cocaine?' No, no, and no again.

'So what, in the name of all that is Holy, led you to the conclusion that this young woman had taken so much cocaine, it killed her?' asked Sir Leonard. 'A conclusion so firm that you told the attending police officer there was no need for a post-mortem examination.'

Dr Spink was brick-red by now and perspiring freely. 'There was a box containing cocaine by her side; she had been suspected of taking cocaine previously, and her pupils were dilated,' he said.

Sir Leonard leaned forward. 'Please explain to the court the significance of this sign.'

Dr Spink seemed relieved to have something medical to explain. 'Cocaine causes the pupils of the eyes to dilate, so that the iris is barely visible, and the pupils look very large,' he said. 'The dilation of her pupils confirmed to me my initial theory that cocaine was the cause of death.'

'And what else might cause this, Dr Spink? Is cocaine the only drug that will affect a person in such a way?'

'Well... No, there are other causes,' said Dr Spink, slowly. 'Pupils dilate naturally in low light, of course. And there are eye drops, which are used by my ophthalmologist colleagues to allow for a thorough eye examination.'

Sir Leonard was following this keenly. 'And is it possible that low light – such as would be expected in a bedroom with the curtains drawn – caused the pupils to dilate to the extent you observed?'

Dr Spink shook his head. 'Not to that extent, Sir Leonard.'

'Eye drops, then. Explain what they are,' said Sir Leonard.

Dr Spink seemed to realise he was on shaky ground. 'Atropine, Sir Leonard, an extract of the nightshade plant. Belladonna. As I said, atropine is used for eye examinations. The drops should be restricted to medical use, in my opinion. But they are also used for cosmetic purposes. Some of the modern girls have got it into their heads that large pupils are attractive. They use atropine drops as they would lipstick, or rouge on the cheeks. Most unwholesome, in my opinion.'

'Thank you, Dr Spink. If I require your opinion, I will ask for it. Right now, I am interested in the medical facts of the case.'

Sir Leonard counted the facts off on his fingers. 'Miss Caldwell was found dead with a box of cocaine next to her. She had exhibited none of the usual symptoms of cocaine poisoning. Her pupils were dilated, which could have been a sign of cocaine poisoning, or could have been the result of cosmetic eye drops. On this basis, you assumed that the death was caused by heart failure brought on by cocaine poisoning and advised the investigating police officer not to order a post-mortem examination. And you have come here today to the court which seeks to establish the cause of her death and expect me to be satisfied with your conclusions. Is that correct?'

'Yes, Sir. No. I... I mean, Your Lordship may or may not be satisfied... I simply wanted to protect the family. And do what seemed best to me. Avoid any unnecessary unpleasantness,' stuttered the doctor.

The reporters were scribbling away frantically. The girl to my right crunched into another boiled sweet, as if she was at the pictures.

Eventually, Sir Leonard allowed Dr Spink to step down. He conferred for a moment with his clerk, then addressed the room.

'Ladies and gentlemen, I am very sorry for this. However, I see no other way. I cannot proceed with this inquest when the cause of death has not been medically confirmed,' he said. 'I am therefore adjourning the hearing until a post-mortem examination report is available. I apologise for the additional distress this delay may cause to Miss Caldwell's family. I shall be writing to the relevant authorities to explain my great dissatisfaction with this situation.'

'All rise,' called the clerk, and Sir Leonard walked from the room.

The seats around me exploded into noise.

'That's a turn-up,' said the reporter, shoving his pen and notebook in his jacket pocket. 'I'd better get outside; they won't let me interview anyone in here. I'll grab them on the street. That policeman and doctor, though. What a shower, eh?' He grinned and clambered over the other reporters to join the rush for the exit.

Desperate to confer with Mrs Jameson, I pushed past the sweet-chomping girls and made my way to the back of the room to wait for her. But as I reached the door, I saw Mr Li rise from seats in the back row. Bother. I would have to keep my distance from Mrs Jameson until he had gone.

'Good day, Miss Swallow. What did you make of that?' he asked. He was wearing a black Astrakhan coat with a cream silk scarf and carried a black Homburg hat. He looked very suave.

I shook my head. 'I'm not sure what it means, apart from more delay,' I said. 'I mean, I suppose the post-mortem will confirm that it was cocaine.'

'Perhaps not,' he said, thoughtfully. 'Perhaps she had taken something to help her sleep. A sedative.'

'Like Billie Carleton?' I hadn't thought of that. Billie Carleton was a young actress who died the morning after the Victory Ball of November 1918. It had been all over the newspapers. She was thought to be addicted to cocaine, and her associates had been arrested for supplying her with drugs. However, some journalists argued that she had taken an accidental overdose of the sedative veronal, which had been prescribed to her for sleeplessness.

'Exactly.' Mr Li's gentle smile held the seeds of hope. 'Perhaps the answers to her friends' questions about Daisy's death are closer to home than to the Harlequin after all, Miss Swallow. Now, had you not better join your other employer?'

I started guiltily. 'My other...'

'Come now, Miss Swallow. I make it my business to know about my employees. And your sudden appearance was too much of a coincidence. I know that Ambassador Caldwell is a friend and compatriot of the esteemed detective Mrs Jameson. Her involvement in the dreadful murder in Bloomsbury last year was well-publicised.'

He'd seen right through my flimsy mask. I felt bad for deceiving him. I supposed that was the end of my nightclub career; just when I was starting to find things out.

'I'm so sorry, Mr Li. We thought it would be a good way to find out what had happened to Daisy,' I said. 'I suppose you want me to leave the Harlequin now?'

He smiled. 'On the contrary. I would like you to continue your investigations. As you know, I am concerned about the influence of the Armstrong brothers on the Harlequin. Edward Armstrong seems to have taken a liking to you. If you can get into his confidence, without putting yourself in harm's way, that would be very helpful.'

I considered this. 'But I do have to report to Mrs Jameson first,' I said.

He inclined his head. 'Of course. But my terms for your continued employment are that you tell me everything it is in my interests to know. I am paying you a rather good salary, after all.'

That was true. Along with the tips, and on top of the salary from Mrs Jameson, I was earning more money than I'd ever dreamt of. His proposal seemed rather reasonable.

He held out his hand and I took it. We shook hands on the agreement.

Chapter 23

There was a stir in the courtroom as Ambassador Caldwell walked heavily towards the door, eyes straight ahead and Mrs Jameson on his arm. John Franklin and Felicity followed, with Harriet behind. The four Americans looked like a family, and I supposed any casual observer would assume Mrs Jameson was the ambassador's wife.

'I must go,' said Mr Li. 'I have business to attend to.' We followed the crowd outside.

Mr Franklin pushed the Caldwell party through a throng of reporters calling for the ambassador's thoughts on the unexpected events of the morning. He got them into a taxi-cab, and I heard him give directions for Prince's Gate before the vehicle disappeared. Well, I would take the bus. It didn't do to get too reliant on taxi-cabs, after all. I wondered when Mrs Jameson would do as she'd proposed a couple of times and buy a motor-car. And if so, whether she would let me drive it.

'Where are you off to, Miss? I usually 'phone my copy back from the Lyons café across the road.'

It was the reporter who had been next to me in the court, emerging from the scrum as the Caldwells' taxi departed.

'Fancy a cuppa? The name's Field. Jonathan Field, reporter

with the *Westminster Gazette*. I might be able to give you some tips.'

I supposed it would do no harm to find out what the press planned to write about the affair. We sat in the window and ordered tea and buns. The café was stuffy and full of people who'd attended the inquest, the windows steamed up with drips running down. The general mood was of disappointment. People had come to hear about Daisy Caldwell's scandalous behaviour and downfall, not medical arguments about post-mortems and dilated pupils.

'The old man will have a fit,' said Mr Field. 'He was expecting to fill three columns with this morning's proceedings. He's not going to be pleased. I'd better string it out a bit.'

I watched him scribble in his notebook, flipping back and forth to find the exact quote or phrase he needed. His shorthand was better than mine, although he did ask to check the occasional word against my notes.

'There. Coroner's outrage at police and medical incompetence halts inquest into American society beauty's drug death. Or something like that. The subs will mess up the headline, no doubt. Excuse me while I go and use the 'phone.'

'Do you remember Billie Carleton's death?' I asked him.

He paused, half out of his seat. 'Course I do. Not likely to forget it.'

'They said it was cocaine then, but some people thought it was veronal, didn't they?'

He sat back down. 'Go on.'

'Well,' I turned the morning's evidence over in my mind, 'what if that doctor had prescribed her a sleeping draught, for example? And she'd taken too much and died. But then he got panicky when she was found dead, so he said it was cocaine.

And he said there was no need for a post-mortem, or else it would have come out.'

Mr Field grinned. 'You have a very suspicious mind, Miss Swallow. An excellent thing in a newspaper reporter. I might run that line past the editor. We could hint at a medical cover-up. The readers would like that.'

While he used the telephone, I drank my tea and thought. There had been eye drops in Daisy's wastepaper bin. I hadn't looked at the label, but what if they had contained atropine? If Daisy had used them before we went out – but no, surely they would have worn off by the next day? I tried to remember if she'd had wide pupils that evening. Her eyes had seemed big and sparkling, especially after she'd gone to the powder room. But then, that could have been cocaine…

I was going around in circles.

Mr Field sat back down and poured another cup of tea. 'I should be getting on. They want me to go over to Prince's Gate, try to get an interview with the ambassador or his wife. But she looked like a right tartar – did you see? Like she eats reporters for breakfast.'

I smothered a laugh at this description of my employer. 'She did look quite stern,' I said. 'You'd better be careful.'

He swallowed a mouthful of tea. 'Tell you what, though. I've been thinking about what you said. What if she'd taken opium? That makes your pupils go tiny, like pin-pricks. I saw it once, after my editor sent me to Limehouse to investigate an opium den. Horrible place. But then, the doctor gives her those eye drop things, so it looks like cocaine. Like you said, a cover-up.'

My head was spinning now. Limehouse. Opium. Why would Dr Spink be connected, though? Unless, of course, he was somehow involved in the supply of opium. Did doctors still prescribe it, now that morphine was available?

My thoughts wound back to Limehouse.

'Do you know anything about two brothers called Edward and Vincent Armstrong?' I asked.

He pushed back his cup and saucer. 'Do I? You don't want anything to do with the Armstrong brothers, Miss. Nasty pieces of work, they are. They're the ones behind that opium house I went to. Vince is just a thug, but Ted's vicious. After I wrote my Limehouse story, they posted a parcel to the news room, addressed to me personally. It had a dead rat inside, with its throat cut. Stank the whole place out. You wouldn't catch me going back to Limehouse, Miss. Not for nothing.'

I shivered. 'How horrible. Have you heard about them coming up West, though? I've heard they are trying to take over the West End clubs.'

He gave me a sharp look. 'Are you sure you're not a reporter? You sound pretty well-informed. You're not with the *Post*, are you?'

I tried to blush. 'I wish. I just find crime very interesting. And I read all the newspapers, anything about murders. The *Illustrated Police News* and that.'

He laughed heartily. 'Well, if you believe what you read in that rag, you'll believe anything. Look, I've got to get over to Prince's Gate. Do you want to come?'

I finished my tea and picked up my handbag. I wasn't sure how I would gain entrance to the ambassador's residence without being seen, but I'd think of something.

Chapter 24

We took the 'bus; the number 2 to Hyde Park Corner, then the 33 along Knightsbridge to Prince's Gate. It was freezing outside on the top deck, the sharp wind making my eyes water as we trundled along beside Hyde Park. Even so, I could see that there was already a crowd of reporters outside the railings of number 14. The curtains of the ground floor windows onto Henry Caldwell's office were firmly drawn.

Mr Field clattered down the steps as the omnibus drew to a halt. 'Well, good luck to you, Miss Swallow. Here, take my card. Get in touch when you've finished your course and I'll tell you if I know of any openings for reporters. Let me know if you hear anything more about the Armstrongs. I'd better see what I can manage here. Bit of a scrum, but it can't be helped.'

He disappeared into the throng of reporters. They seemed to be taking turns to approach the policeman standing outside the door with pleas for him to pass on notes scribbled on pages torn from their notebooks. I thought for a minute, remembering my previous visits to Prince's Gate, then walked back along Kensington Road and into Ennismore Gardens, trying to look inconspicuous and respectable. My despised floppy black hat was doing good service today.

As I'd hoped, there was a spot just beyond the grand mansion of Kingston House where all that stood between me and the Prince's Gate Garden was a row of railings. I looked around to check there was no-one in sight, then scrambled up with help from a nearby tree and jumped down the other side, my descent cushioned by piles of dead leaves.

I strolled through the private garden, smiling benignly at a chilly-looking nurse with two muffled-up charges who were playing at riding wooden horses on the lawns. Trying to keep my bearings, I turned north to locate 14 Prince's Gate, the end of the terrace looking out onto Kensington Road. It was easy enough to spot and the wall separating its private terrace from the garden was low. I hopped over without too much difficulty, feeling rather pleased with myself.

'Oi! What do you think you're doing? If you're one of those blooming reporters…' A furious-looking man in mud-caked boots and a gardener's apron stamped across the terrace towards me.

'I'm not,' I protested. 'Honestly. I'm Mrs Jameson's assistant. She's in there now with Mr Caldwell. I didn't want to have to go through all the newspaper people at the front door, so I came around the back.'

'Wait there.' He still looked suspicious. I waited on the terrace, where the man had abandoned his rake on a pile of dead leaves. Momentarily, the sun came out from behind the heavy clouds. Something glinted against the bare earth of the flower bed where the man had been working. I stooped and brushed the remaining leaves away.

At first, I thought it was Daisy Caldwell's gold box. But it couldn't be. The police had taken it away. This looked very similar, though. It was the same size and colour, with the same scallop-shell design.

I pulled on my cotton gloves, then scooped it into a paper envelope and stowed it in my handbag. I wasn't sure of its significance, but I knew Mrs Jameson would want to see it as soon as I could get her alone.

The gardener came back with the housekeeper, who nodded, although she was looking none too friendly. 'Yes, I recognise her,' she said. 'You can come in. Mrs Jameson and Ambassador Caldwell are in the drawing room. Mind you wipe the mud off your shoes.'

I followed her through the kitchen and down the corridor to the green baize door. As we turned the corner, Harriet clattered down the back stairs, her rosy cheeks pinker than ever and her cap askew.

'Oh! Sorry, Mrs Desborough.' Her eyes were bright, and she was a little out of breath. 'Didn't mean to run into you like that. I had to get changed after we came back from the court.'

The housekeeper gave her a look. 'Put your cap straight, girl. And take that smile off your face, or I'll take it off for you.' She shook her head in distaste.

I glanced up the stairs. A pair of legs was visible from the knee down, clad in smart black suit trousers and shiny black shoes. The legs retreated silently, backwards up the staircase. Harriet had been wearing her uniform in court, I remembered. She hadn't needed to change her dress. So what had she been doing?

Thomas the footman showed me to the drawing room. I needed to get him on his own, I remembered. But with Mrs Desborough holding us under her beady eye, I didn't dare say anything.

The ambassador was slumped in an armchair with a whisky and soda in his hand. Mrs Jameson, sitting next to him, looked up at my arrival.

'Oh, there you are, Marjorie. I had begun to think you had got lost. Henry is rather despondent about this morning's debacle – all the fault of that ridiculous policeman, of course. But I thought it was most interesting.'

'The bit about the eye drops…' I began.

'Yes, exactly. And, as I observed last week, the lack of evidence of the usual symptoms of cocaine poisoning. It rather throws open the whole case, until the post-mortem has reached its conclusion. What is it, Marjorie? You look like you want to say something.'

'I had tea with one of the newspaper reporters,' I said. 'I thought it would be a good idea to find out what they are going to write. Which is pretty much what you would expect, I'm afraid. But then we got talking about possible alternatives to cocaine. I suggested veronal. And he suggested opium, because that causes the pupils to contract, but eye drops would reverse that.'

Mrs Jameson looked startled. 'Well, that's true,' she said. 'But where did he get the idea of opium from? Henry, was Daisy prescribed sleeping draughts? Veronal, laudanum, that sort of thing?'

He roused himself from his reverie. 'No, I don't believe so. She never wanted to see the doctor. She always said she was perfectly healthy, even when she was under the weather and Myrtle urged her to consult Dr Spink.'

Mrs Jameson frowned. 'When was Daisy unwell?'

'A couple of weeks ago, I think. Too many late nights, too much champagne. Too much of that damned cocaine, probably. Anyway, I don't see where this is getting us,' said Ambassador Caldwell, his voice impatient.

'The reporter said he'd been investigating an opium house in Limehouse,' I explained. 'Which was run by the Armstrong brothers. So, I wondered if they might have been involved with Daisy's death, because they've been going to the Harlequin.' As I said the words, it sounded far-fetched. 'Sorry. It's probably nothing,' I admitted.

But Ambassador Caldwell had brightened up. 'Who are these devils? If they've been getting innocent girls hooked on opium, I want to see them hanged. We've had no end of trouble with opium gangs in New York. And don't tell me the Chinese aren't involved.'

I opened my mouth to defend Mr Li, but Mrs Jameson shook her head to warn me to keep quiet.

'We'll investigate, Henry,' she said. 'I will ask my friends in the Metropolitan Police what they know about these gangsters. And Marjorie will be back at the club on Wednesday night. If the Armstrong brothers are bringing in opium, we'll find out about it. Now, I think we should be getting back to Bedford Square.'

'Of course. Franklin will see you out.' The ambassador rang the bell and the man appeared. I glanced at his shiny black shoes and sober black suit trousers. Hmm. Had that been him on the stairs with Harriet? What had they been up to?

Mrs Jameson was very quiet in the taxi-cab going home. She tapped her chin rhythmically with her index finger, gazing out of the window onto the dreary afternoon with eyes that saw nothing. I was used to her moods by now and recognised this as one of deep thought.

Usually, I would wait until it passed, but I was keen to show her what I had found on the terrace. I opened my bag and unwrapped the box.

'I found this,' I said. 'I thought you'd want to see it before I mentioned it to anyone else.'

Mrs Jameson stared at it a moment. 'Where?'

'It was in a flower bed by the terrace at the back of the house. The gardener had been sweeping up, and I think he'd uncovered it from the leaves.'

She nodded slowly, as if she had already put this piece of the jigsaw in its place. 'So, it could have been dropped out of Daisy's window,' she said. 'Her bedroom was on the back of the house.'

'I suppose so.'

She clicked it open. There was a tiny trace of powder still inside. But it wasn't fine white crystals, like the other. It was coarse, slightly lumpy, and a greyish colour. It might have looked the same at first glance, I supposed.

Mrs Jameson closed the box and put it back in the bag. 'Well done, Marjorie,' she said. 'Please say nothing about this for the time being. I think I know what this is. But I will have it analysed.'

'And fingerprinted?' I asked.

She meditated a moment. 'Yes. Although I think it is very unlikely that we will find fingerprints on this box. Unless they belong to Daisy herself.'

Chapter 25

By Wednesday night, life as a hostess at the Harlequin had taken on a routine. I rested in the afternoon, then walked to Wardour Street at eight o'clock. The fifteen minute walk took me from a respectable garden square in Bloomsbury to the heart of the rackety West End, passing gangs of young men and women out for a good time, and policemen trying to keep order. I was no longer shocked by the street girls and their customers in the Soho alleyways, although I still distributed a few pennies to the ragged children and limbless soldiers who begged on street corners.

As I approached the club, a slim figure wearing a trilby hat and long overcoat detached itself from the lamp-post at the corner of St Anne's Court and let out a piercing wolf-whistle. I put my head down and hastened my steps. Being accosted by men was all too common in this part of London.

'Oi, Marj!' I turned. 'I thought you wanted to talk to me.'

I laughed. 'Frankie! I thought you were… Never mind. How are you?' I'd written to Frankie on Monday to ask what she knew of the Armstrong brothers.

She lit a cigarette. 'I'll live. Are you going to ask me in for a drink, then?'

I found Frankie a bottle of bitter from the bar, then changed into my Pierrette dress in the powder room. My mother had mended and altered it so it was a perfect fit.

Frankie took a swig from the bottle. 'Very nice.' I wasn't sure if she meant my costume or the beer. 'Right-oh. The Armstrong boys. Like Graham told you, they're a nasty lot. Reckon they're the kings of Limehouse. They've got a finger in everything. Illegal betting syndicates, skimming off a percentage from the docks, smuggling untaxed booze. You can't mess around with them, Marjorie. My Auntie Clara knows old Ma Armstrong from way back, so they mostly leave me and my family alone.'

'Opium?' I asked.

'Yeah, that too. If you can make money from it, they're involved. Ask anyone in Limehouse.'

'If everyone knows about it, why don't they tell the police?' I asked, dabbing eye-black on my lashes.

Frankie rolled her eyes. 'Everyone knows about it, including the police. They're not going to war with the Armstrongs. Especially when they make such generous donations to the Limehouse Police Station's Benevolent Fund.'

She finished her beer as Miss Crumb popped her head around the door.

'Mind yourself with the Armstrong boys, that's what I'm saying. They're bad news. Right, I'm off to Caravanserai. Hot date tonight. Can't keep her waiting.' She winked at Miss Crumb and sauntered up the stairs. The notorious Caravanserai club, which I had visited in memorable circumstances the previous autumn, was a five minute walk away in Ham Yard.

Miss Crumb watched her go with raised eyebrows.

'All right, Miss Swallow? Ready for battle?'

'All ready, Miss Crumb.'

She hesitated, then sat down on one of the pink velvet stools. She pulled out her dark red lipstick. 'Listen, I know what Mr Li said about drugs in the club. You've probably noticed...' she paused and stretched her mouth wide, tracing the colour around her lips, '...some of the girls pep themselves up a bit, towards the end of the night,' she said into the mirror. 'It's just to keep them going. The band, too. If you feel like you need it, let me know, or Miss Tierney. Nothing stronger, mind, and only a pinch. And obviously, keep it quiet.' She turned to me with a bright smile, but her eyes were troubled.

I tried not to look shocked. 'Thank you, Miss Crumb. I'll remember that.' I hesitated, then thought I might as well ask. 'Where does it come from? Do you get it from the Armstrong brothers?'

'Hush.' She looked nervously towards the door. 'No, I'd never do business with them. Taio would kill me.'

'Taio?'

'Mr Li. That's his Christian name. Well, not Christian exactly, but... you know. His given name.' She picked at the velvet on the stool, which was starting to fray.

'The thing is, Miss Swallow, I'm worried about what might come out at the inquest. Taio has been along, and he said he saw you there. I did give Daisy Caldwell a paper wrap once. But I swear I hadn't given her anything for weeks. I only handle very small quantities, and usually just for staff. She must have been getting it somewhere else. And I never gave her enough that would have killed her.'

I buckled up my satin shoes, feeling rather sad. I'd liked and admired Violet Crumb. She'd always seemed so in control. She was not the dope-dealing fiend of Ambassador Caldwell's imagination. But I knew I'd have to report back to Mrs

Jameson about her confession. And what about Mr Li? What would he do if he knew the manageress was selling cocaine in the club? I hated the thought of getting her in trouble, but I had promised to tell him anything I thought he should know.

'I do understand, Miss Crumb,' I said, trying to reassure her. 'Anyway, she might not even have died from cocaine. They said at the inquest that they don't know for sure. She might have been on something stronger. Opium, for example.'

She brushed her shining dark hair and shuddered. 'You wouldn't get me touching that stuff. Taio has told me enough horror stories about what it does to people back home in China. Did you know it came from India originally? And the British brought it to be sold in China? There was a war about it. Two.'

I didn't. But I was more interested to know who might have brought it to be sold to Daisy Caldwell.

'I talked to one of the reporters who was covering the inquest,' I told her. 'He reckons the Armstrong brothers are involved in the opium business. He'd visited their opium den over in Limehouse and written a story about it. He gave me his card.' I showed her Mr Field's business card. 'Said to tell him if I heard anything more about them.'

'Well, for goodness' sake, don't tell him anything about the club,' said Miss Crumb sharply. 'We don't want the Harlequin in the newspapers for the wrong reasons.'

I could hear the band tuning up outside. I put the card in my coat pocket, just as the powder room door burst open, and the Misses Proudfoot, Tierney and Potts all arrived together. From then on, we were in our usual rush to get everything ready.

Seated in my place at the foot of the stairs, I couldn't help staring at Freddie as he ran through scales on the piano. Did he take cocaine to keep him going? He did sometimes get a wide-eyed, slightly manic look towards the end of the evening. I'd put it down to excitement combined with the beer that the band drank freely through the night.

'You like him, don't you?' said Miss Tierney, nudging me. 'That piano player.'

I felt my cheeks redden. 'He's friendly,' I said. 'And he plays very well.'

She snickered. 'And he's a looker, ain't he, despite that scar he tries to hide? Admit it. You've got a pash for him.'

I tried to laugh it off. Was it true, though? I had found myself thinking about Freddie more than usual since starting work at the club. Perhaps it was seeing him in his element, doing what he did best. He was a different person on stage. It was hard to remember him as a shell-shocked patient in the Maudsley Hospital, four years ago.

My romantic musings got no further, however. Edward and Vincent Armstrong sauntered down the stairs and headed straight for us.

'Evening, Miss Swallow, Miss Tierney. Would you care to have a drink with me and my brother?' asked Edward. 'We'd like to get to know you better.'

Now was my chance to find out about their involvement in the opium trade. I'd much rather be able to report back on the Armstrong brothers than incriminate Miss Crumb.

'Likewise,' I said, flashing a bold smile. 'Shall we?'

Chapter 26

Miss Tierney and I followed them to their corner table. Edward ordered champagne. 'And you leave the bottle with me,' he said. 'I know your tricks. If I pay for it, I'm damn' well going to drink it. Begging your pardon, ladies.'

The rather dubious house champagne cost thirty shillings a bottle, and the club bought it for twelve, according to Miss Tierney. The bar staff upped the price to two pounds a bottle after legal licensing hours. I was amazed anyone bought the stuff. You could get a perfectly nice new dress for that.

'I want to dance,' said Vincent, somewhat aggressively, swallowing down a glassful.

Reluctantly, I half-rose, but Edward put a restraining hand on my arm. 'Dance with Miss Tierney, Vince. I want to have a chat with Miss Swallow here.'

Throwing me a nervous glance, Miss Tierney led Vincent Armstrong to the dance floor.

'I like you, Miss Swallow,' said Edward. 'You've got a bit of class, you have. Not like that blonde tart or those uptight Geordie bitches. And my brother has taken a shine to you, too. Where are you from?'

I smiled, choosing to ignore the insults to my fellow Harlequinettes. 'I'm not anything special, Mr Armstrong.'

'Call me Ted, why don't you? I think you're pretty special, Marjorie.'

I blushed. Despite all I knew about him, he was rather charming when he wanted to be.

'Well, I grew up in Catford, south of the river. My dad's a shopkeeper.'

'Is he, now? I'll have to look up his shop, one of these days. What does he sell?'

I felt a cold clutch of fear. I'd been an idiot. Why hadn't I pretended; used a different name or given a different town? Would my parents be receiving a dead rat through the post?

'Bicycles,' I said, wildly. 'Perambulators and bicycles. The shop's in Bromley High Street.' I hoped that was far enough from Swallow's Drapers and Fancy Goods on Rushey Green to put him off the scent.

'And what does a respectable shopkeeper's daughter from Catford do to end up as a dance hostess in Lucky Li's club, eh?' He winked as he topped up my glass. I would have to keep an eye on how much I was drinking.

'I've always been keen on dancing,' I said. 'Miss Crumb was kind enough to give me a chance of doing that professionally.'

He laughed, not a nice laugh. 'If you say so, Miss. I know what you girls are like. And you can't resist that Chinaman, can you? You know where you'll end up.' He leaned his face close to mine. He smelled of lavender soap and sour champagne. 'On the boat to Shanghai, bound for a Chinese whorehouse.'

I recoiled. But I wanted to find out more about the Armstrong brothers and their business. I wasn't likely to get a better chance. I took a gulp of champagne for courage. It really was quite nasty.

I forced myself to laugh.

'You seem to know a lot about China,' I said. 'I suppose there are quite a lot of Chinese people in Limehouse. I've read in the newspapers about opium dens and the like. Have you ever seen one?'

'How do you know we're from Limehouse?' he asked.

Bother. I was giving myself away. 'One of the girls must have told me. But you are, aren't you?'

Vincent Armstrong and Miss Tierney returned to the table. Miss Tierney was looking rather flushed, her hair disarrayed.

'I must dash to the powder room,' she said. 'And I should say hello to the Colonel. He's just come in with his niece. Will you excuse me, gentlemen?' She fled, leaving me alone with the Armstrong brothers.

'The lady wants to know about Limehouse and the opium trade, Vince,' said Ted. 'What do you think? Should we take her out East and show her around sometime?'

Vincent roared with laughter. 'That's a good 'un. Show her around.'

Edward leaned closer to me again. 'Me and Vincent would be happy to show you our humble abode, Miss Swallow. And I'm sure we could arrange a tour of an opium den for you, since you're so keen on seeing one.'

I could hardly believe my luck. This was my chance, but it would be dangerous. I'd agree to meet them, but make sure I had back-up from Scotland Yard. Mrs Jameson's friend Inspector Chadwick would be very interested in that Limehouse opium den. I imagined how impressed he would be when I told him.

'That would be so kind of you,' I said. 'Perhaps we could go on Friday morning.' I hoped that would give the police enough time to prepare a raid.

He grinned. 'Perhaps we could. I'll have a look at my engagement diary.' He pulled his pocket-watch from his waistcoat and checked the time. 'Why don't you and Vince have a little dance, now? Vincent's very keen on jazz dancing.'

He might have been keen, but Vincent Armstrong was an even worse dancer than Felicity Caldwell. He lurched around the dance floor, holding me as if I was a sack of coal he was manoeuvring around a goods yard. I tried to steer him away from collisions with other dancers. Although it was still early, I'd started to feel dreadfully tired. Each step was an effort. There's nothing more exhausting than dancing with a man who doesn't know how.

He ended the dance with a flourish, throwing me over his arm. To my horror, I found my heels slipping. I struggled, but I didn't seem to have full control of my legs. Embarrassed, I landed on my bottom on the floor in front of the band.

'Oops-a-daisy!' called Vincent, pulling me up. But my legs barely held me, and my head had started to spin. What was happening? I'd had barely a glass of champagne, but I felt as if I'd had a bottle.

I heard the piano falter to a halt, and Freddie's voice.

'What's going on?'

'She's had a glass too many,' said Ted, taking my other arm. 'You carry on, matey. We'll look after this one. She needs a bit of air.' They lugged me away from the dance floor.

'Miss Crumb,' I slurred. 'Where's Miss Crumb?'

'We'll take you up to her office,' said Ted. 'Come on, Miss Swallow. Lean on my shoulder.'

Overcome with shame at my condition, I let them lead me out of the club and up the stairs. At the top, Johnnie looked at me in alarm.

'Are you all right, Miss Swallow?' The burst of cold air brought a moment of clarity. I hadn't had too much to drink. I'd been drugged. The brothers must have slipped something into my champagne.

'No,' I said. 'No, Johnnie, tell Miss Crumb…'

A motorcar drew up next to the kerb and Ted Armstrong pulled open the door. 'Get in,' he said. They shoved me into the back seat. The last thing I heard before I passed out was the roar of the London traffic.

Chapter 27

When I awoke, it was dark as pitch and my head felt fuzzy. I was uncomfortably curled up on a leather seat in the back of a moving vehicle, squashed next to a man's leg.

'What's happening?' I asked, confused. My throat was sore, my mouth dry.

'She's waking up,' said the man next to me. A voice with an East End accent. I rubbed my eyes, trying to remember. I knew that voice, and I didn't like it. Why did I feel so sleepy?

'I only gave her half a grain,' said another voice. 'No point in wasting it. I want her awake.'

My eyes snapped open. Edward Armstrong. And the other voice was his brother, Vincent.

I lay still, willing my mind into alertness. Brief snatches came back – the Harlequin, talking to Ted about Limehouse and opium dens. Dancing with Vince. I shuddered, remembering how I'd fallen on the dance floor, and they'd carried me out.

I swallowed, and fear flooded my mouth. Where were they taking me? What did they want? I remembered Ted's words about ending up on a ship bound for Shanghai. But he'd been teasing me, surely. I struggled upright, keeping as far from Vincent Armstrong as I could. I couldn't see much out of the windows: the streets were unlit, and no moonlight had made it through the cloudy sky.

I pulled the window down with the strap.

'Are you going to throw up?' asked Ted. 'Do it out the window. I don't want you messing up my car.'

I wasn't, but the cold, damp air blew away the fuzziness in my brain. I sniffed. No mistaking that dank salt smell: we were by the river. I listened, heard a deep creaking sound, like tall trees swaying in the woods. Masts, perhaps, of sailing ships moored at the docks. A sudden strong smell of horse manure, a whistle and roar of a passing train. We rattled over a bridge, and I had a glimpse of water and boats. To my right was the wide sweep of the river, shrouded in mist; to the left, the Regents Canal Basin crowded with coal barges, their lights twinkling in the darkness.

The view of the water was quickly obscured by the backs of warehouses as we plunged down a narrow street, crowded on each side by dock buildings and public houses. We were heading into the heart of Limehouse.

'What do you want?' I asked, trying to make my voice firmer than it felt. 'Why have you brought me here?'

Ted laughed nastily. 'You asked for it, Missy. A Limehouse opium den, you said. Well, your wish is our command. Isn't it, Chang?'

The man driving the car also laughed. In the gaslight as we passed a narrow-fronted pub, I saw his face. For a second, I thought it was Mr Li, but of course I was wrong. This face was coarse, the smile gap-toothed as he laughed, a harsh bark of a sound.

. The car swung left, away from the river. The warehouses were replaced by mean-looking terraced houses crammed together. We went under the railway line and the buildings changed again: boarding houses and food shops; tall houses whose purposes I could not divine. We rattled over cobbles and splashed through puddles where the road had broken up.

The car turned again into an entrance so narrow, it could barely pass between the coal-blackened brick walls. I caught a glimpse of the sign: Ming Street.

'Get out,' said Ted. 'Don't be stupid enough to run away. You have no idea what the people in these streets would do to you. Unless you fancy taking your chances in a boarding house full of unemployed sailors, dressed in that carnival outfit?'

I got out. Vince gripped my arm. I shivered, wishing I at least had my coat over my flimsy Pierrette dress. The car drove on.

Ted rapped on a nondescript door. It was opened by a Chinese woman in a tatty ivory silk wrap. Her eyes widened at the sight of me, held captive on either side by the Armstrong brothers. I stared at her, trying to send an appeal with my eyes, but she dropped her gaze quickly and beckoned us in.

Chapter 28

A heavy, sweet smell hung about the place, making my nose itch. From the darkened rooms leading off the corridor came drowsy murmurings, the occasional giggle. Someone was singing softly, a song with no particular melody that went on and on. Red-glass oil lamps hung from the ceilings.

This was it then. A proper Limehouse opium den. I'd been curious to see one, but now I wished myself anywhere else. Would they force me to take the drug? In my mind's eye I saw lurid pictures: myself being held down and injected with the horrible stuff or hypnotised into smoking an opium pipe. I'd never even smoked a cigarette.

The woman showed us into a room with low couches and cushions on the carpeted floor. A small fire burned in the grate, its warmth barely penetrating the chill. The floor was unswept, the cushions grubby and stained.

'You want something?' she asked Ted.

'Not now. Maybe later,' he said. 'Just leave us here quietly, all right? No interruptions.'

'I don't suppose I could have a cup of tea, could I? I'm chilled right through,' I said, rubbing the gooseflesh on my arms.

Ted laughed. 'Go on, then, Annie May. Bring her a cup of tea. Might as well make us a pot.' The woman hurried away.

He took a seat on one of the couches. The red lamp flickered, giving his face a satanic glow.

'Sit down.' Ted pointed at the couch next to the fire. I took it, moving as close as I could to the flames. I was shivering hard.

'How long's this going to take?' asked Vincent, slouching against the mantelpiece. 'You promised.'

'Shut up, Vince. It'll take longer if you keep yapping,' said Ted. There was a gentle tattoo on the door and Annie May came back in, carrying a lacquered tray with a small iron teapot and three porcelain beakers. She poured the tea. No milk, no sugar. No matter: I drank the fragrant hot liquid gratefully.

'Ooh, that's lovely. It smells of jasmine. Thank you.' The briefest flicker of a smile passed over Annie May's face. 'Won't you have a cup?' I asked her, hoping to make a friend. She might be my only connection to the outside world. 'I'm Marjorie. Marjorie Swallow.'

But she didn't look back as she left. The door closed behind her.

I took a deep breath. What now?

Ted sipped his tea. 'You'll get no help there. We own her. Now, what are you really doing at the Harlequin? I mean, you have a nice cosy job as secretary to Mrs Jameson, don't you? Mrs Jameson, the private detective who also happens to be a close friend of Inspector Chadwick of Scotland Yard.'

I stared at him in dismay. How did he know all that?

'You're not the only one with connections in the Metropolitan Police, you know. When people ask questions about me, I like to know who I'm dealing with. And my friends like to keep on my good side. So, I'm asking again, what are you doing at the Harlequin?'

'I... I wanted to dance,' I began, lamely.

He sighed. 'Marjorie, you've got a pretty face.' He reached in his pocket and pulled out a vicious-looking short knife, the blade stuck into a cork. He removed the cork. 'I don't want to have to spoil it, but I promise you, I will if you lie to me one more time.'

The glint of the knife in the firelight chilled me to the stomach. I had no doubt that he was telling the truth. Would I be able to disarm him in time, if he came for me? My jiu-jitsu training had included how to take a knife from a man, and I'd managed to throw his brother, but Ted was sharper than Vince. And, of course, there were two of them. One could hold me down while the other... I shuddered. It wasn't just the thought of the damage to my looks. I wasn't sure I could bear the pain.

'Then I will tell you nothing,' I said, defiantly.

Ted crouched in front of me, holding the blade right before my eyes. 'Then, Marjorie, I will leave you here with my brother. Like I said, he's taken a right shine to you. He won't care if you talk or not. All the same to him. And when I come back in the morning, I'll carve his name right across your face, so everyone knows who you belong to.'

I stared at him, hardly able to believe that such evil could come from his mouth. He seemed completely unperturbed by the nature of his threats and was no doubt ruthless enough to carry them out. I had few enough cards to play. I might as well play one now.

'I'm investigating the death of Daisy Caldwell,' I said. 'On behalf of the American Ambassador to London, with the full knowledge of Scotland Yard, who will have followed me here. I'm going to find out who supplied her with cocaine, or opium, or whatever killed her. Was it you?'

He laughed, rocking back on his heels. 'Oh, Marjorie. You are a joker. I'm not some tin-pot small-scale dope-dealer. I'm insulted that you'd think I would bother.' The blade flashed in the firelight and a hot pain flared on my left cheek. I gasped and clutched my face. It was wet.

I understood what I was dealing with now. These men were ruthless beyond anything I'd met before. Even if I told them everything about our investigation into Daisy's death and the Harlequin club, I had no doubt that they would still carry out their evil threats. Would I even make it out alive, now I'd seen where they operated? There was only one chance left. I would have to fight.

I sprang to my feet, grabbed his knife hand, and twisted his wrist back the way I'd learned. Taken by surprise, he shouted out and dropped the blade. I kicked it into the hot coals.

'Help me, Vince, you idiot!' yelled Ted.

His brother, who had been watching us vacantly as if he'd been at the Saturday morning pictures, grabbed my arm. But I'd been expecting that, and let him pull me close to him, before stamping on his instep with my heel. He yelled and fell back against the fireplace.

Ted had freed his wrist and was onto me again, pinning both arms behind me. I struggled and twisted, but I had no purchase against him. I needed to make space, to give myself a place to lever his weight. I couldn't find it.

'Knife, Vince,' said Ted, his voice tight beside my ear. 'Show her what's in store for her.'

Vincent pulled a blade from his jacket and took the cork from the tip. He looked at me, then at his brother.

'Seems a bit of a shame,' he said. 'Don't it?'

'There'll be others,' Ted Armstrong said.

Chapter 29

Footsteps sounded outside in the corridor. I could hear whispering, then a tap on the door. The brothers looked up.

'Keep your mouth shut,' Ted warned me, his voice low. 'Vince, see what's happening. Tell them to get lost.' He took the blade from his brother and held it to my throat.

I heard the door open, and tried to twist my head to see what was happening. 'You stay still,' warned Ted. Cautiously, I moved my elbow back. There was a bit of space now that he couldn't use both hands to pin my arms. But with the knife against my neck, I didn't dare use it.

'Sorry to disturb, Mr Armstrong,' said a soft Chinese-accented woman's voice. Annie May? 'There's a girl here asking for you. She says it's about your mother, very urgent. Miss O'Grady, she says you know her auntie.'

O'Grady? Could it possibly be...

It was.

'Your mum's very sick, Vince. She sent me to get you and your brother,' called Frankie from the corridor. 'My Auntie Clara's with her now. She says she hasn't got long.'

Ted relaxed his knife hand and turned towards the door. 'What do you mean, not long?'

I saw my chance and took it. I elbowed his arm away and

147

ducked under the blade.

'Careful,' I shouted. 'He's got a knife.'

The next few seconds were a bit of a blur. Vince doubled over, although I didn't see Frankie's blow. I grabbed Ted's little finger and pulled it back until it broke, forcing him to drop the knife. It skidded across the floor. Both Ted and I dropped to our knees to scramble after it. I saw a red silk slipper close over it, and looked up. Annie May stood impassive, her foot covering the weapon. Ted hadn't seen. She began to inch her way towards the door, pulling the knife with her.

I started to rise, but Ted launched himself on top of me, trying to get an arm around my neck. I dropped one shoulder, and he lurched forward, but maintained his grip.

'You little devil,' he gasped. Seconds later, there was more commotion at the door.

'Let her go.' I looked up in shock. It was Freddie, trying to drag Ted off me by his shirt collar. Oh, goodness. I wasn't sure if he'd be more hindrance than help. But I'd forgotten he'd been a soldier.

He pulled Ted up by brute force and punched him on the jaw, sending him crashing across the room. Frankie and Vincent were tussling on the floor, with Frankie getting the better of it. Then Chang, the Chinese man who'd driven the car, appeared in the doorway, his face panicked. He pulled Annie May into the corridor and shut the door. Both Ted and I saw the knife at the same time and dived for it.

We each got a hand to it. I yelled to Freddie for help, and he dragged Ted back by the hair, then knelt on his chest while I prised his fingers from the knife. Frankie looked up from where she had Vincent Armstrong in a head-lock.

Three of us, two of them. We had the upper hand, but

we were on their territory. No doubt Chang would call for reinforcements. Gang members from all over Limehouse might be arming and assembling as we struggled.

'We need to get out of here,' said Frankie. 'Now.'

I heartily agreed. I held the knife gingerly in front of me and opened the door. The corridor was deserted and quiet. The sounds from the opium-smoking rooms that I'd heard as I came in had stopped; the doors to the rooms were shut, keys protruding from the keyholes.

I saw with relief that the key was still in the door to our room.

'Quickly,' I said. 'Get out.'

Freddie landed one more punch on Ted, taking more pleasure than perhaps was necessary, and ran to my side. Quick as a snake, Frankie jumped away from Vince and followed. We pulled the door shut and I turned the key, just as the combined weight of the Armstrong brothers crashed against it.

We ran along the corridor to the front door and threw it open.

Chang stood on the street, facing us. He had a vicious-looking foot-long machete in his hands. Either side of him were more men, some Chinese, some white and a few from Africa. They held a variety of weapons – knives, lengths of piping, coshes. There were perhaps twenty of them, and a more terrifying-looking crew I hope never to see.

'Keep behind me, Marjorie,' said Freddie, his voice shaking.

Frankie breathed an unrepeatable curse.

'You should all go home while you still can,' I called out. 'The police will be here any moment.' I hoped to goodness that was true. Surely Frankie and Freddie would have called the police before they came after me? But how long would they take to get here? I remembered how the Harlequin had received warning of the raid from Vine Street, and that Ted had 'friends' in the Met. What if the police agreed to turn a blind eye to the Armstrong brothers' activities?

One of the men laughed and spat on the ground. Chang took a step forward. I swallowed hard. My invocation of the police did not seem to have deterred him.

'We're going to have to run for it,' murmured Frankie.

She took a step down from the lintel. The men surged closer. I held my breath.

A shot splintered the silence. I jumped a foot in the air and looked to see who had been injured. The three of us all seemed intact.

'Let them through,' said a clear voice. 'Or the next one won't go over your heads. I've got you right in my sights, Mr Machete.'

It was Violet Crumb. I could have kissed her.

The men fell back, hesitant.

'Go,' shouted Miss Crumb, a service revolver in one hand. She pointed. We went, and she followed close behind us, holding the gun on the men until we reached the end of the narrow street.

I could hardly believe it. A Rolls Royce motor car, royal blue paintwork gleaming in the gas light.

'Get in the back,' said Miss Crumb. She turned a stern look on me. 'Don't you forget this, Marjorie. You owe me.'

Freddie, Frankie and I piled in. I saw a glimpse of the driver: Mr Li, looking terrified. Violet Crumb took the seat next to him and the car charged off through the streets of East London.

'Where are we going?' asked Miss Crumb. 'Not the Harlequin. Too dangerous. I've told Miss Potts to close it up and see the girls get home.'

'Bedford Square,' I said. It was the only place I could think of that felt like safety. And Mrs Jameson would call Inspector Chadwick, and all would be well.

'All right,' said Mr Li. 'Hold onto your hats.'

Chapter 30

We flitted through the empty streets like a phantom, Mr Li showing a surprising enthusiasm for speed. I was also keen to put as much distance between ourselves and Limehouse as possible.

'What's he done to you?' asked Freddie, turning my face with gentle fingers. He'd draped his jacket over my shoulders and had one arm around me. I was shivering so hard I didn't protest.

I touched my hand to my cheek. The blood seemed to have dried. Would I be scarred? It was different for men, I thought, seeing the outline of Freddie's own shrapnel scar running from his eye to his hairline. So many former soldiers bore scars that it seemed almost normal, except for the poor devils who had lost half their faces. But on a woman, it was a shocking sign of violence.

'I don't think it's too bad,' I said, with a sick feeling in my stomach. 'It's stopped bleeding, anyway.'

'I'll kill him,' said Freddie, his voice low and fierce.

I shivered. It was rather more likely that Ted Armstrong would kill Freddie. I kept the thought unspoken.

'Sorry to interrupt you lovebirds,' said Frankie. 'But I think we're being followed.'

I twisted around and saw a black car, lights off, career around a corner in our wake.

'We should get this motor off the streets,' said Frankie. 'It's much too recognisable.'

'Where are we?' I asked. I rarely had reason to come to the East End and didn't recognise the surroundings.

'Whitechapel High Street. We'll be in the City of London in five minutes,' she said. 'Mr Li, what do you think? I've got a mate who keeps a motor garage off Finsbury Circus. He'll look after your Rolls for you, and we can transfer to something less fancy.'

Mr Li glanced around. 'I can outpace them for a while. You tell me which way to go, Miss O'Grady.'

The car swung right. 'Bevis Marks,' said Frankie. 'Look, there's the synagogue.' I caught a flash of a handsome square brick building with arched windows. 'Straight over the junction, Mr Li.'

I closed my eyes as he sped up to shoot over a road, busy with traffic even at this time of night. Miraculously, we didn't hit anything. Looking out of the back window, I saw the car in pursuit had been forced to stop.

'Good work. Take the next right onto Blomfield Street, then left where you see the garage sign.'

He swung the Rolls Royce through the coach gate she pointed out and skidded to a halt on the cobbles. Frankie was out of the car before we had fully stopped and banging on the door of the mews.

'Dan! Emergency. Can you help us out?'

A man came down from the flat above in his shirt sleeves. 'Blimey, Frankie. What's all this about, eh?'

He opened the coach house and Mr Li drove straight in.

Only when Dan had shut the big wooden gate behind us did I breathe more freely.

'Don't relax yet, Marjorie,' said Miss Crumb. 'We need to get somewhere safe, and to have a doctor look at your face.'

By the time I emerged from the garage, my legs shaking so hard that Freddie almost had to carry me, Frankie was behind the wheel of a small van.

'Come on,' she called. 'You two get in the back.' We piled in, Miss Crumb and Mr Li taking the seats beside Frankie in front, and Freddie pulling the tarpaulin closed over the two of us.

This journey at least was uneventful. We pulled into Bedford Square, parking at the far side from Mrs Jameson's house in hope of avoiding notice.

It was a strange party that rang the bell for Graham Hargreaves. He scanned the five of us, his gaze alighting on me and his face creasing with concern.

'You're back early, Miss Marjorie. Looks like you've had some trouble. You'd better all come inside.'

Mrs Jameson exclaimed in dismay as I stumbled to the sofa in the drawing room. To my astonishment, the clock on the mantel said it was barely eleven o'clock. I felt as if I had been away for weeks.

'Marjorie, what on earth has happened? No, don't talk. Sit down here. Graham, call my doctor. And ask Jenny to bring warm water and clean cloths.'

She turned to the rest of the party. 'Perhaps one of you can tell me what is going on?'

Mr Li spoke up, over the babble of voices from Frankie, Freddie and Miss Crumb.

'I owe you an apology for allowing your secretary to be

put in such danger, Mrs Jameson. I am Li Chen Taio, owner of the Harlequin club. This is my wife, Mrs Violet Li, who manages the club on my behalf. I am afraid that two of our least welcome customers took Miss Swallow by force from our premises tonight. I fear my request to her to investigate their activities may have prompted this outrage.'

I was staring at Miss Crumb, or rather Mrs Li. She blushed and shrugged. 'We've been married for two years,' she said. 'But I thought the customers wouldn't like it, so I kept my maiden name. And anyway, Vi Li? It sounds like a music hall joke.'

'Fortunately, Mrs Li and Mr Gillespie,' Mr Li, ignoring his wife, inclined his head to Freddie, 'were quick-thinking enough to find out where they might have taken her. And Miss O'Grady, with her knowledge of the Limehouse district, was able to help us retrieve her.'

Jenny came in with the water and helped bathe my face. 'Oh, Miss,' was all she said. But I knew that wasn't good.

'Is it very bad?' I asked.

She hesitated. 'It's not deep,' she said. 'I don't know. See what the doctor says, eh?' Her kind words and gentle hands brought tears to my eyes.

Graham put his head around the door. 'The doctor is on his way, Mrs Jameson. I took the liberty of telephoning Scotland Yard. Inspector Chadwick will be with you very soon.'

I tried to smile, but it hurt my face. Inspector Chadwick was a great friend to Mrs Jameson, and to me. We had been through plenty of adventures during our last case of the Bloomsbury blackmail murder. I always felt safe when he and Graham were around.

'Thank you, Graham. That's a relief. Now, Miss O'Grady.

Can you or Mr Gillespie tell me how you found Marjorie?'

I'd been wondering that myself, but our fight and flight had given me no chance to ask questions. They both started talking at once, but Freddie gave way.

'Right you are,' said Frankie. 'Well, Marjorie had told Vi here about this newspaperman she'd got pally with, who had told her about running a story on the Armstrong brothers' drugs den. She had his card in her coat pocket, so when Johnnie on the door told Vi that Marjorie had been dragged off, Vi rang the reporter. He wouldn't go with us – said he was never crossing them again. But he gave us the address, Ming Street in Limehouse.'

Freddie burst in. 'I wanted to get a taxi out there straight away, but Miss Crumb – Mrs Li – said we should talk to Mr Li first and come up with a plan. He was awfully decent; came straight over in his motor. But I'd been thinking – Marjorie had told me that Frankie was from Limehouse and knew some of the...' he hesitated. She glared at him. 'Knew lots of people there.'

'Vi knew I was at Caravanserai, just round the corner from the Harlequin,' continued Frankie. 'They picked me up on the way. And it's true, some of my family do know the Armstrongs. You can't help it, living in Limehouse. So, I went in and told them their mum was sick. Then Freddie helped, and we got Marjorie out.'

'Wait!' I exclaimed. 'None of you actually called the police?'

The Lis exchanged looks. 'The thing is,' said Vi, 'we know the police. We work with the law enforcement, as much as we can. But the Armstrong brothers own half the policemen in East London. Maybe your Inspector Chadwick is different, but in our experience, you can't rely on the police where the

Armstrongs are concerned.'

On cue, Graham showed in the inspector. He took in the assorted company with his alert gaze, then came and crouched in front of me.

'Who cut your face, Miss Swallow?'

'Edward Armstrong. And his brother Vincent was going to do worse,' I said. 'At a place where people were taking opium, in Limehouse.'

He looked at the ground for a moment and expelled his breath in an exasperated rush.

'And you were at an opium den with the two most vicious thugs in London for what reason?' he asked.

'Because they drugged me and took me there. I was working undercover at the Harlequin club in Soho,' I explained, glancing apologetically at Vi. From the roll of her eyes, I realised this was not news to her. 'Investigating the death of Daisy Caldwell.'

He sat back, looking troubled. I expected him to spring into action and order a raid to arrest the brothers. But he said nothing.

'Ambassador Caldwell asked me to investigate his niece's death,' said Mrs Jameson, somewhat abashed. 'It was Marjorie's idea to get a job at the club. I had no idea it would end up like this.'

Inspector Chadwick rose and picked up the telephone. 'Scotland Yard, please. Put me through to D division.'

He turned his back and spoke cryptically to whoever answered the 'phone. 'We need protection for a private residence in Bedford Square. Armed officers, for the next twenty-four hours at least. I'll speak to the commissioner in the morning.'

He turned back to us in the room. 'Miss Swallow, there are

parts of London where the rule of law means little. If I send men to Limehouse to arrest the Armstrong brothers tonight, we will have a war on our hands. I promise you, their destiny is to swing at the end of a rope. But I will need to take this step by step, putting the pieces together before we act. My first concern is for your safety, and that of your companions. Now, tell me everything, from the start.'

Chapter 31

I could have slept for a week. But I'd made Mrs Jameson promise to wake me in time to attend Daisy's inquest, which reopened on Thursday morning. The doctor had dressed my wound and assured me the cut was not deep enough to need stitches. With luck, it would heal completely. Even so, I felt self-conscious about the gauze tied around my face and was grateful when Mrs Jameson found a hat with a heavy veil for me to wear.

Inspector Chadwick had arranged protection for Mr and Mrs Li at their flat on Jermyn Street. It was thought unwise for Frankie to go home to Limehouse, so she had stayed at Bedford Square and was comfortably ensconced in the kitchen, boots up on the fender, drinking tea and swapping family gossip with Graham Hargreaves. Freddie had gone back to Brixton, which Inspector Chadwick deemed too far from the Armstrong brothers' influence to be dangerous.

A policeman accompanied us to the court. I saw Jonathan Field among the reporters, but he didn't recognise me under my veil as I filed through the company to sit at the front with Mrs Jameson and the Caldwell party. I should thank Mr Field, I thought, for passing on the address in Ming Street. If he hadn't done so, Freddie and the others might not have found me in time.

My thoughts kept returning to Freddie: his fury as he punched Ted Armstrong and the tenderness with which he had looked after me as we fled in Mr Li's Rolls Royce. Since nursing him in the hospital, I'd thought of Freddie as I would a younger brother; someone who needed my protection and care. Last night, that had been upended. I wasn't sure how I felt about that.

All in all, I was not at my sharpest when Sir Leonard Tebbings resumed his seat at the front of the court. He called the first witness, the Home Office pathologist Dr Peregrine Manning. Dr Manning stepped up to the witness stand with alacrity, his waxed moustache a trifle wider than is respectable and a red carnation in the buttonhole of his striped suit. It was clear that he was a man who liked an audience.

'Please give me the salient points of your examination, Dr Manning,' said Sir Leonard. 'I have read your report, but it would be helpful if you would summarise for the benefit of the court.'

Dr Manning's voice was like that of an old-fashioned Shakespearean actor: resonant and deep. He smiled around the court and began.

'The deceased was a young woman in excellent health, with no signs of chronic illness,' he said. 'She was also with child.'

Sensation in court, as the newspapers say. Ambassador Caldwell inhaled sharply and closed his eyes. Felicity gave a little cry and clapped her hand over her mouth. Beyond her, John Franklin compressed his lips and stared straight ahead, and on the other side of him, Harriet the maid cast her eyes down demurely with a flush on her cheeks. Mrs Jameson, next to me, did not stir. I got the impression that she was not surprised by the news.

'Her pregnancy had advanced towards the end of the first trimester,' continued Dr Manning, 'around ten to twelve weeks, by my estimation.'

Sir Leonard leaned forward to intervene. 'Most interesting, Dr Manning. However, this had no bearing on her cause of death?'

'Indeed not, Sir Leonard. The cause of death was very clear. Analysis of the liver demonstrated that the deceased had ingested a large dose of morphine shortly before her demise. This would have led to heavy sleep, respiratory suppression, coma and eventually death.'

Morphine. Not cocaine, not even veronal or opium. Where on earth would Daisy have got hold of morphine?

Sir Leonard intervened again. 'Thank you, Doctor. This court had previously been advised that Miss Caldwell had been a habitual user of cocaine. Was there any medical evidence to support the theory that cocaine poisoning had been the cause of death?'

'There were indeed some signs of cocaine use on analysis of the liver of the deceased, but at a low level. I would not expect such an amount to be fatal to a habitual user. However, the dose of morphine was more than sufficient to cause death.'

Sir Leonard nodded, thoughtfully. 'And what was the route of administration, Dr Manning?'

The doctor gazed around the courtroom. 'People addicted to taking morphine often inject themselves with a solution of morphine salts, but there were no injection marks on the body of the deceased. For medical use, it may be prescribed orally as tablets or in an alcohol solution, as laudanum. However, from the residue in her respiratory tract and nostrils, I should say she had taken the drug by the nasal route. I would suggest that the deceased had inhaled ground-up morphine tablets. It is an unusual route of administration, but not unknown among drug addicts.'

I stole a glance at the Caldwells. The ambassador had broken into a sweat and was wiping his face with his handkerchief. Felicity had begun to weep softly. Mr Franklin stared ahead still, his gaze stony. And Mrs Jameson, bright eyes glued to the pathologist, was tapping her forefinger on her chin.

'One more question, Dr Manning. Would it be possible for the deceased to have taken an overdose of morphine by accident? For example, if she had intended to take cocaine – which I understand is more usually taken nasally?'

Dr Manning nodded briskly. 'If she had thought she was taking cocaine, then it would explain why she had taken such a large dose. Grain for grain, pure morphine is more toxic than pure cocaine. If the deceased had taken the amount she was accustomed to taking, but had mistaken morphine for cocaine, she might well have taken an overdose without intending to do so.'

The next on the stand was the unhappy Dr Spink, who was perspiring even before he was asked the first question. Sir Leonard was quietly merciless.

Did Dr Spink know that Miss Caldwell was with child? He did not. Did he not notice this when examining her after her death? He did not think an intimate examination to be necessary. Did he not suspect morphine poisoning? He did not – morphine overdose was known to cause the pupils of the eyes to contract to pin-points, whereas Miss Caldwell's pupils were enlarged. Yet this could have been the result of the use of eye-drops? It could.

Sir Leonard next turned to the powder in the box found by Daisy's bed. Why was the doctor so certain it was cocaine?

'I have seen the drug many times, Sir Leonard, in the course of my medical career. It was widely prescribed until very recently. I know what it looks like and tastes like.' No, he said. There was no chance at all that he had mistaken morphine for cocaine. The box contained cocaine, and analysis by the Metropolitan Police had confirmed this.

Had Dr Spink ever prescribed morphine to Miss Caldwell for any purpose? He had not.

Sir Leonard leaned forward, his spectacles catching the light so that his eyes behind them seemed blank.

'And what of the rest of the household, Dr Spink? Have you prescribed morphine for anybody in the Caldwell residence?'

Dr Spink hesitated and cleared his throat. He looked utterly miserable. He nodded.

'Speak up, Dr Spink.'

'Yes, Sir Leonard. I prescribe morphia tablets for Mrs Myrtle Caldwell, who suffers from neuralgic headache. I understand she has taken the medicine for several years.'

Chapter 32

After the sensational medical evidence, Felicity Caldwell was called to the witness stand. Poor Felicity tried hard to do what was required, but was clearly overcome by what had been revealed already. Her voice shook and she had to be asked several times to speak up.

Sir Leonard was patient, leading her through the events of the morning that led to her discovery of her cousin's body. He was particularly interested to know at what point she had heard Daisy snoring.

'If only I'd gone to wake her!' she said, her voice soft. 'I don't think I will ever forgive myself.'

'There is no need to blame yourself,' said Sir Leonard, kindly. 'You say the snoring was unusual, and quite heavy?'

Felicity nodded. 'That's why I mentioned it to my maid. I don't recall Daisy snoring like that before. But we'd all been out late, so I supposed she was just sleeping heavily.'

'And the time, as exactly as you remember?'

'After nine o'clock. Harriet usually comes in at nine, but it was more like half past the hour. I'm sorry I can't be more exact.'

Sir Leonard tactfully elicited the events at lunchtime, when she had gone to call her cousin.

'What was the first thing you noticed?' he asked.

'That the door was locked. She'd been locking it since... for a couple of weeks. I had to get the key from my bedside drawer. I knocked on the connecting door and unlocked it. The curtains were shut, so it was hard to see. But she was just lying there, one arm out. And... and then...'

'Take your time, Miss Caldwell. We appreciate how difficult this is.'

'I touched her arm, and it was cold. I think I screamed. John came in – Mr Franklin – and then Harriet and Papa. He pulled back the curtains and said we should call the doctor, and I remembered that I'd taken Dr Spink in to see Mamma, so he was probably still there. I think Mr Franklin went to get him.'

Sir Leonard leaned forward again. 'And you saw something on the bedside table, Miss Caldwell?'

She nodded. 'Daisy's gold box. She took it everywhere. She said it was for powdering her nose, but...'

'But what, Miss Caldwell? You are not to blame for your cousin's indiscretions, you know.'

She looked uncertainly at her father. 'The thing is, I'd seen her use it before. She sniffed up powder from it. I told Papa, because I was worried. And then Dr Spink tasted it and said it was cocaine, and that's what killed her. But now you say that wasn't the case, so I don't know what to think.'

Sir Leonard smiled kindly. 'There is no need for you to think anything, Miss Caldwell, only to remember. You have been very helpful. Can you remember seeing any other box or container, on or near the bed?'

Felicity shook her head. 'I'm sorry,' she said. 'I don't remember anything else. Daisy's room was always quite cluttered.'

He coughed gently. 'One more question, Miss Caldwell. I am sorry to have to ask you if this involves betraying confidences, but did you know your cousin was with child?'

Felicity shook her head, looking down with pink cheeks.

'And you have no idea who might be responsible for her condition?'

She looked up again then and I saw a curl of disdain in her mouth. 'I haven't the slightest idea.'

'Thank you, Miss Caldwell. You may stand down.'

Sir Leonard looked at his pocket watch. 'I will adjourn for luncheon,' he announced. 'One hour. The inquest will resume at two o'clock.'

Chapter 33

The ambassador put his arm around his daughter and hurried her from the courtroom. John Franklin again led the way through the crowds and procured a taxi for Felicity.

'We need to stay here, Felicity,' said Ambassador Caldwell. 'But you can go home, darling. Well done; you were a brave girl. Rest up this afternoon and we'll talk this evening.'

The reporters were close around us, calling out questions. 'I need a whisky,' muttered the ambassador. 'Franklin, get us another taxi. Let's lunch at my club in Whitehall.'

The invitation included Mrs Jameson and me. Harriet looked rather put out as we left her on the pavement. I supposed she'd have to fend for herself in the Lyons.

I'd never been in a gentleman's club before and was rather taken with the dining room's handsome, masculine fittings and sombre decoration. It seemed appropriate for the solemnity of the occasion.

'Good Lord, what happened to you, Miss Swallow?' John Franklin looked in dismay at my bandaged face as I removed the hat and veil.

'It's not as bad as it looks,' I said. I glanced at Mrs Jameson, unsure how much to share.

'Marjorie had an adventurous night in pursuit of the opium

gangs of East London,' she said. 'I fear we have stirred up a bit of a hornets' nest there, Henry. But given the medical evidence from this morning, perhaps further pursuit of that particular hare is unnecessary. If you'll excuse the mixed metaphors.'

He swallowed down his whisky and soda. 'I can't believe Spink's incompetence,' he said. 'I suppose Daisy must have got hold of Myrtle's medicines, somehow. He probably left packets of the stuff all over the house.'

'I think not,' said Mrs Jameson, cautiously. 'I spoke to Myrtle last week about it. She is prescribed half-grain morphine tablets in bottles of twenty. Dr Spink delivers them himself and they are immediately locked in the medicine cabinet in her room. She is quite particular about it.'

Mr Franklin intervened. 'Although, of course, the doctor's bag might contain more. And he is at the house quite frequently. I suppose Daisy could have abstracted some tablets while his bag was unattended.'

Mrs Jameson turned her unblinking grey eyes on the young man. 'That is a possibility,' she said, inclining her head.

The food arrived – plain, old-fashioned nursery-style food, but well-cooked and tasty. Sometimes steak and kidney pudding is just what you need on a cold day. I tucked in with relish, as did Mrs Jameson and Mr Franklin. Ambassador Caldwell seemed to have little appetite, but ordered another whisky.

'And then there's the other thing,' he said, gloomily. 'Damn it, how did the girl get into such a mess?'

I remembered the letter that we had retrieved from Daisy's wastepaper basket. Would Mrs Jameson tell him about it? 'There's no use crying over spilt milk,' Daisy had written. 'Uncle Henry will come around.' But who was the letter addressed to?'

Mr Franklin coughed apologetically. 'Perhaps Miss Swallow's investigations at the Harlequin club could look in that direction,' he said. 'From the little I saw during our visit, the club hosts some disreputable characters. There's the owner, of course, and one of the musicians playing that jazz stuff is black. You know what sort of reputation they have when it comes to white women.'

'T-bone is my friend. He wouldn't do anything like that,' I said, hotly. 'He's married and sends all his money back to his family in Harlem. You have no reason to accuse him.'

Mr Franklin smiled. 'I can see this "T-bone" has made an impression on you, Miss Swallow. You probably don't have the experience in London that we've had in the United States. I'm not saying it was one of them. But I'd start looking there.'

Ambassador Caldwell put down his glass and thumped the table. 'Enough! I won't have my niece's name dragged through the mud like this. Franklin, I'm surprised at you.'

Mr Franklin held up his hands. 'I apologise. I was trying to help. I'll say no more.'

Mrs Jameson had watched the whole exchange through narrowed eyes. At one point, I thought she was about to intervene, but she touched her finger to her lips and said nothing.

The ambassador looked like a man whose whole world was falling apart.

'The trade talks begin on Monday, don't they? I need you to focus on that, Franklin. I've had telegrams from the White House asking if I need to take leave of absence. The chief of staff has threatened to send someone over to relieve me. It's vital we get on top of the situation.'

'Of course, Ambassador. I have the papers for next week in my dispatch case. I'll work on them in the waiting room outside the court. I'll be close enough if they need to call me.' Mr Franklin wiped away a sheen of sweat from his upper lip with his napkin. The previously harmonious relationship between the ambassador and his chief aide seemed to be unravelling under the strain.

'Henry, you know you can trust my discretion,' said Mrs Jameson. Her voice was softer than usual. 'Marjorie and I will see what we can find out about Daisy's personal circumstances. You can be sure we will do so with delicacy, and that we will report to no-one but yourself.'

He nodded his thanks and took out his pocket watch. 'We must go. The inquest will resume shortly. Franklin, please ask the desk to summon a taxi. Are you coming with us, Iris?'

She shook her head. 'Marjorie will attend and take notes for me. Henry, how is Myrtle today? I should like very much to visit her if you think she is well enough.'

Chapter 34

The afternoon at the inquest was less sensational than the morning. First it was Harriet's turn on the stand. She kept her eyes cast downward, all traces of pertness suppressed. Her voice was demure as she was sworn in.

'When was the last time you saw Miss Daisy Caldwell, Miss Jones?' Sir Leonard's voice was fatherly, as it had been with Felicity.

The girl raised her eyes. 'I helped her to get ready for her night out, Sir. We started at about six o'clock, I suppose. It took quite a long time because Miss Daisy was very particular about how she looked. She said she wanted to be a sensation.'

There was a ripple of laughter in the court. Sir Leonard looked up sharply and frowned. It subsided.

'So, you did not see her on her return from the club?'

Harriet shook her head. 'I got Miss Felicity ready for bed when she came up at about midnight. But I was very tired. Miss Daisy had said before that there was no need to wait up for her when she was that late. I went straight to bed after seeing to Miss Felicity, then slept like a log all night. I didn't see Miss Daisy again until… afterwards.'

'But you did hear her in the adjoining room, with Miss Felicity Caldwell, in the morning?'

Harriet smiled, and there was the hint of a smirk again. 'Yes, Sir. About half past nine. I was a bit later getting started than usual that morning, what with the late finish.'

I wondered what the housekeeper would have made of that.

Sir Leonard pushed his spectacles up his nose and leaned forward. 'Miss Jones, were you aware that Miss Daisy Caldwell was pregnant?'

The girl flushed and looked down. When she looked up again, her eyes were sparkling with defiance. 'I was. It would have been difficult to keep it from me, to be honest. But I didn't say anything to anybody. It wasn't my place.'

'Indeed not. And did you know the identity of the father of the child?'

Harriet's gaze swept around the courtroom, lingering over the ambassador and his secretary. I held my breath. There was a spark of mischief in her expression, as if she was enjoying exercising her power. Was she about to name the guilty man?

She shook her head decisively. 'No, Sir. She didn't tell me,' she said. All the same, I thought, Harriet knew.

Sir Leonard had few further questions. A minute later, Sergeant Borden was recalled to go over his evidence again, in the light of the new revelations. He had nothing to say that I had not heard already, although I diligently recorded his evidence in my notebook. The courtroom was warm, and I was unable to stop yawning. Once or twice, I was on the verge of nodding off as the coroner's quiet voice took us again through events I was already familiar with.

At four o'clock, Sir Leonard called a halt to proceedings. 'Ladies and gentlemen, we will reconvene tomorrow. I hope that we will be able to conclude our hearing before the end of the day.'

I packed up my notebook. All I could think of by that stage was getting a nice cup of tea and retiring early to bed. But as I walked towards the exit, a young man with freckles and a snub nose stood up in the back row, a troubled expression on his face. It took me a minute to place him, then I realised. It was Thomas, the footman from Prince's Gate.

As I watched, he hurried after Harriet Jones and caught at her arm. She spun around. I wasn't close enough to hear what they said, but she seemed angry. She shook off his hand and stalked to the door.

I followed. Harriet called out and John Franklin turned quickly with a frown. He gestured to her to hurry up, and she trotted to his side.

'Blooming heck,' muttered the freckled young man beside me.

I turned to him with my brightest smile, pushing aside the veil. 'Hello, Thomas. Do you fancy some tea across the road? You look a bit fed up.'

Under the influence of a steaming cup of tea and a Lyons teacake slathered in melting butter, Thomas quickly shed his professional discretion.

'I am fed up, to be honest, Miss,' he said. 'I don't understand why a girl would tell a fellow that she liked him if she didn't. I don't see what's in it for the girl, I mean. If she doesn't like a fellow, why doesn't she blooming well say so? Why leave a fellow hanging around like a fool?'

I gave the poor boy a sympathetic look. 'Sometimes girls change their minds,' I said. 'But it's not very nice for the fellow, I suppose. Is it Harriet?'

He looked miserable. 'She was nice as pie until that Miss Daisy arrived. Then it's all giggling in corners and taking messages between Miss Daisy and… and him. And then she starts getting keen on him herself. And now she won't even look at me. And it's not right, standing up and saying stuff that isn't true.'

I leaned in quickly. 'What did she say that wasn't true, Thomas?'

He shoved back his cup and saucer. 'She says she went straight to bed and slept all night after she'd seen to Miss Felicity. Well, she blooming well didn't. After I'd turned in, I remembered I hadn't set out Mr Caldwell's boots for the morning. I'd left them in the kitchen after cleaning them. So, I went down to get them, and I heard her on the back stairs, giggling.'

'Going up or down?' I asked. 'And what time?'

He shrugged. 'Don't know. It was really late. After two o'clock. I'd been awake because I had a toothache.'

'And who was she giggling with?'

He raised his blue eyes, and I could see his hurt pride. 'I didn't see him. But who do you blooming think?'

Chapter 35

Back home, Graham plied me with tea and buttered crumpets in the drawing room.

'Got to keep your strength up, Miss Marjorie. The doctor said you should be resting.' He glanced reprovingly at Mrs Jameson's back. She was at her desk, immersed in a medical textbook.

'Thank you, Graham.' I was overcome by another fit of yawning. 'I would quite like a nap, Mrs Jameson.'

She looked up and I could see her mind was abstracted on the puzzle. 'Yes, of course. Was there anything of interest to report from the afternoon?'

I ran through the main points of Harriet's evidence and my conversation with young Thomas.

'She's clearly hiding something. And no matter what she said, I'm sure she knows who is the father of Daisy's child. So that's two things she lied about to the coroner.'

'Interesting. What makes a girl cover up something like that, Marjorie?'

I considered. 'I suppose she was worried she'd get into trouble for being out of bed so late – and for consorting with John Franklin, if Thomas is right. Of course, we don't know what they were doing, but that's the second time they've been seen together on the stairs.' I was now in no doubt that the legs I had seen belonged to the ambassador's secretary. 'I think she kept quiet about Daisy's baby because she likes the power of knowing.'

Mrs Jameson smiled, as if she completely understood that pleasure. 'Indeed. Thank you, Marjorie, that's most helpful. Off you go, now. Get some rest.'

I took a candle – the electric light did not reach to the attic – ascended to my room and took off my shoes. It was my retreat from the world, and I'd made it cosy: a rag rug from home on the floor, a white-painted bookshelf stacked with detective novels (much thumbed), school prizes and books recommended by my friend Evelyn (less thumbed). I'd bought a posy of snowdrops from a flower girl in Piccadilly Circus the previous morning and they still looked fresh and pretty on the table.

I just managed to pull off my clothes and slip into my comfortable bed before sleep claimed me. It was a troubled sleep. I dreamed I was running, trying hard to move arms and legs that seemed stuck in place, while figures dressed in harlequin suits pursued me with flashing knives. I woke with a start, my heart pounding hard. I had no idea whether I'd been asleep for minutes or hours.

Someone was knocking on the door. 'Miss? Miss Swallow?' It was Jenny's voice.

I struggled to throw off the rags of my dream. 'Yes?'

She opened the door a crack, holding an oil lamp. The light flickered across the whitewashed walls. I sat up and glanced at the clock on the mantelpiece. It was almost midnight. I must have been asleep since about six. My head felt thick, and my limbs ached.

'I'm sorry to wake you, Miss. Mrs Jameson asked me to call you. There's a young man downstairs. He seems in a bit of state, to be honest.'

I swung my feet to the floor. 'I'll be right down. Did he give a name?'

'Mr Gillespie, Miss.'

Freddie. I jumped up and dressed. What had happened to bring him here? My mouth dried. We'd thought he would be safe in Brixton, I remembered. Had the Armstrong brothers found out who he was and pursued him there? What had they done to him?

I flew down the stairs and into the drawing room. He was standing by the windows, wearing the evening suit he wore to play with the band. Of course, he would have been playing in the club that evening. I stopped, saw what looked like blood smeared across his white shirt. His hair was sticking up, his face was streaked with soot, and he looked quite wild. I admit, my heart rather skipped a beat.

'What's happened? Are you all right?'

He seemed at a loss to know how to begin. My heart sank as I recognised the look he'd had in the hospital, the way his mouth worked as if he couldn't bring himself to speak the words.

'Oh, Freddie.' I'd thought he was recovered. He'd seemed so happy, carefree even, in recent weeks. I took his hands, as I had done many times on the ward, sitting with him when the nightmares got bad. 'Quietly, now. Breathe nice and slowly.'

He clung to my fingers, hands shaking.

'They've wrecked it all,' he said, when he could get his words out.

Mrs Jameson came in. 'There you are, Marjorie. Freddie,

I've called the inspector. It's not his jurisdiction, but he will do what he can. He's going to talk to the commissioner about the need to clamp down on the gangs. Whether that will translate into action remains to be seen. Now, which police station have they been taken to?'

I tried to make sense of this bewildering mass of information.

'What's actually happened?' I asked.

Freddie gulped and tried again. 'There was a raid. The police came, but we'd had no warning. They searched us all. They arrested Vi and Mr Li. They've taken T-bone, and Miss Tierney.'

'Golly. What for?' This was sad news.

'Alcohol licensing violations,' said Mrs Jameson, briskly. 'Miss Tierney had a wrap of cocaine in her handbag. And unfortunately, your trombonist friend had a tiny bit of reefer in his tobacco pouch. Which won't do him any good if he has overstayed his work permit.'

'Oh, Freddie. I'm so sorry,' I said.

He was shaking his head. 'That's not all. After the police left...' he broke off and gazed wildly at the ceiling. I waited until the spasm had passed.

'Sorry. After the police had left, the Armstrongs and their men came. We – me and the band – got the girls out the back way. But there was fighting. Sid Harpo was stabbed. He's in hospital.'

I exclaimed in horror.

'And then they set fire to it. The whole place burned down, Marjorie. Me and Sampson hauled Harpo out the window and through the yard of the shop next door. We were on the pavement, calling out for a doctor. Miss Potts was trying to stop the bleeding. Then we smelled smoke.'

He put his face in his hands. 'By the time the doctor came, the place was burning like billy-oh. No fire brigade, of course. Not until it was too late, anyway. I reckon someone slipped them cash to dawdle. They had to evacuate the buildings on either side. The place went up like a tinder-box.'

He started to gasp again, his breath coming too fast and his eyes staring. One shoulder rose and his back twisted. I guided him to a chair and sat him down, then kneeled in front of him. The trauma had sparked off his old trouble.

'All right now, Freddie. Nice, slow breaths. Count four in, and five out. You're safe here,' I said. I wished I believed it. Was anyone safe in a London where such things could happen, and the police do nothing? I counted with him and slowly his breathing returned to normal.

Mrs Jameson had been watching in silence. She gave me an odd smile, as if I'd finally done something to impress her, and a nod of approval.

'Do you know if Mr Li and the others were taken to Vine Street, Freddie, or Bow Street?' she asked. 'I think it would be wise for Inspector Chadwick to let the custody sergeant know that he is interested in their welfare. I have heard too much about accidents occurring to people in police cells.'

He shook his head. Speech was beyond him yet.

'Very well,' said Mrs Jameson. 'We will find out, and I will bail them out first thing in the morning. It was my interference that brought this trouble to the Harlequin. I will make it my business to repair that trouble as well as I can. Now, where is Jenny? Make up a bed for Mr Gillespie in one of the spare rooms, dear. I think it's best if he stays the night with us.'

That made two house guests because of my tangling with

the Armstrong brothers. I realised I had not seen the other one since I left for the inquest in the morning.

'Where's Frankie?'

Mrs Jameson smiled her secretive smile. 'Out. She has been gathering intelligence for us. She has some singular networks of informants, that young woman.'

I heard the front door open. 'Indeed, I think that must be her now. Miss O'Grady, would you care to join us? We are holding a Council of War. We need to neutralise the Armstrong brothers, before they cause more damage.'

Chapter 36

At eight o'clock in the morning, a raiding party swept into Bow Street police station: Inspector Chadwick, Mrs Jameson, Freddie, and I. Frankie had recovered Mr Li's Rolls Royce from her friend's garage in Finsbury Circus and opted to stay outside with it, rather than leave it to the depredations of the Covent Garden market boys.

The desk sergeant, who looked like he might be happy to amuse himself at the expense of Freddie and me, soon changed his tune when the inspector pulled out his warrant card and Mrs Jameson her cheque book. The prisoners were promptly brought up from their cells.

Mrs Li and Miss Tierney looked exactly as one would expect two hard-working women to look after a sleepless night in a police cell. They'd done their best to repair the damage with a spot of powder and paint, but were decidedly bedraggled. Mr Li, by contrast, looked as fresh and dapper as if he'd just been pressed and brushed down by his valet after an excellent night's sleep and a good breakfast.

'Don't look at me,' murmured Vi, shielding her face from the harsh electric light of the police station waiting room. 'I feel too ghastly. Taio, how do you manage it?'

T-bone caused the most difficulty, having not just the matter of the reefer (whatever that was) in his tobacco pouch, but his over-run work permit. I suspected that prejudice from the custody sergeant also played a part. Eventually, Inspector Chadwick had to get him to sign T-bone over into his own custody, to aid with his inquiries. The tall man looked exhausted and rumpled. But his first question was for his instrument.

'You got my trombone, man?' he asked Freddie. Freddie shook his head and looked anguished. Oh, golly, I thought. All the band's instruments would have been in the club when it burned down.

'Let's go across the road and get some breakfast,' said Mrs Jameson, diplomatically. 'There's a lot to tell you all.'

We repaired to the Market Porter public house, next to the great floral hall of the Covent Garden market. The fresh green scent of the market competed for a moment with the smell of fried egg and bacon. The bacon won. Frankie joined us, having come to an arrangement with the leader of a small gang of market urchins. She would give him a ride around the block in the Rolls Royce, and maybe let him sit in the driving seat, but only if it was in pristine condition and the horn had not been audibly tooted.

When Mrs Jameson explained about the fire, Mr Li shut his eyes for a moment, his face the colour of ivory. Then he exhaled slowly, opened his dark eyes again and nodded.

'It is over,' he said. He took Vi's hand. 'It lasted well. Eight years. It brought us great success, my love. It is time to move on to other things.'

'The instruments?' asked T-bone, his tone urgent.

Freddie shook his head. 'I'm sorry. I don't know. We had to get Harpo to hospital. It was burning, T-bone. We couldn't get close.'

Mrs Jameson looked at her wristwatch. 'You can go and have a look after this, can't they, Peter?' she said to Inspector Chadwick. 'Perhaps you could go with them, inspect the scene of the crime. I must go to Horseferry Road, however. The inquest into Daisy Caldwell's death is due to conclude today. Marjorie, do you want to go to the Harlequin, then join me later?'

I agreed. While I was sad about Daisy, my immediate sympathies were with my friends from the nightclub. What would the dance hostesses do if the club disappeared? What other things would Mr Li and Vi go on to? And worst of all, what would happen to the band if they'd lost all their instruments – not to mention their lucrative regular engagement?

Bacon and eggs dispatched, we walked solemnly to Soho, leaving Frankie to reward the guardian of the motor car, and then bring it over to Wardour Street. The acrid smell of the burned-out building assailed us as we approached. Vi clung to Mr Li's arm. Freddie and T-bone marched ahead with Inspector Chadwick, looking grim.

'I don't know what I'm going to do.' Miss Tierney was sniffing into a handkerchief. Her colourful ribboned frock looked tawdry and incongruous in the daylight. 'I'll have a criminal record now. No-one's going to take me on in another club. I won't get chorus work. And I'll never see my Mr Duckworth again. He was getting so keen, too. I half-expected him to propose.'

'You'd have married him?' I asked, amused.

'Well, I don't know what sort of proposal it would have been,' she admitted. 'But you never know.'

The club was in ruins. The windows of the building above were broken and blackened. The Italian grocery store next-door was badly damaged too; the owner dragging crates of ruined foodstuffs out of the door.

'Twelve years,' he said, with tears in his eyes. 'Twelve years of working every day, and it's all gone.'

Mr Li clasped his hand and I saw his wallet come out of his pocket.

The metal steps down to the basement area looked rickety, but Freddie tried them, nonetheless.

'I think they'll take my weight,' he said. 'T-bone, you stay up here. I'll see if I can find anything.'

He carefully picked his way down to the debris-strewn area and pushed at the door, once the enticing red portal to the delights of the Harlequin. The blackened wood splintered and gave way.

'It's too dangerous, Freddie,' I said. 'Don't go in.'

'Please don't put yourself in danger,' said Mr Li. 'I will do what I can to help you recover your losses.' Although he looked pretty sick himself, I noticed.

'I would advise against it,' said Inspector Chadwick. 'I need to look myself, once it's been assessed as safe. Why don't you wait for that?'

I recognised the obstinate set of Freddie's jaw. 'I'll be fine,' he said. He ducked his head and pushed through the door.

'I'm going too,' said T-bone.

'You're not,' said the inspector. 'You're in my custody, and that's a crime scene. You're staying where you are.'

We waited anxiously. There was a squawk, and I jumped. Moments later, Freddie emerged, three charred instrument cases in his hands and a kitten sitting on his shoulder.

'I found them,' he said, with a triumphant grin. His face looked his own again, as if his act of bravery had beaten down his demons. 'The piano's so much firewood and I couldn't see anything left of the drums. But here's your trombone, T-bone, and this is Goldberg's trumpet.' He set the third case down. 'I only hope Harpo's clarinet has survived.'

The kitten, a tiny black ball of fluff, jumped down from his shoulder into my arms.

'This little fellow was scratching at the back window,' said Freddie.

'It must be one of Shadow's kittens,' said Vi. 'I suppose she took the rest of them away. It must have got left behind.'

The creature began to lick the soot from its bedraggled fur, then paused and sneezed, wrinkling its pink nose.

'It's adorable,' I said. 'Hello, Sooty. I wonder if Mrs Jameson would let me keep you.' I determined to take it back and find it a place in the kitchen. It settled down in my arms and began to purr.

T-bone took his instrument case and opened it up on the pavement. He lifted out the trombone and gave it an experimental toot. His face split into a wide grin.

'Good work, Fred. Thank you, man.' He packed it away and pumped Freddie's hand.

'I am pleased,' said Mr Li. 'Perhaps you will be able to play in my restaurant, the Lucky Lotus.' He seemed determined to put a brave face on things. Vi Crumb was taking her lead from him, her chin raised and her face set. But I could see she was trembling.

'Will you be all right, Vi?' I asked quietly.

She shot me a rather brittle smile. 'Taio will look after us,' she said. 'He's a good businessman. And a good sort. He'll see the other hostesses get work, even if it's just as waitresses until they get back on their feet. Although I understand you already have another position, Marjorie.'

I flushed. I'd not had the opportunity to explain to her about my decision to go undercover as a dance hostess.

'I'm sorry that I misled you,' I said. 'The idea was to find out about poor Daisy Caldwell's death. All this business with the Armstrong brothers – I wasn't expecting any of that.'

Vi shrugged. 'They were already circling the Harlequin. It's hard, but nightclubs are always vulnerable to the gangs.' She hesitated. 'I was sorry about Daisy. I liked her. She was very generous to the staff, and so friendly. She always looked like she was enjoying herself, and that's good for business too.'

I was touched. 'Thank you. I liked her too.'

Vi walked us a little away from the others. 'You wanted to know where the cocaine came from. Taio doesn't know about it, and I'm going to stop now. Please don't tell him. It was only ever a small thing. There's a chemist in Lisle Street, Mr Woolridge. He sells it without a doctor's prescription if you go with a recommendation from a friend. I told Daisy about it. You say it's for your nerves.'

A chemist shop. I remembered Mrs Jameson's words when I first suspected Mr Li of supplying the drug. 'If he wanted to supply cocaine, he'd be better off opening a chemist shop.' She'd been right all along, and my investigations of the criminal world had been wrong.

'I promise not to let anyone know you used it,' I said. 'But I might need to tell Mrs Jameson that Daisy got her cocaine from there. She'll need to tell the ambassador.'

Vi nodded. 'There's something else. It came out at the inquest, so I might as well tell you. Daisy told me she was pregnant. She asked if... if I knew anyone. To sort it out. But then the next time I saw her, she said to forget about that – she'd decided to go through with it. She was going to tell her boyfriend and make sure he did the right thing. She said her uncle would help her, if she told him.'

I clutched her arm. 'Do you know who the man was?'

She shook her head. 'I don't know his name. But when you came to the Harlequin with Daisy's cousin, she told Miss Tierney she was going to have it out with him that night. The night before she died.'

'Here.' I passed her the kitten. 'Give Sooty to Frankie to take back to Bedford Square. I'd better tell Mrs Jameson right away.'

Chapter 37

I slipped into the courtroom, desperate to tell Mrs Jameson what I'd learned. She nodded at me and raised her finger to her lips. Henry Caldwell was in the witness box.

'And your wife had been prescribed morphine for how long, Ambassador?' asked Sir Leonard.

'For about six months, as far as I know. She'd been having painful headaches,' said Mr Caldwell. 'Dr Spink thought it would help.'

'And the tablets were kept locked in her medicine cabinet?'

'Yes.' Ambassador Caldwell looked terrible, his eyes red and his cheek marked by dried blood from a shaving cut. 'Daisy must've got hold of the key somehow.'

'And had your wife missed any tablets?'

'I don't know.'

The coroner took a moment to speak to his clerk. 'Ambassador, it would help us materially if we knew the answer. Would you be amenable to me sending a police constable to your residence to find out? I understand your wife is an invalid and I do not wish to either discommode her or prolong the inquest longer than is necessary.'

He nodded his assent. 'As you wish. I just want to know what happened to my niece,' he said, heavily.

'Ambassador, please tell us about the last time you saw Miss Caldwell.'

He closed his eyes for a moment and pinched the bridge of his nose. 'My niece and my daughter had gone dancing at the Harlequin club, which was a favourite haunt of Daisy. I'd persuaded my secretary, Mr Franklin, to accompany them. Sometime after midnight, the young people came home together. I had been working late in my study. My daughter kissed me goodnight and went straight upstairs. Mr Franklin asked if I needed his help, and I told him I was through for the night. I invited him to have a whiskey with me while we discussed the... some important meetings I had scheduled for the next day.'

He sighed heavily. 'My niece insisted on joining us. I felt she had probably had enough to drink already, but she seemed in high spirits and insisted. Eventually, I left the pair of them to it and went to bed.'

The coroner leaned forward again. 'So, the last person to see Miss Caldwell that night would have been Mr Franklin?'

'That's right.' The ambassador frowned. 'I heard their voices when I returned to my bedroom after checking on my wife.'

'You heard their voices?'

Mr Caldwell nodded, his gaze seeking out Mr Franklin. 'I did. I remember thinking it was past time for everyone to call it a night.' Suspicion dawned in his eyes.

'And where were you at the time?'

'Upstairs, crossing past the stairway from my wife's bed-room,' he said.

Sir Leonard pushed down his spectacles. 'Would the voices have been raised, for you to hear them from that distance?' he asked.

Mr Caldwell hesitated. 'I… I suppose so. I didn't hear what was being said, but yes. They sounded like they were having… a discussion, I suppose.'

'An argument?'

'Perhaps.' The ambassador shut his mouth like a trap and clenched his jaw firmly.

Sir Leonard nodded thoughtfully. 'Thank you, Ambassador Caldwell, you may stand down.' He looked at his watch. 'We will have a short break of ten minutes. I am anxious to conclude the inquest today, if possible.'

I scribbled in my notebook and passed the page to Mrs Jameson. She glanced at my note and nodded. As we filed out, she touched Mr Caldwell on the arm.

'We will join you in one moment, Henry.' She steered me towards the ladies' cloakroom.

'What is it, Marjorie?' Her grey eyes were penetrating.

'Daisy told Miss Tierney that she was going to have it out with the father of her child the night we went to the Harlequin,' I said, breathlessly. 'She said she was going to tell him to do the right thing, and that Ambassador Caldwell would make sure he did.'

She nodded. 'So that would explain the argument between Daisy and Mr Franklin?'

'It sounds like it. And it would also mean Harriet had something against Daisy, wouldn't it? I mean, if she knew Daisy was going to force Mr Franklin to marry her, and Harriet was involved with him herself. We know she didn't stay in her room all night, and she was in Daisy's confidence about the baby.'

Mrs Jameson narrowed her eyes. 'Motive… and with the door key, opportunity. But let's not get ahead of ourselves. We shall see what Sir Leonard makes of Mr Franklin. He's to take the stand after the break.'

Outside, we found Henry Caldwell and Franklin waiting for us. The atmosphere between the men was tense. Franklin was covertly looking at his reflection in the window and smoothing down his hair with his manicured fingers. The man was vain, I realised, wondering how I had failed to spot it before. Dandified, even, to use Vi's phrase about Daisy's boyfriend.

The ambassador stared glumly out of the window at the rain.

'Where is Felicity?' asked Mrs Jameson.

'I thought it best for her to stay away,' said Mr Caldwell. 'Giving evidence yesterday upset her very much. I'm wondering if I should send her home for a spell. She could stay with friends, get away from all this unpleasantness.'

Mrs Jameson nodded. 'Perhaps that would be wise. The press coverage is bound to make uncomfortable reading.'

He grunted. 'I've banned the newspapers from the house. I won't have the servants reading about the household. Not in my own residence, anyway. The serious newspapers are delivered to the Embassy, and Franklin or one of the others goes through them for anything I need to see.'

Mrs Jameson turned her gaze on the secretary. 'That must be a distasteful task for you, Mr Franklin.'

He looked a little irritated. 'Not especially. I only read the sections that seem relevant to our diplomatic work. Not the gossip.' His tone was sharper than usual. He must have been anxious about giving evidence. As indeed he should be, if our suspicions were correct.

The break over, Sir Leonard leaned forward and fixed John

Franklin with his eyes.

'Please tell us what happened in the early hours of Thursday January 11, after you returned from the Harlequin club, Mr Franklin,' he said, in his deceptively quiet voice.

Franklin cleared his throat and smoothed back his hair. 'I went to see if I could help Ambassador Caldwell,' he said. 'He was working late in his office, and we had important meetings scheduled for the next afternoon.'

The coroner gave a faint smile. 'Very commendable. Why did you not go to bed when the ambassador retired for the night?'

'I hadn't finished my drink. And Daisy – Miss Caldwell – wanted another,' Franklin said, stiffly.

'So, you decided to keep her company? Was that usual, a late night tête-a-tête between you after the household had retired?'

He flushed. 'Not particularly, but it would have been impolite to leave her when she wished to talk. Miss Caldwell liked to talk,' he said, sounding impatient again.

Sir Leonard looked delighted that he'd been offered such a smooth opening for his next question.

'And what did Miss Caldwell wish to talk about that night, Mr Franklin?'

Franklin's flush faded, as if he'd seen too late the path he was set down. 'I don't remember. Nothing of consequence,' he said. 'Probably about the music at the club. Daisy liked to dance.'

That was the second time he'd accidentally used her first name, I noticed. So did Sir Leonard.

'Come, Mr Franklin. Mr Caldwell says he heard raised voices, a discussion or argument. This was the last time you saw a young woman who died the next morning. A woman with whom you were apparently on first-name terms. Do you really expect me to believe that you cannot remember your conversation?'

Franklin took a deep breath and looked straight at Sir Leonard. He opened his eyes wide, presumably aiming for an expression of candour.

'I hate to blacken her name after her sad passing,' he said. 'But I felt the need to remonstrate with her about her behaviour. I was concerned that her antics were making the ambassador's household the subject of scandal and gossip. This was not helpful to the ambassador's mission.'

'Her antics?' Sir Leonard's eyebrows almost disappeared into his wig. 'Dancing, talking... are these the antics you refer to?'

Franklin swallowed and stared back at his inquisitor. 'Dancing like... like a show-girl. Drinking gin. Taking cocaine. Flirting with all manner of people at nightclubs. I was not, of course, aware of her... unfortunate predicament. I did not know she had gone so far. But I warned her she should not presume on Ambassador Caldwell's goodwill forever. I had made up my mind to speak to the ambassador if she did not moderate her behaviour. I saw the way the newspapers reported on Miss Caldwell's social activities, and I was worried it would undermine the seriousness of our mission.'

He wiped his hand across his mouth, dislodging the sheen of sweat that had broken out on his upper lip. He looked defiant, as if challenging the coroner to dispute what he had said.

On the other side of Mrs Jameson, Ambassador Caldwell sat stonily, gazing at the floor with his jaw set. Sir Leonard's eyes strayed to the ambassador for a moment, before returning to his prey.

Sir Leonard took Mr Franklin through the events of the next day, from his awakening to Felicity's scream and the arrival of the doctor. Then he removed his spectacles and rubbed his eyes.

'And how did you feel when you knew she was dead? Did you care for Miss Caldwell, Mr Franklin?' he asked.

Franklin blustered. 'I was shocked and upset, like everyone in the house. I care about the ambassador's household, and that included Miss Caldwell, of course.'

Sir Leonard did not take his eyes off the young man. 'There is another explanation for the argument you had with Miss Caldwell on the night before she died. Is it possible, Mr Franklin, that you were the father of Daisy Caldwell's unborn child? When you answer, please remember that you are under oath.'

Franklin turned brick red. 'Certainly not,' he said vehemently. 'I'm offended to be asked such a question.'

Sir Leonard nodded slowly. 'You may stand down.'

Franklin stalked out of the room. I wondered if he would return to sit with us. The ambassador had not flinched at the question to his aide, I noticed. He had clearly admitted the same suspicion himself.

Chapter 38

Sir Leonard closed proceedings with a promise to bring in a verdict or to reopen the case within the next month. It had been, he said, an unsatisfactory process and he felt there were still many questions to be answered about the sequence of events that had led to Miss Caldwell's death. He would be writing to the commissioner of the Metropolitan Police to make clear his feelings about the lackadaisical approach that his officers had taken to presenting evidence to the inquest. He apologised to Ambassador Caldwell for the continued anxiety that this would be likely to cause to the family.

Outside, Mr Franklin was nowhere to be seen. We managed to force a path through the swarming newspaper reporters. I got a glimpse of Mr Field, looking surprised to see me with the Caldwell party as we piled into a taxi and returned to Prince's Gate.

'I can drop you at Bedford Square,' said Mr Caldwell. 'I have to talk to Franklin. It may not be pleasant.'

'I will just drop in to see Myrtle and Felicity, if you don't object,' said Mrs Jameson. 'Don't worry; we'll keep out of the way.' She laid her hand on his arm. 'I am sorry, Henry. It's been beastly for you.'

He sighed. 'It's been hellish. But I should have taken more

notice of the girl. I let her run around on her own. She was probably missing home. I thought she'd just fit in like a sister to Felicity, and we would carry on as before. Felicity has never been any trouble. But with Myrtle so sick, there was nobody to perform a mother's role for poor Daisy – and she clearly needed it. I feel badly, Iris. I let that girl down, and I let my brother down too. He's arriving next week, you know, to see to the funeral arrangements.'

Mrs Jameson took from her handbag the fragment of pink paper we had found in Daisy's wastepaper basket.

'You should see this, Henry. It was in Daisy's room. Marjorie has discovered from her friends at the nightclub that Daisy was planning to "have it out", as she said, with the father of her child. And she planned to enlist your help to ensure that the young man married her.'

Henry took the paper, with its lines about spilled milk and facing the music. He read it, face impassive.

'Why didn't the little fool come to me?' he asked. He tucked it in his inside pocket.

Mrs Jameson sighed. 'She wasn't the first one to be deceived by him. Henry, I've had a letter from an old friend in Paris. I wrote to ask her about Mr Franklin. She says it was a similar story with his last posting. Only it was the ambassador's wife. That's why it was hushed up.'

When we arrived at Prince's Gate, the orderly residence was in uncharacteristic chaos. Servants stood around looking scared, although they jumped to attention when the ambassador strode in. We could hear banging and crashing from upstairs and a dreadful wailing sound from the drawing room.

Felicity was weeping as if her heart would break, her face buried in her mother's lap. Mrs Caldwell, pale and thin, was stroking her daughter's auburn hair.

'She's been like this half the morning,' said Mrs Caldwell. 'Henry, what on earth has happened? John Franklin is upstairs packing his bags. He says he's leaving at once and going back to the States on the next boat.'

The ambassador ran his hands over his thinning grey hair. 'I need to talk to him,' he said. 'Felicity, sweetheart, calm down. You'll set off one of your mother's heads. What's the matter?'

'He said…' gulped poor Felicity. 'He said we'd get married. He promised. But all the time he liked Daisy better than me. And now he's going away, and I'll never see him again.'

'You're well rid of the lousy cad,' said Mr Caldwell, his voice grim. 'Stay there. That fellow will be out of this house with my boot-print on his backside and no chance of another job in the service.'

He stalked out, slamming the door behind him. Felicity threw herself on the sofa and resumed her sobs. Mrs Jameson and I exchanged glances, then sat on either side of the weeping girl.

'Now then, Felicity. When did Mr Franklin ask you to marry him?' asked Mrs Jameson.

She looked up, her eyes pink and her nose running. I passed her my clean handkerchief, which she took with a tearful smile of thanks.

'He never exactly asked…' she quavered. I was reminded of Miss Tierney and her Manchester industrialist's non-proposal. 'But he said one day, when he'd got established in his career, I would make an excellent diplomatic wife. And he said Daisy would never make anyone a wife.'

'Well, he was right about that,' remarked Mrs Jameson, a touch callously. 'But why do you say he liked Daisy better?'

She pulled a face. 'Harriet told me.'

'Harriet? What does Harriet know?' asked Mrs Caldwell, her voice sharp.

'While she was doing my hair this morning, we talked about what they said in court yesterday, about the baby. And she admitted Daisy had told her. She said... she said she thought it was Mr Franklin's fault.' Felicity's cheeks were pink, and she looked down at the handkerchief. 'So that means John liked Daisy best after all.'

Mrs Jameson sighed. 'Oh, Felicity. If only life was as simple as that. But a man who throws a girl over and refuses to take responsibility for his actions is never going to make a good husband. You are well rid of him.'

Mrs Caldwell called her daughter to her. 'Iris is quite right,' she said. 'Stop crying, Felicity. I should have been more careful about Daisy's conduct. I'm afraid your cousin was rather weak and silly. And Mr Franklin is very wicked.'

Felicity sniffed. I could have told Mrs Caldwell that men's wickedness is no barrier to young women falling in love with them.

Mrs Caldwell gripped her daughter's hands. 'Felicity, listen to me. Did that man ever try to get fresh with you? Is there anything between you I should know about?'

A fresh burst of tears from Felicity. 'No,' she wailed, before she buried her face in her mother's peignoir. 'He didn't even kiss me!'

A schoolgirl crush, encouraged by a vain man who liked to have women's regard, but had no interest in the consequences. I remembered the look of rapture on poor Felicity's face when she danced with Franklin at the Harlequin and felt indignant on her behalf.

We heard doors banging above our heads and a man's voice – Henry Caldwell – shouting. Mrs Jameson and I moved as one to the door into the hallway. Harriet stood at the foot of the stairs, her chin raised and a defiant look on her face.

'What's happening?' I asked her.

'He's getting what's coming to him, that's what,' she said, her voice sharp with spite. 'After all I done for him, Miss. I wish I'd named him in court, the devil.'

'What sort of things have you done for him?' Mrs Jameson asked.

Harriet bit her plump lip and turned her sideways gaze on us. 'Kept his blooming secrets. Covered up when Miss Daisy was in his room one time. Told him where the key to the wine cellar was kept. What more do you want to know?' Tears glittered in her eyes.

I put a hand on her arm. 'But why did you do all that for him, Harriet?'

She gave me a look. 'Blimey, Miss. I don't have to spell it out for you, do I? I liked the bloke. And he said he liked me. He said I could be a movie star, with my looks.'

'Are you all right?' I asked, keeping my voice low. 'Not in any trouble?'

She shook her head, but her tears overflowed, and she wiped them away quickly. 'Not me, Miss. I'm not as daft as some. But that devil made me promises. He said he'd take me to America with him, introduce me to some film producer he knew in Hollywood. I wanted to be in the movies, Miss. And now I never will be.'

Chapter 39

Shortly afterwards, John Franklin came down the stairs, his valise in one hand and his head held high. His colour was heightened, but his eyes were flint-cold.

He nodded to me and Mrs Jameson, standing in the hall like sentinels. His eyes lingered on me for a moment.

'Goodbye, Miss Swallow. Pleasure getting to know you,' he said, with just the hint of insult in his tone.

I felt my cheeks grow warm. I said nothing as he crossed the chequered floor and saw himself out. Thomas the footman closed the door behind him with a look of great satisfaction. Harriet gave a strangled sob and ran along the corridor to the servants' quarters.

Henry Caldwell walked slowly down the staircase, his tread heavy. He stood beside Mrs Jameson and me, gazing at the front door.

'Sir Leonard was right, it seems. Franklin was a cad of the worst order. I can't believe I was fooled. I've sent him away, of course. It is most inconvenient, but I cannot retain him in my household.'

'You did the right thing, Henry. Although...' Mrs Jameson paused, and her eyes took on the glazed look that sometimes came over her when she was thinking.

'Although what?'

She shook her head and smiled. 'Nothing. I wonder if the police officer has been to talk to Myrtle yet.'

We repaired to the drawing room where Mrs Caldwell sat alone, looking exhausted.

'What a business!' she exclaimed. 'Felicity has gone to her room. Thank heavens she was not seduced like her cousin. That dreadful man, after all you had done for him.'

Mr Caldwell was looking at his watch. 'We should eat,' he said. 'I need to get onto the embassy to find me a replacement secretary. I will have to work this afternoon and at the weekend too, if I am to begin to make up the ground.' He looked as tired as his wife.

Lunch was not a success, although the poached salmon was up to the residence's usual high standards. Felicity came down, but ate almost nothing. She had drawn her hair back into a tight bun, which along with her simple black dress and expression of injured pride made her look like a martyred saint in an early renaissance painting. The ambassador ate mechanically, but his mind was clearly not on the meal. Even Mrs Jameson was quiet, her eyes once more veiled. Twice, I saw her pause with a laden fork halfway to her mouth, her lips moving as if she was about to speak. Then she gave herself a little shake and continued with her meal.

The plates were being cleared away and coffee brought in when Thomas interrupted.

'There's a policeman at the door, Sir. He says he's come to look at Mrs Caldwell's medicine cabinet?'

'I'd forgotten to tell you, Myrtle.' Henry explained quickly to his wife. 'I'm sorry, darling. I thought it would be better than them calling you to give evidence.'

His wife rose. 'Of course. No, you stay there, Felicity. I'll take the policeman up.'

The interruption did not improve the atmosphere. Felicity poured coffee. Both Ambassador Caldwell and Mrs Jameson had lapsed into silence, their thoughts clearly elsewhere. Felicity and I seemed to be the only people present in the room.

'Your father said you might be going back to America for a while,' I said, more to break the silence than anything else. 'Will you be pleased to be home, after all this?'

She raised her pale green eyes, opaque as sea glass. 'Home is wherever Mamma and Papa are. I shan't go back to the States without them.'

Her words penetrated the ambassador's abstraction. 'That's very sweet, my dear, but I think it would be wise. Just for a couple of months, until this whole business blows over.'

Her brows drew together. 'I don't want to,' she said. Her jaw clamped shut in a way that reminded me of her father giving evidence in court. 'I want to stay and look after Mamma.'

I happened to be looking at the door just then, which was when Mrs Caldwell and the policeman re-entered. For a fleeting second, I saw something unexpected on Mrs Caldwell's face: fear. It was quickly smoothed over as she came into the room. Perhaps it had just been her normal expression of anxiety.

'Henry, it looks as if there are tablets missing,' she said, returning to her seat. 'We opened the cabinet with my key and counted out the contents against the prescriptions Dr Spink had given me.'

'How much?' asked Mrs Jameson, her attention back in the room.

'Mrs Caldwell believes there is one bottle of tablets missing,' said the policeman. 'I'll need to get back and report to the coroner's office.'

'It would have contained twenty half-grain tablets of morphine hydrochloride,' said Mrs Caldwell.

Mrs Jameson's eyes narrowed. 'According to Dr Manning's evidence, three grains of morphine would have been sufficient to cause death. That suggests Daisy took perhaps six ground-up tablets.' She looked at us over her coffee cup. 'The question now is, where are the remaining fourteen tablets of morphine?'

Chapter 40

'Are you absolutely sure?' the ambassador asked his wife.

She nodded, twisting her hands together. 'I'm sure.'

'That's a hell of a lot of morphine to be lying around the house,' he said. 'We need to find it. Before there are any more accidents.'

'Marjorie is good at finding things,' said Mrs Jameson, her voice bright. 'Why don't we conduct a search?'

I felt most uncomfortable at the thought of searching through the Caldwells' things while they looked on. But of course, if the alternative was to call in the police and ask them to do it, the family might prefer my services.

'I've thought of something rather dreadful,' said Felicity, slowly.

We all turned to look at her. She was swirling the remains of her coffee around in the cup, staring into the grounds.

'What are you talking about?' asked Mrs Caldwell, rather sharply.

Felicity raised her eyes. 'It's probably nonsense. It's just... everything we've discovered since Daisy's death. About Mr Franklin, and about her baby. It's all so horrible. And it made me wonder if it was even worse than we thought. If John... Mr Franklin... had been so worried about Daisy telling Papa about the baby, he tried to get rid of her altogether.'

Ambassador Caldwell's jaw fell open. 'You mean… he gave her the morphine? What, in her drink or something?'

Felicity shook her head slowly. 'I don't know. Perhaps that was how it was done. I don't have any idea about how whisky tastes, or morphine.' She looked at Mrs Jameson. 'Perhaps Aunt Iris can help?'

Mrs Jameson switched her luminous gaze to Ambassador Caldwell.

'Morphine hydrochloride dissolves tolerably well in alcohol,' she said, slowly. 'If you were to drink your whisky neat, you might not notice it. Six tablets are a lot, though, to dissolve in one glass.'

'We don't know how much of the stuff he gave her,' said Mr Caldwell. 'I don't know how long they sat up talking after I'd gone to bed. But…' His face gave a spasm, and he clenched his fist. 'When I passed by the top of the stairs, I heard Daisy saying she would talk to me in the morning, and John telling her she'd be sorry if she did. I thought it was some squabble about a crazy plan of hers. I almost came down to find out. I wish to hell I had.'

Mrs Jameson rose. 'I think we should take a look at Mr Franklin's rooms,' she said briskly. 'Marjorie, come with me.'

The attic rooms were panelled in dark oak. First came a small dressing room with a plain dark wardrobe, a bureau under the window and a looking glass placed prominently on it. Several drawers had been pulled half-out of the chest and one lay on the floor. The wardrobe door hung open. Mr Franklin had not troubled to tidy up after himself.

Beyond was the bedroom, faded red curtains parted to let in the dreary January light. Like my room in Bedford Square,

Mr Franklin's chamber had a view of grey slate rooftops and the alleyway at the side of the house. Mrs Jameson opened the window, which was stiff with damp, and looked out. Perhaps the view from a servant's room was a novelty to her.

I began with the bed; pulling the grey wool blankets and white sheets off and shaking them, then folding them up and giving them to a maid to take outside. They were very clean, with a slight hint of lemon-scented hair oil.

Nothing under the pillow or the mattress. I wanted to say that if Mr Franklin had stolen the morphine from Mrs Caldwell, he surely would have taken it with him. But perhaps he might have left it behind in his haste. I checked under the rugs and looked for loose floorboards. Nothing.

Back in the dressing room, I found a single gold cuff link and a stiff collar in the chest of drawers, a couple of hair pins under the rug and an empty bottle of bourbon whiskey in the back of the wardrobe. I showed this last to Mrs Jameson. She raised her eyebrows.

'That's Henry's brand. So, the man wasn't above filching a bottle for his own use.'

I knelt before the grate in the fireplace. 'Look at this,' I said. I picked out a few charred fragments, brushing the ashes from my fingers. The scraps were the same pink writing paper that we had found in Daisy's wastepaper basket. Only one word was still visible: 'Darling'. The handwriting was the same.

Mrs Jameson took them. 'He really is a nasty piece of work,' she said, her voice sharp. 'Check the bureau again, Marjorie.'

I rifled through the pigeon holes, then pulled out the shallow drawer and turned it upside down. I peered into the space left by its removal, then reached in a hand. There was something white – an envelope. I pulled it out.

The envelope was an old one, addressed to the American Embassy in Grosvenor Gardens with American stamps and a postmark from the previous month. It had been folded over, and there was something lumpy inside.

I laid it on the blotter.

Mrs Jameson's eyes glinted. 'Henry,' she called. 'You'd better come and look. We've found something.'

Henry Caldwell and Felicity must have been waiting just outside. They crowded around as Mrs Jameson opened the envelope.

Inside were three small tablets of a grey-white substance.

'Those look like Mamma's tablets,' said Felicity, her hand at her throat. 'How dreadful.'

Mrs Jameson closed the envelope up again and snapped it into her crocodile handbag. 'I will have them checked,' she said. 'Henry, had you missed any whiskey recently? We found an empty bottle of bourbon in the cupboard.'

He was staring around the room in disbelief. 'The fellow stole my whiskey and my wife's medicine, and used them to poison my niece? And we're just letting him walk away?'

Mrs Jameson gave a sudden gasp, and stared at him as if she'd never seen him before. 'You're right, Henry. There is no time to lose. Where did he go? Did he leave a forwarding address? We need to find him immediately.'

He thumped his fist into his hand. 'I don't know. Dammit, I told him I never wanted to see or hear from him again. I don't know where the hell he went.'

I slipped down the back stairs in search of Harriet. I soon found her: all the staff were eating their midday meal together in the kitchen. Her eyelids were pink, but her appetite seemed to be unaffected by her upset.

'Where's he gone?' I asked, breathless. 'They need to find him.'

'I didn't ask, and I don't care,' said Harriet. 'Good riddance to him.'

'Please,' I urged. 'Does anyone know? It's important.'

'Try the Palace Gate Hotel,' called Thomas across the table. 'It's a scrappy place over by the Cromwell Road. He boasted about it once, told me he took women there. If you see him, give him a poke in the eye from me, Miss.'

Chapter 41

Mrs Jameson telephoned Scotland Yard and summoned Inspector Chadwick.

'I know it's not your usual jurisdiction, Peter. But there's murder in the air. I can smell it. We shall need your expertise and authority.'

The inspector was waiting in his motorcar outside the Palace Gate Hotel when Mrs Jameson and I arrived. The footman's description had been accurate enough; despite the pillars and porticoes, the place had a neglected, scrappy air with yellowed lace curtains in the windows, broken railings in front of the basement area and green water stains running down the white stucco from the guttering.

The manager, a balding middle-aged man in a greasy black suit, didn't look terribly surprised to find a police officer on his doorstep. He showed us in, heaved a great sigh and reached for one of the keys on the board behind the reception desk. A smell of bad drains drifted from the basement as he led us up the narrow stairs.

He paused before a closed door with chipped black paint. 'Number twelve,' he said, and rapped on the door. No answer. He handed Inspector Chadwick the key.

'He arrived a couple of hours ago; I haven't seen him go out.

I'll be downstairs if you need me,' he said, disappearing rapidly down the stairwell. I got the impression he had seen more than he would have wished of hotel rooms that required the attention of the police.

'Please wait outside,' said Inspector Chadwick. 'The fellow might be violent.' He turned the key, shouted a warning of 'police!' and flung the door open.

'Damnation.' He crossed the room to the single bed in a couple of strides.

John Franklin lay on his back in his shirt-sleeves, his eyes staring open. His limbs stretched out across the pink candlewick bedspread. There was a smell of vomit, and a dark patch on the pillow.

Inspector Chadwick checked his neck and wrist for a pulse, then shook his head.

'Too late,' breathed Mrs Jameson. 'I should have realised sooner.'

We stepped cautiously into the dreary little room. On the small bedside table was a bottle of bourbon, almost empty. He didn't seem to have used a glass.

'I should preserve that and have it analysed,' said Mrs Jameson. 'Check for morphine.'

The inspector nodded. 'Although the blighter probably just washed the tablets down with the whiskey,' he said.

'Perhaps,' said Mrs Jameson.

The inspector stepped cautiously around the bed, taking in the rest of the room.

Mr Franklin's valise lay open on a straight-backed wooden chair. He hadn't bothered to unpack his belongings. A small case of clothes; rather pitiful to think this was all that remained of the man. He must have parents somewhere, I supposed.

Brothers and sisters, perhaps friends who would miss him. His leather wallet and room key lay on the bedside table next to the bottle. At the foot of the bed were his shiny black shoes, lined up neatly next to each other.

'Why would he do such a thing?' I asked. His career was finished, his reputation muddied, it was true. But he had not seemed remorseful when he left. 'I don't suppose you can see a note, Inspector?'

He turned over the few items on the desk. 'Nothing.'

Mrs Jameson was standing very still, tapping her chin with her fingers. Eventually, her gaze cleared, and she looked briskly around the room.

'Well, there we have it. Peter, what's your reading of the situation? Given everything we've told you about Mr Franklin and his potential involvement in the death of Daisy Caldwell.'

He hesitated. 'I usually find that the simplest explanation is the most likely,' he said. His voice was not as firm as usual. 'Which, in this situation, would be self-destruction. We know from what you found in his room in Prince's Gate that he had acquired morphine tablets and bourbon from the Caldwells. He had been at the inquest into Daisy's death. He knew what constituted a fatal dose of morphine.

'Whatever his culpability for Daisy's death – and it looks as if that will never be fully ascertained now – he would know that his career in the diplomatic service was over. Ambassador Caldwell would make sure of that. And perhaps he did feel regret, remorse for what had happened to Daisy Caldwell. Whether or not he had a hand in her death, he had clearly had an intimate relationship with her. When she died, so did his unborn child.'

He broke off and looked at Mrs Jameson, with the hint of a

question in his eyes. She nodded very slightly.

The inspector continued. 'So, he comes to this anonymous hotel, armed with the agents of suicide. He doesn't waste time in unpacking his possessions. Perhaps there is no-one he wished to read a final note. He lies on the bed, takes the tablets, and drinks the whiskey, hoping for a painless death.'

They looked at each other for a long time without speaking.

'Yes,' said Mrs Jameson, eventually. 'That does seem the most likely explanation.'

Chapter 42

Frankie stuck her head around the drawing room door at eight o'clock on Saturday night. 'It's time, Mrs J.' Her eyes glittered behind her black eye-mask. Mrs Jameson rose and reached for her own mask.

'Ready, Marjorie?'

My stomach was knotted with anxiety. I wished I'd eaten less at dinner, but I'd always operated on the principle that you might as well go into action on a full belly. I rose to my feet.

'I'm ready,' I said, settling my mask into place. I hoped my voice was reasonably steady.

The van that Frankie had borrowed from her friend at the garage was parked outside in Bedford Square under a gas lamp. Mrs Jameson and Frankie sat in the front, while I climbed into the back. Five young women with black eye-masks, all dressed like me in harlequin pyjama suits, shuffled up to make room.

'All right, Marjorie?' asked Lily Rose, flashing me a smile from the corner.

'I suppose so.' My mouth was dry, and I tried to slow my breathing. It would take us at least half an hour to get to Limehouse. The plan that Frankie and Mrs Jameson had hatched to disarm the Armstrong brothers was audacious.

I was not sure it would work. The girl gang of pickpockets and thieves, recruited from Frankie's wilder days, looked far too few to go up against the gangsters.

'What if they don't show?' asked one of the girls.

'They'll show,' said another. She patted a canvas duffel bag on the floor next to her. 'They won't want to risk this getting into the wrong hands. It was well-guarded, believe me. Took me no end of trouble to get it. And Sissie delivered the note to the Red Lion at seven o'clock. She said Vince Armstrong was frantic.'

Ten minutes later the van came to an abrupt halt. I looked out of a gap in the tarpaulin and saw we were outside the garage in Finsbury Circus. Two more women climbed in the back, tall and slim in their harlequin suits.

'Howay, Marjorie.' My surprise must have shown in my face. 'You didnae think I'd miss this, did you? Those radgies have been on my hit-list since they threatened our Edie last year,' said Hester Proudfoot.

Edith smiled primly and opened her handbag.

'I brought this along just in case, like. Count Rostokovich gave it to me. Canny, eh?' A diamond-encrusted pistol twinkled among the powder-compacts and handkerchiefs.

I stared. 'Let's hope you don't need to use it.'

There was little more chat before we clattered over the swing bridge at the Regent's Canal Basin. The last time I'd crossed that bridge, I'd been a captive, trying to fight off the effects of the veronal the Armstrong brothers had slipped in my champagne.

Lily Rose sensed my anxiety.

'Don't you worry, Marjorie. Frankie's got it all in hand. And your Mrs J won't let anything go wrong.'

The truck parked up. We'd been warned to stay out of sight until called. After a few minutes, Frankie pulled back the tarp.

'Quickly as you like, girls. Down the side and into the hall.'

We piled out of the van, which was backed up against an alleyway. We trooped down the alley and in through a side door to a big brick building: the Methodist Mission Hall. Frankie lit a couple of gas lamps. Chairs were stacked up around the whitewashed walls and heavy blue curtains hung at the windows. We ran around, pulling them closed.

Mrs Jameson stumped up the steps to the stage at the end of the hall. She checked her wristwatch and rapped her cane on the floor for silence.

'Thank you, ladies. You all know what to do. Keep out of sight behind the curtains or at the side of the stage until you are needed. I think our first guests should be arriving soon... ah, that must be them now.'

Frankie ran to answer the firm knock on the door at the front of the hall. Two ladies came inside. Both were in their fifties or sixties and their faces bore lines of hard work and laughter. One wore a patched worsted coat and a hat that had seen plenty of service; the other a surprisingly good fur coat and hat. The lady in the patched coat hugged Frankie tight. I noticed the purple, green and white ribbon on her lapel. This must be Frankie's suffragette aunt.

'Always in trouble,' she said. But her tone was proud, not disapproving.

'All right, Auntie Clara? How are you, Mrs A?' Frankie led them to the stage.

'Welcome,' said Mrs Jameson. 'Please, take a seat in the wings.'

Lily Rose and I went around extinguishing all the gas lights except for the ones that illuminated the stage. Frankie carried a wooden chair into the middle of the stage and sat on it, propping up her feet on the duffle bag.

'All right,' she called. She took a pack of cigarettes from her pocket, flared a match, and lit up a Woodbine. 'You can unlock the door. I'm ready.'

The time was nine o'clock exactly. The room cleared. I slipped behind the curtain across one of the windows. It was pitch black outside. I could hear noise from the docks; masts groaning and water slapping against the basin walls. A seagull began to cry, that weird sound like a baby mewling. Would they come?

A crash from the front door, as it swung open. My heart began to beat faster, double-syncopated like Mr Sampson's drums. Heavy footsteps approached. There was the sound of a man hawking, then spitting on the floor.

'Evening, lads.' Frankie's voice sounded bright enough, but she must have been scared.

Ted Armstrong's voice was low, controlled, and terrifying. 'I thought I'd leave you with Vince for a while, but he don't like blokes,' he said. 'So, I'm going to cut you up until not even a doctor can say what you really are.'

'I thought you'd want this back first,' said Frankie. 'I mean, you wouldn't want to get blood on it, would you, Vince? That'd be a shame.'

'Get it,' said Ted.

I peeped out. I could see the brothers' silhouettes against the light from the stage. Frankie was still smoking, looking remarkably cool. Vince walked up to the front of the stage and made a grab for the bag.

'Let's all have a look, shall we?' Frankie got to her feet and held it above her head.

That was our cue. We emerged from behind the curtains.

'What the...?' Edward Armstrong looked around. An army of harlequins, masked and silent, lighting the lamps and converging on the stage.

'You bleeding rubster. You think I'm scared of a bunch of women?' he yelled.

Vince was still trying to grab the bag from Frankie. 'Give it back,' he whined, like a small boy outnumbered in the playground. Frankie tossed it to one of the Proudfoot sisters, who held it high above her head.

'Why, let's have a look, Vince,' she said. 'Shall I get it out?'

'No!' he roared. 'It's mine!'

'You are dead meat,' hissed Ted, still staring at Frankie. 'You even used our mum. You told us she was sick.'

The two older ladies emerged from the wings, arm in arm, and advanced to the front of the stage. The woman in furs pointed her finger at Ted.

'I am bleeding sick,' she yelled. 'I'm sick of you and your brother behaving like a pair of gorillas, ain't I? I'm sick of you picking fights with my neighbours and acting too big for your boots, Edward Armstrong.'

She turned her gaze to her second son. 'And you, Vincent, are a bleeding disgrace. I know it ain't all your fault. I know your Dad,' – she paused to spit off the side of the stage – 'God rot him, messed you up as a kid. Knocked something wrong in your head, I reckon.'

Vincent had stopped jumping after the bag and stood, head bowed, looking like he might cry. We were all standing in a tight circle around Ted Armstrong now, watching the drama. Mrs Armstrong drew breath and continued.

'But you, Edward, need to get yourself in order. Your uncles were satisfied with the turf. They made a decent living on the racecourses, without all this messing around in nightclubs. Look at you. Going up West, picking up floozies, pretending you're the big man. Well, you're not. You're my boy still, Edward, and you need to look after your little brother.'

'I do look after him,' yelled Ted. 'It's all I bleedin' do.'

'Then do it more quietly,' said Mrs Armstrong. 'Stop this racket in the West End. Stick to your own.'

Frankie's Aunt Clara squeezed Mrs Armstrong's arm. 'We're all friends here,' she said, her voice comfortable. 'Our Frankie did what she did to rescue an innocent girl what had got in too deep. We don't want to make enemies. Me and Peg Armstrong has been friends since we was at Sunday School together. I want you boys to promise not to hurt a hair on Frankie's head.'

I wasn't sure now whether I was a floozie or an innocent girl, but I hoped the amnesty might extend to me.

'Step forward, Marjorie,' called Mrs Jameson from the stage. Quailing, I did as she said.

'This young woman was carrying out undercover duties on my behalf,' she said. 'You have done her grievous harm. You owe her an apology.'

I swallowed. A promise not to go after me would have done. Vince hung his head. 'Sorry, Miss.'

His brother looked at me with contempt. 'I don't like narks,' he said. 'But I'll let it go this time. You keep out of our way in future, and we'll keep out of yours.'

I supposed that would have to do. I nodded and retreated behind Lily Rose.

'One more thing, bonny lad.' Edith Proudfoot held up the duffel bag in one hand and her jewel-encrusted pistol in the other. She pointed the gun at the bag. Vincent Armstrong let out a yelp of dismay. 'Mr Li and Vi are the soundest bosses I've ever had in this rotten business. You've destroyed their club. There's never going to be another like the Harlequin.'

Hester stood nose to nose with Edward Armstrong. 'Our Edith's right. You promise to leave them be, Ted. And the band. Or a full account of this evening will be reet round Limehouse before you can blink. How're you going to keep your Boss Man image if everyone knows you were held to ransom by a bunch of lassies in dress-up costumes?'

Ted muttered something.

'I cannae hear you,' said Hester.

'I said, all right. Li can have his restaurants and stuff. I won't go after the band.'

'Promise them, Ted!' called Vincent Armstrong, staring in consternation at Edith and the gun.

She cackled. 'Swear, or the bear gets it!'

'All right,' shouted Ted. 'I swear.'

Edith tossed the bag in the air and Vince lunged forward. Ted caught it and handed it to his brother.

The Armstrongs left, tails very much between their legs, with their mother chivvying them along. Vincent clutched the duffle bag, but not before he'd opened it to check the contents. Edward Bear, a mangy-looking teddy-bear with most of its mohair fur rubbed off, was still intact.

Chapter 43

For two days, everything went quiet. We heard no more from the Armstrong brothers. Frankie returned home to Limehouse, Freddie to Brixton. I paid my usual Sunday visit to my parents in Catford. I told my mother I'd scratched my face on a thorn bush in Bedford Square Gardens, but I wasn't sure she believed me. She'd always thought of me as clumsy, but my recent run of 'accidents' was starting to make her suspicious.

Inspector Chadwick said he'd been given the go-ahead to investigate links between the Armstrong brothers and police officers at Vine Street and in the East End. He warned us that the investigation must be kept top-secret and would take some time.

Despite our success in the Caldwell case and in subduing Ted and Vince Armstrong, Mrs Jameson was restless and twitchy. She sat up very late on Sunday night, reading through all our notes from the case. When I came down in the morning, the table was piled high with medical textbooks, copies of the *Chemist and Druggist* and the *British Medical Journal*, and papers covered in Mrs Jameson's distinctive, clear handwriting. I saw she'd made a list of questions still unanswered. I read them over, frowning. Perhaps the case was not quite closed, after all.

Over breakfast, Mrs Jameson asked me to make a tour of all the jewellers in the region of Kensington and Knightsbridge. She produced a photograph of the gold box that had been on Daisy's bedside when she was found. I remembered the twin of it that I had found on the terrace behind Prince's Gate, which Mrs Jameson had said she would send for analysis.

'I want to know who sells these boxes, Marjorie. Are they turned out by the dozen, or are they bespoke? Who has bought one since Daisy arrived in London in September? Did Franklin buy one as a present for Daisy, and if so, did he buy two at the same time?'

I foresaw a long and tedious day traipsing up and down Knightsbridge and Kensington High Street. And, of course, there was no reason why they should have been bought there. They could have come from anywhere in London. They could even have arrived with Daisy from the States. I tried to remember if Daisy had told me anything about hers. Was it a gift, or had she bought it herself? I couldn't remember. I laced up a pair of stout walking shoes and set off.

My fears were quickly allayed. As I hopped off the 'bus on the Brompton Road at Knightsbridge, a small display of knick-knacks in Harrods' window caught my eye. The display included three golden trinket boxes, each embossed with a different pattern. One had a sun-ray pattern, one a spiral shape and the third had a scallop shell. They were displayed artistically, surrounded by powder puffs, pearls, and curls of pink ribbon.

I stepped smartly through the door, nodding to the doorman in his olive-green uniform and bright buttons. I'd never been inside Harrods before and for a moment, I was overwhelmed by its size and grandeur. The entrance hall glittered with mirrors and pillars painted in oriental designs. The food hall was to one side, with poultry hanging from hooks and vast cheeses piled up. There were signs for sporting goods, for silver and cutlery, pianos, men's hats and gloves. However would I find what I was looking for?

With relief I spotted an information desk, where a smartly dressed young woman was able to answer my question about the boxes in the display.

'Of course, Miss. Second floor, ladies' toiletries and fancy goods,' she said. 'Take the moving staircase from the hall.'

The escalator was far grander than the wooden affairs that carried passengers on the London Underground, with a sloping leather floor and mahogany handrail as well as glass walls that gave a rather unnerving view of the floor below as I was raised smoothly upwards.

Finally locating the correct department, I asked about the boxes I'd seen in the window. I took out the photograph to show the superior-looking young woman in charge.

'Oh, we've sold dozens of those,' she said, rather crushingly. 'They're gold plate, you see, which means they are accessible to most budgets.' Her professional glance seemed to assess whether that included my modest means.

'I'm interested in the one with the scallop pattern,' I said. 'Have you carried them for long?'

She looked again at the photograph, squinting a little. Short-sighted, and too vain to wear spectacles, I guessed.

'Not that exact design,' she said. 'It came in a month ago, which was a nuisance because we only had them for two days before Christmas. We'd have sold more if they'd come in earlier. Would you like to see one?'

I said I would. She searched under the counter and unwrapped one from a green velvet bag. I examined it carefully. As far as I could tell, it was the exact same model as that owned by Daisy Caldwell – and the double that I'd found in the flowerbed at Prince's Gate.

I smiled my most winning smile. 'My friend had one just like it,' I said. 'I wonder if she got it here. Poor Daisy. I suppose you heard about her? The ambassador's niece. She died of an overdose. It was in all the newspapers. But she loved that box. I was thinking I might get one to remember her by.'

The woman's eyes grew round. 'Daisy Caldwell? That American girl? Was she really your friend?'

I nodded, glanced around, and leaned closer. 'You know, we went out dancing at the Harlequin club together the night before she died. She had that box with her then. If only I'd known what was going to happen.'

She was avid for information now. 'That's so sad,' she said. 'Did she really have one with her? I remember the day she came in and got them. They must have been some of the first ones we sold.'

This was excellent news. 'Yes, she showed it to me when we were in the powder room. I admired it very much. You remember her, then?'

'Oh, yes, Miss. She's very…' I saw the woman try to find a polite way to put it. 'She was very vivacious. And distinctive, in the way she dressed. I remember she had a pink and yellow hat, a sort of beret thing. Very striking, what with her red hair.'

I smiled. 'A tam o'shanter. Yes, you couldn't miss her in that,' I admitted. 'You said she bought more than one of them, though? Are you sure? I thought she just had the one.'

The woman nodded vigorously. 'Yes, because I remember thinking it was very generous. She said she was buying the second one as a Christmas present. She said you should always buy people presents that you want yourself, so it just made sense to buy two of everything and give one away.'

I couldn't help laughing at this evidence of Daisy's combination of generosity and selfishness.

'Yes, that sounds like her,' I said. 'She didn't tell you who she planned to give it to, did she?'

Chapter 44

Mrs Jameson wasn't usually anxious about entertaining, but she'd been up and down to the kitchen all morning with questions and last-minute orders about luncheon. Even the saintly Graham Hargreaves rolled his eyes when her bell rang yet again.

'She just wants everything to be perfect. The Caldwells have had such a terrible time,' I told him.

He smiled. 'Of course. But it always is perfect, Miss Swallow, isn't it?'

That was true. Graham had the household running like clockwork and our cook (enticed to Bedford Square from one of the grandest families in Norfolk) was the envy of all Mrs Jameson's friends. Mrs Jameson was exacting but fair, paid far better than most English families and had no interest in regulating the servants' lives so long as her domestic comfort was assured. We must have been the last household in London not to complain of the servant problem.

When I went through to the dining room, Mrs Jameson was attempting to instruct Ellen, the under-housemaid, in the art of flower arranging. I had never seen her show any interest in such a thing before. The handsome bronze chrysanthemums, however, were her favourite flowers and looked well in their crystal vase.

'Oh, there you are, Marjorie. Do you have it?'

I took the velvet bag from the drawer in the sideboard. 'Right here, Mrs Jameson.'

'Good. Not a word until I tell you, understood?'

I nodded.

'And you know what to do when we have coffee?'

I did, although I was a little nervous about that part of the plan.

The doorbell rang.

'They're here.' She glanced in the mirror and adjusted her double strand of pearls over her russet-coloured high-necked blouse. 'Come through to the hall.'

Ambassador Caldwell, tall and stooped, seemed to have aged twenty years since I had first met him. Mrs Caldwell looked thin in her black two-piece suit, although she greeted us warmly, her head held erect. Her husband's deterioration seemed to have brought out some inner strength, as if she was determined to support him now that he needed her.

'Thank you so much for inviting us, Iris dear,' she said. 'One certainly learns who one's friends are at times like this. Apart from official visitors, we have been quite abandoned this last terrible week.'

Felicity Caldwell gave a tremulous smile. 'You're very kind, Aunt Iris,' she said. 'Hello, Marjorie. You're looking well.'

To my surprise, so was Felicity. I had been wondering how the girl had coped with the news of John Franklin's death. Even if she had been disabused of her liking for him, it must have been a shock. But she looked less distraught than she had on the day when Franklin stormed out of the house. Her coiled hair and black velvet frock rather suited her pale northern

Madonna looks.

'Come through,' said Mrs Jameson. 'I'm very glad you could all come. Especially when you, Henry, are so busy with diplomatic business.'

He seemed to emerge from a reverie. 'Oh. Yes, I suppose I am, rather. The embassy staff are being very good. They seem to have things in hand.'

Mrs Jameson exchanged a worried look with Mrs Caldwell. Two weeks previously, I remembered, the ambassador and Franklin were sitting up late working on vital talks about war debt repayment and America's role in the League of Nations. Surely that work could not be so easily handed over to embassy employees. He seemed to have lost all interest in his diplomatic mission, since the shock of Daisy's death.

As Graham had promised, lunch was perfect. Mrs Smithson had conjured up a delicious oyster soup, followed by sole meunière. Mrs Jameson waited until we were served with a rich venison casserole before steering the conversation in the direction she wished to explore.

'I wonder if you could recommend a good chemist shop, Myrtle,' she began. 'I have been suffering from sore eyes. I'm sure it is the result of this London soot. I wanted to ask about eye drops. I don't suppose you use them yourself?'

Mrs Caldwell looked surprised. 'Well, no. Some fellow back home recommended I try eye drops for my headaches, but they made no difference. Felicity is good enough to go out for my patent medicines. Dr Spink has recommended a vitamin tonic. I think you go to a place in Wigmore Street, Felicity?'

The girl looked up with a smile, eager to please as usual. 'That's right. John Bell & Croyden. They're very good. They can get most things. I'm sure they could advise you about your eyes, Aunt Iris.'

Mrs Jameson smiled. 'Thank you. I will be sure to mention your name when I go in, Felicity.'

'Oh, I don't suppose they'll remember me,' she said. 'I just pick up the things that Mamma needs.'

'Of course.' Mrs Jameson hesitated. 'This talk of pharmacies reminds me. There is something I should tell you all. Henry, we have discovered where Daisy was buying her cocaine.'

The ambassador's head jerked up and Mrs Caldwell pressed her napkin to her mouth.

'What?' His voice was harsh. 'Why didn't you say before?'

Mrs Jameson spoke placidly. 'Because we only recently came by the information. And because the cause of Daisy's death was not cocaine, so the matter no longer seemed so urgent. Anyway, I have the address of a chemist shop in Soho, close to the Harlequin club, where the proprietor is known to supply small quantities of cocaine without being too particular about a doctor's prescription. Marjorie's inquiries suggest that Daisy was a customer. I have passed the address to the police.'

The ambassador shook his head. 'Well, I'll be...' He tailed off, his previous bluster about the evils of the drugs trade seemingly forgotten.

Mrs Caldwell shook her head. 'So poor Daisy took cocaine bought from a chemist and died by morphine supplied by my doctor. And yet all the newspaper coverage is of her as some kind of dope fiend. It seems very unfair.'

Graham appeared to clear away the plates and bring in the apple charlotte.

'Indeed,' said Mrs Jameson. 'But then until a few years ago, you could buy morphine injection kits in Harrods department store without anyone raising an eyebrow. Harrods seems to sell everything under the sun, doesn't it, Marjorie?'

This was my cue. I took the green velvet bag from the sideboard. 'I bought this in Harrods two days ago. The sales girl said they came in just before Christmas.'

I untied the golden cord and opened the bag. The gold scallop-shell box sat on my hand.

Myrtle Caldwell frowned and reached out to take it. 'Isn't that like the one that Daisy had?'

Mrs Jameson nodded. 'Exactly like it. You don't have one yourself, Myrtle?'

She raised her eyes, puzzled. 'No. Why do you ask?' She turned the box over, flicked it open. 'It's pretty, but I don't have any need of such a thing.'

Mrs Jameson's voice was silky. 'And what about you, Felicity? What happened to the box that Daisy gave you for Christmas?'

Felicity raised her eyes and stared at Mrs Jameson for a moment. 'I'm not sure,' she said. 'Perhaps it's still in my room somewhere. I never really cared for it, I'm afraid. It was rather typical of Daisy, to give you something she wanted herself rather than considering that one might have rather different tastes.'

Chapter 45

We moved to the drawing room. Graham wheeled in a trolley with the coffee pot and cups. Jenny popped her head around the door.

'Sorry to intrude, Mrs Jameson. Cook says could Mr Hargreaves have a word in the kitchen?'

With a murmur of apology, Graham followed her out of the door.

'Felicity, perhaps you and Marjorie would be so kind as to pour the coffee? Thank you, dear. The sugar is on the sideboard.'

Mrs Jameson took a sip of brandy.

'It seems like a good time to reflect on what we have learned about Daisy's death,' she said in measured tones.

'What? Oh, yes. Of course.' Henry Caldwell pulled his attention back into the room from wherever it had been wandering.

'I'm not sure there is much more to say, is there?' asked Mrs Caldwell, her voice sharper than usual. 'That wretched Franklin seduced poor Daisy, then slipped morphine tablets he'd stolen from me into her whisky when she threatened to tell Henry about the baby. And when he was threatened with exposure, he killed himself using the same method. Took the coward's way out.'

'Well, that's certainly one explanation,' said Mrs Jameson. 'But I have to say, it does leave one or two questions unexplained.'

Standing by the trolley, I poured the coffee and added cream. 'Do you or your parents take sugar?' I asked Felicity.

'I don't drink coffee. Mamma has one teaspoon of sugar, Papa prefers his without. Let me do it,' she said.

'Of course. I have two sugars and Mrs Jameson has hers without,' I said. I picked up the coffee for the Caldwells.

'Oh! So sorry.' A few drops spilled into the saucer as I set the cup on the occasional table by Mrs Caldwell's elbow. 'I'll fetch a cloth.' I nipped out to the corridor and grabbed a dishcloth from Graham, who stood waiting with it in his hand. He raised his eyebrows. I nodded and waited a few seconds before re-entering the room to wipe up the spillage.

'What exactly is unexplained?' Mrs Caldwell was asking.

Felicity passed me two coffee cups. 'The left hand one is yours. The other is for Mrs Jameson,' she said. I set them down carefully and seated myself in an armchair next to my employer. Felicity sat opposite us, between her parents on the sofa.

'The most obvious anomaly is the length of time between Daisy drinking whisky with Mr Franklin, and her death the next day,' said Mrs Jameson. 'Henry, you heard them talking at about one o'clock. But we know Daisy was alive at half past nine the next morning, because Felicity and Harriet heard her snoring. The snoring was likely a result of her respiratory muscles beginning to fail. Morphine poisoning is quick; one slips into a coma around half an hour to an hour after ingestion of a fatal dose.'

Henry Caldwell leaned forward, his eyes showing awakened interest. 'Is that so?'

'And the pathologist said that Daisy had powdered morphine in her nostrils and respiratory tract, which would indicate she had snorted it, not swallowed it dissolved in whisky.'

'That's true,' said the ambassador, looking troubled.

'The other question, of course, is how Mr Franklin managed to get hold of the medication. Was he in the habit of visiting you in your sick room, Myrtle?'

Mrs Caldwell was sitting very still, her hands folded in her lap and her eyes cast down. 'Well, no. I rarely saw him. But perhaps he had help. One of the maids…' She trailed off.

'Harriet!' exclaimed Felicity. 'She was very keen on Mr Franklin. And she was in and out of both of our bedrooms.'

'I have considered that possibility,' said Mrs Jameson, firmly. 'That brings us to the other curious thing. The bottle of atropine eye drops I found in Daisy's wastepaper basket.' She reached into her handbag and brought out a small brown bottle with a dropper.

'Now, I wondered why Daisy – who was not a tidy young woman, judging by her bedroom – had applied eye drops, and then neatly disposed of the bottle. Firstly, why did she need atropine? Dr Spink suggested cosmetic purposes. The drops have the effect of enlarging the pupils, so perhaps she used them before the trip to the Harlequin. The effects can last for ten days, so it is hard to be sure when they were administered. However, her vision at the club seemed quite acute. According to Marjorie, Daisy was able to recognise friends right across the dance floor, despite the dim light. Atropine blurs the vision.'

Mrs Caldwell's hands were clenched in her lap. 'I'm getting

rather tired, Iris. I'm sorry, but perhaps you could finish your explanation another time? I would like to go home.'

Mrs Jameson's eyes rested on her kindly. 'I know this is difficult. I'm truly sorry, Myrtle. But I believe it would be as well for you all to hear what I have to say.'

She turned to me. 'I asked Marjorie to visit the chemist shop whose label was on the eye drops, in the hope of finding out whether they had indeed been purchased by Daisy. I received a troubling reply to my inquiries.'

She reached into her handbag again. 'And then, there is this little gold box,' she said, unwrapping it from the brown paper in which it was swathed. She set it on the table in front of her and opened it. 'Which, when Marjorie found it in the flowerbed on the terrace at Prince's Gate, contained traces of what my friends at the Metropolitan Police chemical analysis laboratory assure me is ground-up morphine tablets.'

Henry Caldwell leaned forward and grabbed the box. 'I don't understand.' He looked at his wife, who had closed her eyes and was pale as death. 'Myrtle, what does this mean? Tell me.'

Mrs Jameson's grey eyes fastened on his daughter. 'Felicity, are you going to be a brave girl and tell your papa? Why did you throw your box into the garden?'

Felicity pouted her lips and looked sulky, like a child caught out for some minor misdemeanour. 'I don't know what you're talking about. I just lost it somewhere. Sounds potty to me,' she said.

'And if I drank this cup of coffee, Felicity? What do you think would happen to me then? What if I gave this cup to your mother, or your father? Would you advise them to drink it?'

Chapter 46

Felicity started forward, lunging for the cup. Her father put his hand around her shoulders, holding her in place.

'Dear God, Iris. What are you suggesting?'

Mrs Jameson set down the cup and rang the bell. Graham, stationed outside the door, appeared immediately.

'Please remove this cup and preserve it somewhere safe.'

'Of course, Mrs Jameson. Will there be anything else?'

He withdrew, holding the cup at arm's length in gloved hands. I eyed my own untouched coffee. I was parched with all the excitement, but I wasn't going to take the risk of tasting it. Felicity slumped back on the sofa, holding tightly to her father's arm.

'Henry, I am so sorry. You asked me to investigate Daisy's death. I promised to do so, but I warned you that the results might not be what you had hoped for. This is what I believe happened.

'Felicity had become very fond of your aide, Mr Franklin, who had encouraged her sentiments. She was used to having her parents to herself and getting her own way. When Daisy arrived, all that was upset. Daisy was self-confident, outgoing, fashionable, and popular. She commanded attention. Felicity, with her quiet ways, resented her from the start. Even Harriet,

234

her maid, seemed to prefer Daisy's company. Then Mr Franklin began his dalliance with Daisy. Discreet on his side, but less so on hers. That cannot have been easy for Felicity to watch. Misled by Mr Franklin about the seriousness of his intentions, she must have felt that Daisy was stealing him away.'

'You have no proof of this!' shouted Ambassador Caldwell. 'So what if my poor girl was taken in by that devil? We all were. That doesn't mean she... she...'

Mrs Jameson shook her head sadly. She looked at the girl, who was staring at her shoes, an angry flush creeping up her neck.

'Felicity, what was it that made you do it that night? Was it seeing your cousin and Franklin sitting up late together with your father, in what you felt was your place? You must have feared you were on the brink of losing them both.'

Felicity looked up, her eyes defiant. 'It's a load of rot,' she said, setting her jaw.

Mrs Jameson continued, unblinking. 'The plan was quite ingenious. You knew that Daisy took cocaine from her gold box. You had caught her doing so first thing in the morning to wake herself up after a late night. You knew from Dr Spink the strength of the morphine tablets, and that they were more dangerous by volume than the cocaine that Daisy was used to. And as her nurse, you were the person best-placed to take Myrtle's tablets.

'You ground up the morphine tablets and put them in your box, the identical box that Daisy had given you for Christmas. During the night, while Daisy was sleeping, you unlocked her door and swapped the boxes over.'

'No,' said the ambassador. 'No, I don't believe this. Myrtle, we're leaving now. This is all wrong.' He started to get to his feet, but his wife held out her hand to restrain him.

'Let her finish,' Mrs Caldwell said, her voice weary. 'Hear her out.'

'The next morning,' Mrs Jameson continued relentlessly, 'Felicity waited until she was sure the morphine had done its work before volunteering to go and wake her cousin.' She turned her eyes on the girl again.

'That was a risk, but you had told Harriet to leave her to sleep and no-one else was likely to disturb her. When you found her dead, you applied the atropine eye drops you had bought from John Bell & Croyden, hoping her death would be attributed to cocaine. As it might have been, had it not been for the diligence of Sir Leonard.

'Finally, you swapped the boxes back and flung your box out of the bedroom window into the flower beds beyond the terrace, presumably intending to retrieve and destroy it later. You then raised the alarm.'

'Rot,' said Felicity. 'You can't prove anything.'

Mr Caldwell was shaking his head. 'Iris… you can't possibly believe my daughter is a murderer. She's just a child. Your god-daughter, for Heaven's sake. She loved her cousin. And what about Franklin, and his suicide?'

Mrs Jameson sighed. 'I'm rather afraid that was not suicide, Henry. When Felicity realised that Franklin was responsible for Daisy's pregnancy, and that his promises to her had been so much hot air, she decided to take revenge. She knew from Harriet that Franklin was in the habit of taking the occasional bottle of bourbon from your cellar. While you and he were at the inquest, Felicity used some of the remaining stock of tablets to poison the bottle in his room. She also stashed a couple of tablets in his bureau for us to find. She then suggested he might have poisoned Daisy.'

Ambassador Caldwell looked straight ahead. 'And do you have proof for any of this?' he asked, his voice scornful.

Mrs Jameson sighed. 'I have the coffee cup poisoned with morphine, prepared by Felicity after I hinted at lunch that I had made certain discoveries. I have the testimony of the chemist who sold Felicity atropine eye drops a week after Christmas. We have the duplicate box which belonged to Felicity, and its contents. The testimony of the sales girl who sold it to Daisy, as a present for her cousin.

'And Harriet saw Felicity go into Mr Franklin's rooms on the morning of the day he died. She didn't say anything because, I'm afraid to say, she had previously seen Daisy coming and going from those rooms. She assumed that Felicity too was romantically involved with Mr Franklin.'

Mr Caldwell turned to his daughter, his face like granite. 'Felicity, you've heard what Mrs Jameson has to say. What is your response?'

The girl knuckled her eyes, as if trying to squeeze out tears. 'I can't believe you would think that of me,' she whined. 'She's talking rot, Papa. We should go home. Mamma is getting one of her heads.'

Mrs Caldwell rose, slowly and painfully. 'I am indeed,' she said. She walked to the window and turned to look at her family.

'Felicity, I saw you take those tablets on Christmas Day. You thought I was asleep, but I was awake. Ever since I have feared what you planned to do with them. Now I know.'

'No,' said her husband. 'No, Myrtle, you must have got it wrong.'

She turned to him, tears spilling over her eyelids. 'Henry, I don't know what we did. Perhaps I have not been a proper mother to her. Perhaps it's because she was brought up alone, with no brothers or sisters, and we travelled around so much that she was unable to make friends. She has been too solitary. But much as it pains me, I believe that Iris is right.'

'Stop it!' Felicity was on her feet, her face red. 'How can you say that? After all the time I've spent looking after you. You're horrible and I hope you die. Papa, make her stop.'

Her father grabbed her shoulders. 'Sit down and keep quiet,' he shouted. 'Let me think.' He wore an expression of absolute anguish.

Felicity subsided.

'Your daughter is dangerous, Henry,' said Mrs Jameson. 'I will not tell you what to do. I have not yet brought this to the attention of the police. As you know, you and your family have diplomatic immunity in Britain. If you chose to remove your daughter from this country, the police would not be able to stop you. It is your choice. But if you do nothing, I promise you this. Felicity will murder again.'

Chapter 47

The ambassador stared at his daughter's angry face. His expression showed a terrible struggle as he tried to decide what – and who – to believe.

'You don't know what you're saying, Felicity. The strain has been too much for you. We must take you back to the States. Get you properly cared for.' He squeezed her shoulders. 'You're my little girl, Felicity. I'll look after you. Don't you worry.'

He rose and turned to Mrs Jameson. 'I am taking my family home. We will return to America as soon as it can be arranged. This whole posting has been a very bad mistake.' He took his daughter's arm. 'Thank you for luncheon. I believe the embassy car is waiting outside. I will take my leave of you now, Mrs Jameson.'

She flinched at his use of her surname, and bowed her head.

Mrs Caldwell looked to be on the verge of protest, but her husband's cold look froze her into silence. She pulled her shawl tightly around herself.

Mrs Jameson held out her hands to her friend, her face showing more anxiety than I had ever seen before. 'Myrtle… you can stay here, you know.'

Mrs Caldwell's eyes darted towards her husband and daughter, walking together across the hall. She shook her head, although she looked very frightened.

'Henry will need me,' she said.

The family left the house and climbed into the black motor-car with the Stars and Stripes flag on the bonnet. As it drove away, Felicity smiled, a satisfied little smirk, and waved to us out of the window.

Mrs Jameson and I retired to sit in the drawing room, a little stunned. Graham brought in fresh coffee. He raised his eyebrows in a silent question, and I shook my head. We had not achieved the outcome we had sought. Without being asked, he poured Mrs Jameson a glass of brandy.

'Are you going to tell the police?' I asked.

Mrs Jameson shook her head. 'I can't.'

'But she might…'

'I know.' Mrs Jameson put her head in her hands. 'It's terribly dangerous. But the police cannot arrest Felicity. I had hoped… I thought Henry would come around. Perhaps he will. A secure nursing home, a private asylum. But if it should be too late…'

There was a long silence. 'She might stop now,' I said, hopefully. 'You might have frightened her off. She might settle down in America and live a normal life.'

Mrs Jameson's voice was heavy. 'She has crossed the line. To cross it once – to deliberately take the life of another human being – makes it so much easier to cross it again.' She sighed. 'And Felicity has not stopped at one murder. Just over a week after Daisy's death, she had killed John Franklin. She really would have killed me, you know. And she will reach for that weapon whenever she is crossed, whenever she does not get her own way.'

'In that case, she should be imprisoned for life, or executed,' I said firmly. 'If you say nothing, no-one will know what really happened. And Mr Franklin may be blamed for Daisy's death and for his own. Think of his family.'

Mrs Jameson sipped her brandy. 'I do. I have, I mean. But my loyalties lie with Henry Caldwell. As I told you before, Henry did me a great kindness many years ago. Now it is time for me to repay that debt. I believe Henry knows he has lost his daughter, as well as his niece. I cannot add to his suffering.'

I glanced at her. Now was the time to ask. 'What did happen in Rome, Mrs Jameson?'

She smiled, a small, sad smile. 'I lost my own child, Marjorie. My only son. And I was so angry and afraid that I stepped perilously close to that line.'

I knew Mrs Jameson was a widow, but she had not previously mentioned having a child. The pain in her eyes was overwhelming.

'I'm so sorry.'

She shrugged. 'It was a long time ago. One never forgets, of course. Not even for a day.'

There was a soft mewing and the door seemed to open by itself. Sooty the kitten strolled into the drawing room and pushed his soft fur against my legs. I reached down to rub his tummy, taking comfort from his warmth. Officially he was confined to the servants' quarters, but he had a habit of slipping through the baize door when I needed him most.

I mulled over the second part of what Mrs Jameson had said. Had she just told me that she'd tried to murder someone, or planned to? I shivered a little. But she said she had stopped short of the line. Whatever could cause someone – someone good, like Mrs Jameson – to kill? We had established a list of motives for use in investigations: greed, passion, revenge, and fear. Fear, Mrs Jameson had said, was the most dangerous of all. It was hard to imagine her being truly afraid of anything.

'How is that young man of yours, Marjorie? I suppose he'll be out of a job now that the Harlequin has closed.' Mrs Jameson broke into my chain of thought, her voice deliberately loud and bright. I flushed a little. Was Freddie really my young man?

'Freddie Gillespie?' He'd come over to Catford for our usual Sunday afternoon walk. My mother had started making cakes for him, so he'd had to sit in our front room and drink tea before we could escape for a stroll in Ladywell Gardens.

'He's going to teach piano lessons. And T-bone says they can get work recording jazz music, up in Denmark Street. They'll be on gramophone records.' I was proud of Freddie's talent and resourcefulness. But I knew he needed to play in a band. It had made all the difference to his recovery.

'That's good. Perhaps you would invite him to take coffee with us one morning this week? I have a mind to buy a piano. It would be nice to have a music room with a gramophone, don't you think? And maybe a listening-in device, a crystal wireless set. I love to have music in the house. Perhaps Mr Gillespie could advise me on the best type of piano, and give me some lessons.'

I felt a rush of gladness. Music would bring the big house to life. And it would be good to help Freddie – so long as he didn't mind being subjected to scrutiny by Mrs Jameson. Poor boy, he would feel as if he had two mothers to impress.

'Thank you, Mrs Jameson. I'll write to him right away.' Sooty leapt onto my lap and started to purr.

My employer's eyes were bright again. 'And perhaps, once

we have music, you could show me some of the modern dances you are so fond of. I understand your rendition of The Charleston is quite the thing.'

Chapter 48

'Are you all right, Miss Swallow?'

Mr Li leaned across the table, his smooth face creasing with concern. I struggled for breath, my face beetroot-red and perspiration breaking out on my forehead.

'Drink some water, Marjorie,' said Mrs Jameson, passing me a glass.

I drank gratefully, the cool water soothing my burning tongue.

'I should have warned you,' said Mr Li, with a hint of laughter around his eyes. 'The black bean with chilli has quite a lot of chilli in it.'

There was nothing chilly about the dish. It was hotter than the hottest jazz the All Stars had ever played at the Harlequin. Freddie, T-bone, and Mr Harpo were laughing behind their napkins, tucking in to the food with relish.

'I thought you liked it hot, Marjorie,' said Freddie.

'Very funny,' I said, when I had recovered the power of speech. 'Mr Li, I'm so sorry. I was raised on boiled suet pudding. Spicy food takes a bit of getting used to.'

Vi passed me a dish of green vegetables. 'Water chestnut in Chinese leaves. It'll cool you down. And do have some more of the honey-glazed ribs.'

The food at the Lucky Lotus was quite unlike anything I'd tasted before. Most of it was delicious, but some dishes were unexpectedly fiery. The restaurant too was exotic: the shiny walls painted dark red and gold, with crimson lanterns casting a low light. It was like dining in a Chinese lacquered box.

Mr Li had invited us for a celebration. Mr Harpo was out of hospital and the All Stars were back together again, with the offer of a spot in the Up Town revue at the London Hippodrome. Mr Li had signed the lease on a town house in Knightsbridge, which he planned to turn into a smart hotel, modelled on the one his family ran in Shanghai. Not only that, but Vi was expecting their first child.

'My mother had given up hope,' she'd confided as we tidied our hair in the cloakroom. 'She's so delighted about being a grandmother that she's almost forgiven me for marrying a Chinaman without telling her.' She'd smiled fondly and shown me an enormous emerald ring on her finger. 'Taio says we should have a proper wedding now and invite everyone.'

Mr Li was expounding on his plans for the hotel. It would have a small nightclub in the basement, to be managed by Hester Proudfoot. Edith would be unavailable, having confounded us all by marrying her Russian suitor. The Countess Rostokovich was now comfortably installed in a suite at the Savoy Hotel, where she took much delight in ordering kippers and pease pudding for breakfast.

'Maybe it should have a Russian theme,' said Hester. 'What do you think? There are so many exiled Russian nobs in London now. Edith could bring them all in.'

Mrs Jameson laughed. 'You might attract attention from the wrong sort of Russian, Mr Li. You wouldn't want some anarchist or communist lobbing a bomb through the door, would you?'

We sipped pale jasmine tea from heavy iron pots. For a moment the delicate fragrance took me back to Limehouse, the opium den and my terrifying ordeal with the Armstrong brothers. I closed my eyes and raised my fingers to my cheek. The cut had healed, but I could still feel the slightest raised line.

Warm fingers closed over my other hand, resting on the chair arm. Freddie squeezed gently.

'Don't worry,' he said. 'It hardly shows at all now.'

I turned to him, saw the familiar red and silver scar at the corner of his eye, which pulled his eyelid down slightly as he smiled. His shrapnel wound had been so much worse and could have cost him his eyesight. Mine was just a thin trace of silver, which you could only see in certain lights.

'I know,' I said. 'I was just remembering.'

He squeezed my hand again. 'Yeah. I know all about that, too.'

Now that the spring days were getting longer, we'd begun walking in Regents Park once I was off duty, enjoying the sunshine and flowers. We talked about everything: music, politics, art and books. Freddie had taken me to concerts – not just jazz, but chamber music at Wigmore Hall. I'd shown him my favourite paintings in the National Gallery.

The one thing we didn't talk about was our future. My mother was expecting an announcement any day. But I liked my independence; my own rooms in Bedford Square, a generous salary to spend as I wished. And although Freddie was much improved, I knew he still had relapses of neurasthenia. Neither of us was ready to settle down.

Mr Li tapped his glass to draw our attention.

'I would like to thank you all for coming,' he said. 'And I hope you will not find it misplaced if I ask you to take a moment to remember Miss Daisy Caldwell. She was a good friend of the Harlequin, and her early death was a tragedy. Please raise a glass with me to remember absent friends.'

We did as he said. Daisy's inquest had concluded with a verdict of death by misadventure, Sir Leonard remarking that he was far from satisfied that all the facts had been uncovered. The police had closed their investigation. Poor Daisy had become a byword for the excesses of the flapper generation, held up as a warning to girls who enjoyed life too much.

Ambassador Caldwell had abruptly resigned his post, citing family illness, and the family had travelled home to America by steamship. There had been some trouble on the voyage. Mrs Caldwell had been taken very ill and almost died of a medication overdose. Fortunately, the ship's doctor had been able to save her life, according to newspaper reports when the ship docked in New York. Their daughter Felicity, perhaps because of the strain, had a nervous breakdown and was committed to a private asylum shortly after they arrived.

I was in a reflective mood as Frankie O'Grady drove us home from Piccadilly. Mrs Jameson had caused a scandal by engaging Frankie as a chauffeur, while she was saving up to buy a garage. It seemed to have started a trend; the most daring socialites in London were now taking on 'chauffeurettes' with peaked caps and smart uniforms. Frankie had been in her element, picking out a handsome bottle-green Lagonda with a two-litre engine and hiring a garage in the nearby Gower Mews, with her own rooms above it.

I watched the bright lights of the city streets flash past, parties of revellers out for the night. I felt a slight yearning for the thrill of dancing at the Harlequin, although my days as a dance hostess were firmly behind me.

'You're very quiet,' said Mrs Jameson as we hopped out of the car. 'Did the chilli burn your tongue?'

I smiled. 'I suppose I was thinking about things. Daisy and Felicity. And the Harlequin and the Armstrong brothers.'

She shot me a sharp look. 'Yes. Well, don't look back, that's my advice. Keep looking forward. There's so much happening now, so many changes and advances. Airplanes and airships, listening-in to the wireless, Mr Einstein's deductions about the nature of space and time. No need to get stuck in the past.'

She opened the door and frowned. 'What's that?' She pointed her cane to a card on the doormat.

I stooped to pick it up. It was a picture postcard with a delicate watercolour of a bright blue lily, exquisite in form and colour. I turned it over, read the printed message and the scribbled lines underneath and handed the card to Mrs Jameson, puzzled.

'Welcome to the Himalayan Valley Garden,' she read aloud. 'Join us at the Chelsea Flower Show for the unveiling of the famous Sapphire Lily.' She laughed and waved the card. 'What fun! I know who this is from.'

Then she looked more closely at the script underneath. 'Please come at once to Hawkshill Manor. I fear there is a snake in my paradise.'

She raised her eyebrows. 'Get an early night. We're off to the countryside in the morning, Marjorie.'

'Of course, Mrs Jameson.' I smiled, but the hairs on the back of my neck were raised as I made my way up the stairs to my attic.

CHAPTER 48

* * *

Enjoyed The Soho Jazz Murders?
Read the prequel novella free.

So how did a nice girl like Marjorie Swallow end up working for a lady detective? Read all about Marjorie's interview with Mrs Jameson over afternoon tea at The Ritz, in the series prequel, *Murder At The Ritz*.

The novella is free and exclusive to my Readers Club. Members also get a monthly newsletter with occasional short stories, news about my books, events, recommendations, special offers and promotions. Sign up at my website: annasayburnlane.com.

Historical note

While the story of the Soho Jazz Murders is pure fiction, it has historical roots. Mrs Edith Garrud was a real person and one of the earliest female exponents of martial arts in Britain. She taught the suffragettes jiu-jitsu and was indeed said to have thrown a policeman over her shoulder!

Much information about the London nightclub scene of the 1920s was gleaned from the memoir of Kate Meyrick, *Secrets of the 43 Club*. The 43 Club, like the Harlequin in my novel, had an uneasy relationship with the police and the strict alcohol licensing laws introduced during the First World War. The memoir explains the role of dance hostesses and the economics of the club, including how much they paid for champagne, and the fees commanded by the top jazz bands.

In any account of the 1920s cocaine panic you will come across the name of 'Brilliant' Chang, a Chinese man who ran a restaurant opposite the 43 Club and was thought to be a drug supplier. He was implicated in the deaths of several 'dope girls', including the actress Billie Carleton after the Victory Ball of 1918. But many accounts of him are tainted by racism and I wonder how conclusive the evidence against him really was. In my character 'Lucky' Li I wanted to suggest an alternative possibility.

The legal situation regarding drugs such as cocaine and opium changed rapidly at the start of the 20th century, and they became illegal during the First World War. It's true that you used to be able to buy cocaine at the chemist and heroin at Harrods!

The real American Ambassador to London in 1923 was George Harvey, a former journalist. He didn't live at Princes Gate because although the residence was acquired for the purpose in 1922, it wasn't used as such until 1929. I've taken the liberty of moving my fictional ambassador Henry Caldwell there early, because I'm familiar with the house, which used to be the headquarters of the Royal College of GPs when I worked as a medical journalist.

If you're interested in the history behind my books, I write a blog, The Stories Behind the Story, which you can find on Substack.

Acknowledgements

Thanks to my editor Alison Jack and cover designer Donna Rogers. Thanks to Avril and Geoff for education about 1920s jazz. Thanks to my beta reader team: Radhika, Rosalie, Christina, Madeleine, Jean and Emma. Thanks to Phil for everything.

About the Author

Anna Sayburn Lane is a novelist and journalist. She writes historical cozy mysteries and contemporary thrillers.

Anna studied English and History at university, then began her career as a reporter on a south London newspaper, later moving into medical journalism.

She published her first novel, *Unlawful Things*, in 2018, followed by *The Peacock Room*, *The Crimson Thread* and *Folly Ditch* in 2022. *Unlawful Things* was shortlisted for the Virago New Crime Writer award and picked as a Crime in the Spotlight choice by the Bloody Scotland crime writing festival.

In 2023 she began writing the 1920s murder mystery series of classic detective stories set in 1920s London. *Blackmail In Bloomsbury* is the first in the series, featuring apprentice detective Marjorie Swallow. *The Soho Jazz Murders* is the second book, and *Death At Chelsea* will follow shortly.

Anna lives on the Kent coast.

You can connect with me on:

- https://annasayburnlane.com
- https://www.facebook.com/annasayburnlane
- https://annasayburnlane.substack.com

Also by Anna Sayburn Lane

Step back into the roaring twenties with classic detective novels set in 1920s London. The Soho Jazz Murders is the second in the series featuring plucky apprentice detective Marjorie Swallow.

Blackmail In Bloomsbury

Everyone at the party had a secret. Someone killed to keep theirs…

When a bohemian party ends in murder, there's no shortage of suspects. Half of Bloomsbury wanted Mrs Norris dead – but who wielded the knife?

Was it the handsome but troubled artist? The vivacious young actress? Or the aristocratic lady novelist? Marjorie and Mrs Jameson must find the true killer to save an innocent man from the noose. From the garden squares of Bloomsbury to the seedy backstreets of Soho, they navigate the glamour and peril of Jazz Age London in a thrilling story of secrets and lies. Marjorie needs all her wit, pluck and charm in this perilous hunt for the killer.

This classic murder mystery will keep you guessing to the very last page. The first in the 1920s Murder Mystery series, Blackmail in Bloomsbury will delight fans of Agatha Christie and classic crime.

Death At Chelsea

The prettiest flowers can be deadly…

Mrs Jameson and Marjorie are called to investigate when a renowned garden designer suspects that someone is sabotaging her priceless Himalayan Sapphire Lilies, ahead of the 1923 Chelsea Flower Show.

But soon it's not just the flowers that are dying. Rival gardeners, intrepid plant hunters and even King George V himself are caught up in a poisonous bouquet with its roots deep in the mountains of Tibet.

The Riviera Mystery

Ready for a trip to the French Riviera? This "sunny place for shady people" hides dark secrets. Marjorie and Mrs. Jameson embark on a dream vacation aboard the famous Blue Train, only to be swept into a whirlwind of intrigue, deception, and murder.

Invited to stay at the luxurious Villa Beau Rivage, they're surrounded by diamond merchants, film stars, and artists. But when a tragic death shatters the party's glitz, Marjorie finds herself drawn into a deadly game where no one can be trusted.

Can Marjorie and Mrs. Jameson uncover the truth? Dive into a world of 1920s glamour, mystery, and suspense.

BV - #0114 - 130924 - C0 - 203/127/15 - PB - 9781739514426 - Matt Lamination